Twilight in Paris

by

Guillaume Alexander

ISBN-13: 979-8-218-22325-0

Cover designed using KDP Cover Creator

Printed in the United States of America

DEDICATION

This story is dedicated to my lifelong friend Laurence, whom I met in Paris in 1991 at a cabaret in Pigalle. I wrote the character Valerie after her, hoping to show appreciation for our friendship and gratitude for inspiring me to write this story.

CONTENTS

ACKNOWLEDGMENTS

I would like to thank my friends and family members for their support. Without their encouragement I could not have started or finished this story. I would also like to thank my journalism teachers for showing me how to write like a professional and my French teachers, who helped give me a foundation for the language. Also, a special thanks to Laurence, who is the source of my inspiration for this novel.

PROLOGUE

It's a Sunday, and the city of Boston is seemingly at peace, well after midnight. The church bells haven't begun to ring yet, and virtually no one is left on its streets near the Isabella Stewart Gardner Museum, which had closed its doors around dusk after another long day. It stands next door to the Museum of Fine Arts, across from Fenway Park, where the Red Sox recently lost another game to the Yankees.

March 18, 1990, would not normally be a date anyone would likely remember. Then again, the two young ladies who are about to commit the crime of the century aren't ordinary women either. This typically average day will leave a permanent mark in America's history and create an international spectacle no one will ever forget.

There is a cool breeze which creates a chill in the air. The blanket of snow from winter has mostly melted by this time, but the trees are still bare and dry from the lack of rain and warmth. Inside the museum gallery, priceless works of art hang proudly on the interior walls, including a Rembrandt known as 'Christ in the Storm on the Sea of Galilee.' This painting alone is worth tens of millions of dollars. Astonishingly, these priceless works of art are protected by only two security guards, who have been busy playing dominoes to combat boredom and fatigue.

Tonight, the city of Boston has two unexpected female visitors from Paris, France, who typically spend their late-night hours removing their clothes for a large, yet discreet audience. However, this fateful evening, they are disguised as police officers, and this will prove to be the performance of their lives.

In a stealth manner, the women's black Mercedes van approaches the side entrance of the art museum, and the pair of romantically entangled friends, Valerie and Bianca exit the vehicle, porting fake badges and moustaches. Valerie knocks at the door to gain admittance to the gallery. One of the guards on duty breaks protocol by admitting the two imposters, who ironically claim to be responding to a potential burglary. The moment they're let inside, the two guards are taken by surprise and temporarily knocked out with chloroform, enabling Valerie and Bianca to tie them up and gag them.

In the meantime, the two Parisienne pirates, get busy pilfering thirteen pieces of art from their perches, worth an estimated $200 million: 'The Concert,' by Vermeer, 'A Lady and Gentleman in Black,' 'Christ in the Storm on the Sea of Galilee,' by Rembrandt, 'Chez Tortoni,' by Manet, and 'Three Mounted Jockeys' by Degas, just to name some of the most valuable works of art.

Bianca and Valerie quickly sweep the Dutch Room of its most celebrated masterpieces and load them in the van, just as the two security guards regain consciousness. The men are wrestled to their feet and escorted to the basement of the museum, where they will later be found, without being able to identify their assailants.

After knocking the two guards out one more time, Valerie and Bianca quickly make their escape from the museum, without being compromised. They drive away along Storrow Drive and head to a small airfield where they have a private plane waiting to take them back to Paris.

These two women, who are unknown to the FBI or Interpol currently, have just pulled off the greatest art heist of the 20th century. No one will ever know the truth about what happened to these rare, master works of art decades later, despite a $10 million reward for their return.

I.   Le Théâtre Coquette

It's midnight on a Saturday in Paris. Le Tour d' Eiffel sparkles with flashing lights, which flicker and twinkle through a dense fog, like diamonds along a lady's finger, sending a signal to all those with lonely hearts. The streets in Pigalle are littered with tourists and thrill seekers, despite the bombardment of raindrops from grey clouds, highlighted by a silvery mist. A canary-colored Mercedes-Benz passes by, splashing through glowing puddles of rainwater, illuminated by the moonlight. The occupants in the backseat sip Louis XV champagne from Baccarat crystal glasses, and exchange moments of lustful glances and affection.

They must be on their way to a club or something, Guy thinks, as he promenades alone down the slick, damp sidewalk, along the rue de Clichy. His long, navy-blue raincoat and matching beret shield him from getting soaked. His hands are burrowed deep inside his coat pockets where they stay warm and dry, safe from the storm.

Guy asks himself if he's up for some lively entertainment at the Moulin Rouge or if he prefers a quieter venue at an obscure nightclub, where there are striptease acts, served up with tantalizing conversations with a sexy waitress or an alluring dancer. He chooses a place called Le Théâtre Coquette, which is just down the avenue, a little further past the famous red windmill, where the Cancan first made its debut in the 1830s.

Guy can't comprehend what he's searching for exactly, other than a little distraction from his everyday life. He recently broke-up with his steady girlfriend, Gabrielle – a devoted dark-haired woman of Italian descent, who works for a chocolatier in Saint-Michel. They had been dating for over three years, but Guy still didn't feel ready to ask her to marry him. They got along fine generally, however there was still some ingredient missing in their relationship - perhaps a little spice.

Guy Martin is a handsome real estate investor with dark, wavy hair and grey eyes, standing about 5 feet 11 inches tall. He came to Paris from Strasbourg, which is on the border with Germany, in the region of Alsace-Lorraine. He now lives in a little village called Aubervilliers, just northeast of the heart of Paris, not far from Montmartre.

At age 31, Guy is hardworking and successful, but unfulfilled spiritually. He is an only child, used to being alone and doing things his own way. The idea of being responsible for another person's life, and being under constant scrutiny by a potential fiancée, is not something he cherishes.

As Guy approaches the vermilion iron doors of the cabaret, he senses that his life is about to take a turn in a new direction - one that he could not have anticipated before the evening began. Entering the foyer, he is greeted by Madame Blanche, one of the owners of the establishment. She appears to be about 55 years of age with dyed crimson hair and azure eyes, wearing a plum-colored blazer and cream-colored blouse. Her age lines and crows' feet are covered by heavy L'Oreal foundation and plenty of rouge on her cheeks. Her lipstick is rust-colored, which is a close match to her hair.

"Bienvenue au Théâtre Coquette. J'espère que vous apprécierez votre expérience ici ce soir – Welcome to the flirtatious theatre. I hope that you will enjoy your experience here tonight," says Blanche.

"Merci, madame. Do you have a place for me to hang my wet coat and beret?" asks Guy.

"Oui, bien sûr. C'est là-bas – Yes, of course. It's over there."

Guy walks over to the coatroom where an attractive young lady in a low-cut white silk blouse and a short black leather miniskirt reaches out to take his wet garments from him.

"Merci, mademoiselle," says Guy.

"Je vous en prie, monsieur – You're welcome, sir," the young lady replies.

Guy redirects his gaze toward the corridor, where he focuses his attention on a pair of provocative women, who are wearing skin-tight dresses and designer jewelry. They are talking to a well-fed, older gentleman with grey hair and a mustache. He's wearing spectacles, a dark suit, and smoking a Cuban cigar. One of the women has her foot on a barstool, and the man's right hand has disappeared underneath her dress, resting high against her upper thigh.

"Pardon," says Guy, as he walks past the licentious trio, toward the entrance to the entertainment lounge. As the door swings open, Guy immediately notices a silhouette of a female in dim light, who is curled up on a chair in the center of the stage. The dancer's arms are wrapped around her legs with her head buried between her knees.

Guy stands there for a moment, as the song 'Au Fur et a Measure' by Liane Foly, softly begins playing in the background. A spotlight suddenly illuminates her body, cutting through the darkness and casting a long shadow onto a blood-red velvet curtain, which hangs behind her. The young woman's body is cloaked in a satin magenta robe, as she waits patiently for her cue.

Guy saunters discreetly down the stairs to the lounge below and strolls over to an open seat at a round table dressed in an ivory cloth, in the corner of the room. A cocktail waitress in a sheer-black catsuit laced with tiny rhinestones, approaches Guy's table to ask for his drink order. She appears to be very tall with short jet-black hair and chocolate brown eyes. Her hands have long, burgundy-colored fingernails and she wears scarlet-colored lipstick, along with Chanel #5 perfume.

"Champagne for the gentleman?" the waitress asks.

"No, merci. Cointreau avec glaçon, s'il vous plaît – No, thank you. Cointreau with ice please," Guy replies.

"Tout de suite, monsieur - Coming right up, sir. My name is Chantal if you require anything further," says the waitress.

Guy's eyes can't help but reflexively glance back in the waitress' direction, as she walks toward the bar to fetch him his drink. Then, Guy turns his head back in the direction of the performer on the stage. He takes notice of her silvery-blonde hair, chartreuse-green eyes, and pale complexion. She grips the chair she's sitting on firmly and leans her head back until her frosty locks cascade toward the floor. Then she stretches her legs straight out in front of her before opening them wider, while gripping her inner thighs, revealing a gold-colored G-string undergarment.

Bending her knees, she gently lowers her bare legs toward the surface, and slips her feet into a pair of fuchsia, open-toe high-heels. Immediately afterwards, she launches herself into a standing position with her hands delicately placed over her hips. An embroidered golden dragon from her robe appears to slither over her well-rounded breasts, as she begins to move in a deliberate manner, like a cobra, guided by the melody from a flute player in a public square.

Guy can barely see the other patrons in the room, due to the soft lighting and smoke-filled atmosphere. The men and women in the audience are gradually being hypnotized by this charmeuse Française. Like many others in the audience watching this spectacle, Guy is fully intrigued by this young lady's appearance and talents, as the song continues. It roughly translates: "I unbutton my clothes and undress myself, in a slow and provocative manner," which is exactly what this seductress is doing in front of an eager audience.

At this moment, a tall, bearded man, dressed in a black tuxedo and wearing an ivory-colored chapeau and silk scarf appears from stage right. He's hit by a second spotlight, as he glides smoothly toward his partner, as if he were on ice. She stretches her arms out to receive him and raps her bare leg around his thigh, as they collide centerstage.

They move again together in unison to the rhythm of the Rhumba - the dance of love. As this lady takes delicate steps underneath her partner's raised arm, he pulls on the belt tied around her robe. It abruptly falls to the floor, as she twirls slowly across the stage, revealing a viridescent, snake-like dragon tattoo, which twists around her mostly naked body. Guy gasps, inspired by her magnificent physique and the precision she is demonstrating, floating across the stage.

The two performers reunite once again in an unyielding embrace. Then, the male dancer allows his enchantress to lie back into his arms, while he lightly brushes the back of his hand vertically across her chest, in between her breasts. The lady tilts her head and stares into her lover's eyes, as if to say... *Take me now!* At that moment, the spotlights extinguish, and the dancers vanish into the darkness. The melody of the song fades away as they exit the stage, and the sound of loud applause fills the theatre.

Guy quickly swallows the remainder of his drink, which feels frigid against the back of his throat. It's a welcomed sensation, after feeling a little warm during the performance. Red roses were strategically placed at each table to fulfill a long-standing tradition of throwing one onstage after a particularly pleasing act. However, Guy holds onto his, even though many of the men gleefully depart with their own. He wants to personally hand his flower to the dancer who has just left the stage if he has the opportunity.

Entertainers at this establishment often choose to sit with one of the gentlemen or women in the audience, after their act is finished. At an exclusive club like Le Théâtre Coquette, fraternizing with the clientele is not only encouraged, but expected. Guy hopes that this young lady noticed his presence during her performance and will accompany him after she's dressed. He knows it's wishful thinking, but there's always a chance that it could happen.

Several minutes later, while the next act has already taken the stage, a door slowly opens adjacent to the platform. The woman entering is wearing diamond stud earrings and the same shoes that she had on a moment ago onstage. She's draped in a lavender-colored dress, split down the side with a plunging neckline and bishop-sleeves, giving her ensemble a classy look.

The dancer walks directly over to Guy's table and sits down next to him, without saying a word. She casually opens a small silver purse which she holds in her left hand, removing one of the cigarettes from a compact platinum case with the initials V.F. engraved on it.

"Ignite me," she finally whispers.

Nervously, Guy fumbles inside his pockets, searching for a lighter. He finally finds one, but his hands tremble as he sparks the flame. Despite his desire for this moment to occur, Guy is completely unprepared for this impromptu interlude.

This amazingly sexy woman is sitting here with me, and I'm clumsily struggling to find something clever to say.

"Comment vous appelez-vous, mademoiselle – What's your name miss?" Guy finally blurts out, awkwardly.

"Valerie, et vous – Valerie, and you?" she replies, releasing a cloud of smoke from her nostrils.

"Guy," he replies.

"Enchanté, Guy – It's nice meeting you," says Valerie smiling. "Are you finished with your drink? Would you like some champagne?"

"No, merci," Guy replies.

"Well, I would like some - waitress!" Valerie calls.

Chantal hurries over to their table.

"Oui, mademoiselle, qu'est-ce que voulez-vous boire – Yes miss, what would you like to drink?"

"I would like some champagne, s'il vous plaît – if you please," Valerie replies.

"Tout de suite, mademoiselle – right away, miss."

Guy glances at the drink menu on his table and notices that a bottle of champagne costs 1,000 francs. This is why performers are encouraged to sit with patrons - it coaxes them into spending more of their money. Guy already knows that he will be paying for the champagne. Employees never pay for their own drinks, and this establishment certainly doesn't give them away for free.

"So, what do you do for work?" asks Valerie, as she exhales another stream of smoke into the air.

"I'm a real estate investor," Guy replies.

"Oh, how exciting."

"Pas vraiment - Not really. I buy old buildings in desirable neighborhoods in Paris, fix them up, and then rent or sell them for a profit."

"It sounds lucrative," says Valerie.

"Well, it pays the bills; I can't complain. I really enjoyed your performance and I wanted to offer you this rose."

"That's very sweet," says Valerie smiling.

"I was hoping you would come to my table so I could meet you. I could hardly believe my luck when you decided to sit with me."

"That's very flattering of you to say - merci," Valerie replies, coyly.

"C'est mon plaisir - It's my pleasure."

Just then, Chantal arrives with a bottle of Beau Joie, a very expensive French champagne, along with two crystal glass flutes. She puts a white linen cloth over the bottleneck and pops the cork.

"May I pour a glass for you both?" asks Chantal.

"Oui, merci," Valerie replies.

The cocktail waitress begins to fill both flutes. Then, she dunks the bottle of champagne in a pewter bucket of ice and sets it on the table.

"Is there anything else I can bring for mademoiselle or monsieur?"

"Non, merci," Guy replies.

"Oui," Valerie interrupts.

Here we go! Now, she will try to run up the bill.

"We will have some strawberries with warm chocolate and honey, s'il vous plaît - please," demands Valerie.

"Avec plaisir – With pleasure," Chantal replies.

Valerie notices Guy's eyes trailing the waitress' backside, as she departs to fulfill her request.

Men are so predictable, Valerie says to herself.

"Santé - To good health!" exclaims Guy, as the newly introduced duo lift their glasses for a toast.

"A la bonne fortune – To good fortune," says Valerie.

"Guy, may I ask you a personal question?"

"Oui, bien sûr – Yes, of course."

"Why did you come tonight? I have never seen you here before."

"That's a difficult question to answer," Guy replies, feeling a little nervous again.

"I don't know exactly. Perhaps, a little voice inside my head just whispered to me to have a little adventure this evening."

Valerie smiles.

"I see. Do you have a lady friend?"

"I did, up until a few months ago."

"Oh, je suis désolé - I'm sorry. What happened?"

"Well, I guess my girlfriend grew tired of waiting for me to propose, after being together for three years."

"Je comprends – I understand. Well, you know what they say… "Il y a beaucoup de poissons dans la mer – There are many fish in the sea.""

"Oui, d'accord – Yes, agreed. Perhaps, it's for the best."

Chantal returns to their table once again with their sweets.

"Voila, vos fraises au chocolat et miel – Here are your strawberries, chocolate and honey," Chantal announces.

"Merci, c'est très gentil – Thank you, that's very kind."

"Je vous en prie – You're welcome,"

Chantal replies.

"Ils sont génial, n'est-ce pas? – They are wonderful, are they not?"

"Oui, si tu le dis – Yes, if you say so."

"Oui, je les adore – Yes, I adore them!" Valerie exclaims.

Valerie clutches one of the strawberries with her long-manicured talons. She first dips it into the honey and then bathes it in the rich, dark Belgian chocolate. She lowers it onto her outstretched tongue, while tilting her head back, wrapping her lips around the succulent fruit.

"Mmm, c'est délicieux – it's delicious!" Valerie moans with delight.

This young vixen's actions weren't entirely unexpected, but they still have had the desired effect – to provoke a reaction. Someone like Guy is easy prey for an experienced professional manipulator, like Valerie. She will have him eating out of her hand, then licking her fingers within a matter of minutes.

Valerie is confident that all men have a weakness for sex, and Guy is certainly no exception. Mentally teasing a person is the most titillating aspect of seduction, and Valerie is an expert. She will have Guy spend a lot of his money without protest, and then beg her to stay with him, while he remains at the club.

I might need to sneak away before he leaves, so he won't try to follow me home. On the other hand, he is kind of cute, so maybe I'll give him a chance to get lucky tonight.

"What about you?" asks Guy.

"What about me?" Valerie replies.

"I mean - where are you from, and what do you occupy your time with during the day, when you're not working at the club? Do you have a boyfriend? What's your story?"

"Eh bien – Well, I live in a petit village called Courbevoie, not very far from here."

"I know that town. I've been there on occasion for my work."

"Ah, bon – Oh, good."

"Oui, I look for properties around the outskirts of Paris, so I have been to Courbevoie once or twice to check out some apartment buildings. It seems like a nice little town to live in, since there are bakeries, butcher shops, cafés, and restaurants close by."

"Oui, c'est vrai, c'est génial – Yes, that's true - that's cool! You seem to know my little village."

Guy is so impressed with Valerie that he stops watching the other entertainers on the stage, for the moment. Conversations with his ex-girlfriend were so predictable and boring, and their sex life had become equally insufferable. He is finding this captivating provocatrix to be a breath of fresh air.

Guy unconsciously longs for more excitement and adventure with a new romantic partner. He's thinking that this dancer he just met seems to be providing him with the stimulation he's been craving. Guy begins to imagine that Valerie might be able to satisfy some of his unfulfilled desires. He doesn't expect that this nightclub siren will want to become his girlfriend, but she might be persuaded to spend a little time with him, every now and then, to have a bit of fun.

"I sleep-in most mornings. During afternoons, I paint, write poetry, clean, and go shopping. I don't have a steady lover because I don't want to be tied down by some jealous, controlling, and insecure little boy, who expects me to be like his mother," says Valerie.

"Well, you certainly know what you don't want. How about what you do want?"

"Most of the time, I prefer to be left alone. However, occasionally, I want to have mind-blowing, earth-shattering, life-changing sex! I don't crave commitments, promises or protection. I can take care of myself. I don't need a man to run my life for me or tell me what to do. I also don't want to be judged for what I say or what I do. I want to live my life on my own terms, without criticism or ridicule. I like to drink bourbon, smoke cigarettes, and have sex with both men and women. Is that so terrible or do you want me to leave now?" Valerie continues.

Guy laughs.

"J'admire ta candeur - I admire your candor. No, I don't want you to leave. In fact, I think you're refreshing and very sexy."

Valerie looks at Guy with approval, smiling at him devilishly.

"Bon alors, nous sommes d'accord - Good then, we are agreed," says Valerie.

Valerie and Guy continue to talk and get to know one another over the course of an hour, while enjoying watching the other striptease acts together.

"What about your family?" asks Guy.

"I don't want to talk about my family," Valerie replies.

"Pourquoi pas - Why not?"

"Well, because my father is a self-centered alcoholic, and my mother and I don't get along particularly well. I have no sisters and my brother died in a car accident. Do you still want to talk about my family?"

"No, perhaps we shouldn't," Guy replies, wishing he could retract his question.

"Eh bien - Well, I need to go now, but it's been a pleasure chatting with you, Guy. Thank you for your company, for the rose, and for the champagne and strawberries. It was delightful! You have been a very kind and generous guest."

"Attends - Wait!" exclaims Guy, as he reaches for her hand. "Can I see you again?"

Valerie had anticipated this question and was prepared with a rehearsed answer. However, she suddenly has the urge to be bold, since she has enjoyed Guy's company immensely.

Guy seems to have a pleasant manner, unlike most of the men who I've spoken to at this club. He is polite, articulate, funny, and surprisingly respectful - a real gentleman who has class. I can imagine myself taking this man home with me.

"I'll tell you what, Guy. There is an all-night café just across the street from here called Le Café Noir. Meet me there in about an hour. I have some things I need to do first, but when I'm free, I'll come to meet you, d'accord - agreed?"

"Tu me promets – You promise me?" demands Guy.

"Oui, mon chéri, je te promets; je serai la – Yes my dear, I promise you; I will be there."

Valerie kisses him on both cheeks, as she gets up out of her chair. Then, she disappears through the backstage door. Guy is both thrilled and anxious at the same time. He almost feels like a teenager who has just arranged his first date with a girl from his class. He's still worried that she might disappoint him and not show up.

What if I wait for her for an hour and she doesn't come to meet me? I guess that I will just have to take that chance.

"Voila, l' addition, monsieur – Here you are, the bill, sir," says Chantal, after she returns to his table.

"Merci," Guy replies.

Guy is somewhat alarmed at the total but pays the bill anyway, including a generous tip for the waitress. As he gets up to leave, Guy almost doesn't notice the four virtually nude women still dancing on the stage because his mind is consumed with thoughts of his upcoming tryst with Valerie.

II. Le Café Noir

Guy retrieves his coat and hat from the coat-check girl. The young lady makes eye contact with him and smiles in a suggestive manner.

She must be only about 21 years of age - a little young for me, I think.

Madame Blanche is there to say goodbye.

"Bonne soirée, monsieur – Good evening, sir. I hope you had a delightful time," says Blanche.

"Oui, madame, it was very gratifying," Guy replies.

"I'm pleased to hear it. Come visit us again soon."

"I'm sure I will. You can count on it."

Guy exits the nightclub and descends the wet stairs to the street. It's no longer raining, but there are puddles on the steps. He has about an hour to kill before his rendezvous with Valerie, so he decides to take a little walk to clear his head before entering the café. It's about 2:00 am, but there are still plenty of people roaming about. Prostitutes are noticeable on corners under street lamps, waiting to earn their pay on a stranger's pillow, in a cheap hotel room.

Occasionally, Guy has paid for sex, however his experiences have been mostly unsatisfying, failing to produce the decided effect. The encounters lasted only for a short period of time. There was no thrill of the chase and the orgasms were faked. Only the money pleased the girls. Guy already spent a small fortune at the club tonight, but he received more of a thrill than he ever did from Lola, Violet, Suzette, or Danielle.

Guy prefers to be challenged, and he knows this young dancer will likely put up a bit of a fight. She won't be easily captured or captivated by his good looks and charming personality, or even his American Express gold card. It might be possible to convince her to sleep with him once. However, Guy is sure he will need to find creative ways to keep Valerie intrigued, if he ever wants to see her again after tonight. Perhaps no longer experiencing the thrill of the chase can be blamed for why he lost interest in Gabrielle. Everything felt too easy and predictable. The excitement of the hunt he once felt when they first met had gradually dissipated.

Valerie isn't anything like my ex-girlfriend. She is rebellious, self-assured, and sexually confident. She seems to have no inhibitions or self-doubts. She's not the marrying kind who wants a family with children, and a house in the suburbs. Non, pas de tout – No, not at all. She is a city girl to her corps, but not a salope either. Valerie has class. She's intelligent, charismatic, and seems to have standards of some type, which she isn't willing to compromise. I believe that Valerie is a woman of character and conviction, despite being an exotic dancer.

Eventually, Guy makes his way over to the café, after about 45 minutes of taking in the sights of Paris, during the twilight hours. Pigalle is not his usual scene, but he welcomes a change of atmosphere, every now and then. It's getting close to 3:00 am, and if Valerie decides to meet him, she should be at the café shortly.

Guy doesn't want to be late, otherwise he knows he won't get a second chance. So, he quickens his pace and heads straight for Le Café Noir. Guy doesn't allow himself to be distracted by the beggars, thieves, or the ladies of the night, who are trying to attract his attention. For just a moment, Guy is overcome by nerves and self-doubt, and wonders if he should abort this assignation and go home.

Don't be scared, she's just a young woman like any other, Guy tries to convince himself.

He's aware that believing Valerie is just an ordinary woman is merely a deception. She is a woman - yes, but far from ordinary. She's not like anyone he has ever met before in his life. That's why he's so intrigued and impressed, but also intimidated by her, at the same time.

Guy had always been introduced to proper women in the past, who were a bit prudish and conservative. It took months before those women would sleep with him. Afterward, he always felt empty and dissatisfied, similar to how he felt with the hookers he slept with. He decided that none of them were worth the wait – not even Gabrielle, who was at least better than the rest.

Guy imagines that perhaps there is something wrong with him, because no one has ever satisfied his craving for excitement and adventure or fulfilled him in bed. He's beginning to wonder if anyone or anything in life is truly worth all the fuss. Perhaps, this exotic dancer might be the one to break the mold and monotony of his everyday life. Valerie could be the kind of woman he's been secretly wishing for to be in his life. However, she could also be just like a room filled with smoke and mirrors – only another fantasy or illusion in a magic show.

This is literally one of the few times Guy has ever felt exuberant about seeing someone again. He senses that this rendezvous might be special, because he has never been so nervous before, thinking about a woman. His hands are moist and trembling, his mouth is dry, and he feels hot under his monogramed, Louis Vuitton shirt. Guy starts to wonder if what he's currently experiencing is a panic attack or just a case of the jitters.

Why is this happening to me? What is so special about this young lady? She is simply a dancer in a cabaret, so why am I so nervous? Once I walk through that café door, the dye is cast and there is no turning back. Be cool, Guy - stay calm.

Guy tries diligently to put his thoughts in the back of his mind before reaching for the door. As he enters the coffee house and brasserie, he isn't surprised to see that there are several people having drinks and engaging in casual conversations. An old song by Edith Piaf is playing in the background, which can barely be heard above the boisterous chatter and laughter.

It's customary at many small cafés like this in France to greet everyone in the room, upon arrival. The men shake hands with each other, but all the women expect to be kissed on both cheeks. Guy isn't especially comfortable with this tradition because he's a bit of an introvert and germaphobe, but he knows people would find it insulting if he didn't follow the cultural protocol.

Despite his reservations, Guy still finds it pleasing to greet certain attractive women this way, especially if they are wearing an alluring scent and dressed to provoke. He gradually makes his way around the room, saying hello to everyone, reluctantly. He is somewhat surprised that he doesn't recognize anyone in the room, even though it's not his usual watering hole. He's also never out this late, even on a weekend.

After finishing his rounds, Guy steps up to the bar and introduces himself to the propriétaire, who is busy serving drinks.

"Bonsoir, monsieur, je m'appelle Guy – Good evening, sir, my name is Guy."

"Jacques," the owner replies.

"Qu' est-ce que voulez-vous boire? - What would you like to drink?"

Un café, s'il vous plaît – A coffee, if you please."

"Tout de suite – right away."

Guy decides to ask for a black coffee, instead of ordering another alcoholic beverage. He wants to sober up a little, after all the champagne he drank earlier. Guy is feeling a little less anxious now, after being distracted by the other guests. As it turned out, following café protocol helped to calm his nerves.

Guy looks around the room among the late-night crowd and attempts to see if Valerie has arrived yet. He sees several young people playing Pool and Baby-Foot, (table soccer) cards, dominos, and chess. The rest are either standing or sitting at tables chatting and drinking whisky, rum, or beer. Suddenly, Guy begins to feel anxious again. He glimpses at his Rolex, noticing the time is now 3:15 am, and Valerie is nowhere in sight.

Perhaps she's not coming? If she's not here by 3:30 am, I'll leave and that will be it.

The moment Guy finishes this thought, the front door of the café cracks open, while Guy stands sandwiched next to the counter, alerted by the clang of bells on the top of the front door. A tall black leather boot appears through the opening, followed by the woman attached to it. She appears to be about five-feet-seven inches tall, in heels. The mysterious woman is wearing tight-fit, Calvin-Klein blue jeans, a low-cut black T-shirt, and a cranberry red leather jacket. She's carrying a black leather purse with a sterling silver, chain-linked strap.

The woman begins to fuss with her silvery-blonde, free-flowing hair, running her delicate pale hands through her thick frosty layers. Her fingers on both hands are garnished with gold rings of various designs, and an 18 karat gold, Italian made chain adorns her neckline. Attached to it is a jade pendant in the shape of a Chinese dragon. Her makeup draws attention to her eyes, which appear to be chartreuse green in color, and snake-like in intensity. Guy's heart begins to race with trepidation.

It's Valerie!

Before she notices Guy, Valerie proceeds to make her rounds, kissing everyone in the café. Guy observes her impatiently, stalking her with his eyes, while turning his head like a periscope. It's clear to him that she knows most of the occupants in the room by name. He's thrilled that she has kept her promise to meet him, after all. Guy can hardly contain his enthusiasm. He continues to follow her movements and begins to feel a familiar warm sensation creeping up on him again. Guy nervously rubs his fingers together timorously, in anticipation of their second encounter.

Valerie now approaches the bar where Guy stands paralyzed. He can barely breathe, much less talk. Words elude him, as she makes eye contact and smiles provocatively at him. Now that she has captured his attention, she instigates a kiss - first on the cheeks and then on the lips of an extremely attractive woman standing next to him, while still holding her gaze upon him. Guy can't help but find this gesture surprisingly erotic. He can't decide if he is a little jealous or turned-on watching Valerie perform this ritual.

"Salut Guy – Hi Guy," says Valerie, finally, as she touches his shoulder and stretches her neck to kiss him. Guy is hoping for a kiss on the lips, but Valerie tactfully turns her head slightly, allowing him access to only the corner of her mouth, and nothing more. She lingers long enough for Guy to inhale the scent of her pricey, Cartier perfume. It's intoxicating and makes him close his eyes for a moment, as she presses her lips against his cheek. Valerie is aware of what she's doing to him and smiles with great satisfaction. The dance is only just beginning. Guy tries to lead with an obvious question, but Valerie remains firmly in control.

"Would you like a coffee?" asks Guy.

"Non merci, but I will take a whiskey with ice, s'il te plaît - please."

Guy is a little startled by Valerie's desire to continue drinking so late. Never-the-less, he asks the bartender for a glass of Johnnie Walker Black on the rocks.

"Would you like to sit down?" asks Guy, trying to be polite.

"If you prefer," Valerie replies.

Valerie and Guy take their drinks over to an open table, after he leaves a tip for the bartender. The song 'Rouge et Noir' by Jeanne Mas begins to play next through the speakers on the wall.

"I'm very happy to see you again, Valerie. I wasn't certain you would come."

"Let me tell you something about myself, Guy. First, I keep my promises, as you can see. I'm not an unreliable woman. Secondly, I'm neither a pretentious, bourgeoise femme, nor a salope. I'm a simple woman, who enjoys her independence and solitude. I told you before that I'm not looking for a boyfriend. However, I enjoyed our conversation earlier, so I thought we could be friends."

"Just friends?" asks Guy.

"Don't get cute - you know what I mean. You're an attractive man – successful and ambitious. You seem to know what you want. Just because I haven't attended La Sorbonne, don't make a mistake, believing I'm a fool," says Valerie.

17

"I understand you perfectly," Guy replies, a bit intimidated.

"Bon, I'm glad we got that out of the way."

Valerie opens her purse and retrieves a cigarette from her silver monogrammed case. Guy struggles once again to find his briquet to light her fag.

"Merci," says Valerie, as she inhales, then blows a stream of smoke into the air.

"So, do you have any ambition, other than being an entertainer? Perhaps you want to own your own club someday?" asks Guy.

Valerie exhales another puff of smoke before speaking.

"I thought about that, honestly. Owning my own cabaret is appealing to me. However, I have another idea in mind."

"What's that?"

"You have to promise not to laugh."

"I wouldn't think of it," Guy replies.

Valerie takes a sip of whisky from her glass, at the same time Guy reaches for his coffee.

"Mmm, that's good!" she says.

"Eh bien - Well, I was thinking about studying to become a lawyer."

"Really! That is surprising – wow! How old are you, if you don't mind me asking?"

"Non, j'ai vingt-septs ans – No, I am 27 years old. It's not too late for law school, don't you think? I know I have waited a long time considering it, but I couldn't afford the tuition when I was younger, after attending art school. I know it's a silly notion, but it's something I think I would like to do. You probably think I'm being ridiculous."

"Non, pas de tout – No, not at all. It's a noble quest. I admire your determination."

"Merci. It may never happen, but we all need our dreams, right?"

"Oui, c'est vrai – Yes, that's true."

"You're the first person I told who's taking me seriously, other than my closest friend, Bianca."

"I understand what it means to want something badly. Forgive me, but you must be tired after a late night at the club."

"Oui, mais, ça va – Yes, but I'm fine. I usually sleep late, as I've told you."

Valerie takes another drag from her cigarette, then turns her head to blow the smoke away from Guy's direction.

"How about you - are you doing okay? I see you're drinking coffee. Are you trying to stay awake or sober?"

"A little bit of both. I'm not used to being up this late on weekends. Friday, Saturday, and Sunday nights, I usually try to catch up on my sleep. Coming out to your club tonight is out of habit for me."

"Je te comprends – I understand you. You craved a little excitement. Every now and then, people need a change of scenery and a chance to mix things up."

"Oui, exactement – Yes, exactly."

Valerie is enchanted by Guy, but she still isn't sure if she will take him home with her. She knows that's what he wants, so it almost makes her choose to do the opposite, just to prolong his agony and build his desire for her.

The dilemma for Valerie is that denying Guy will also extend her own frustration and interfere with why she decided to come to meet him at the café. She hungers to have sex with her new prospect, but she thinks that maybe she should wait for another time – perhaps only give him her phone number. However, that's not really what she wants to do.

Guy isn't entirely sure why he decided to meet Valerie at Le Café Noir tonight.

Boredom, perhaps? No, that's not it. Excitement? Maybe. To get to know this night club dancer better? Certainly. Perhaps, as a challenge or even a distraction from his everyday life? That seems to be closer to the mark. Perhaps, it is simply to have sex with a hot mysterious stranger? Bingo!

"Everyone seems to know you here," says Guy.

"Oui, bien sûr – Yes, of course. I come here often after work, especially on weekends to unwind a little before going home. You could say that these are my friends, especially Jacques. If anyone gets fresh with me here, he will throw them out on their ear. So, you'd better watch yourself, monsieur. I have an army in here ready to defend my honor."

Guy laughs.

"You've made yourself immeasurably clear."

There's something about this man that I like. I'm not quite convinced about what it is yet, but I'm certain that I want to find out, Valerie thinks to herself.

Valerie decides to throw caution to the wind out of curiosity and because she is in the habit of taking risks.

"Guy, did you bring your car here tonight?" asks Valerie.

"No actually, I took the metro. I knew I was going to be drinking and I wanted to be responsible."

"Do you take the metro very often?"

"No, not really."

"Well Guy, I hate to be the bearer of bad news, but apparently you aren't aware that the metro stops running at 2 am."

"Mon Dieu – My God, I completely forgot about that!"

"Alors – So then, what are you going to do?" asks Valerie, facetiously.

"I suppose, I will have to take a taxi."

"At this time of night, it won't be easy to find one. If you do, it won't be cheap if you must travel far."

"Yeah, well, I'm beginning to realize my predicament. How did you get to work tonight?" asks Guy.

"I rode my motorbike. Unlike you, I know the train will have stopped running by the time I'm ready to go home."

"That's right, kick a man when he's down."

Valerie laughs, snidely.

"I'll tell you what, Guy. I have a proposition for you."

Guy raises his head with renewed interest. He suddenly becomes alerted to the fact that his situation may be more of a stroke of good luck than a dose of misfortune.

"If you like, you can ride home with me to Courbevoie and spend the night at my apartment. Then, you can take the train home in the morning. However, you will have to sleep on my couch and not with me, d'accord - agreed? Tu m'as compris – You have understood me?"

"Oui, d'accord – Yes, I agree. Merci, c'est très gentil – Thank you, that's very kind."

This is not exactly what I had in mind, but okay. At least, I will have a chance to spend more time with her.

"Bon – Good. Are you ready to go now then?"

"Oui, allons – y – Yes, let's go," Guy replies, eagerly.

Guy is feeling quite elated and satisfied with himself. This outcome is entirely unexpected. He went to a club this evening to forget about his troubles and to be distracted by beautiful women on a stage. Although Guy had been feeling lonely, he still didn't anticipate hooking up with anyone tonight.

Meeting Valerie was a stroke of luck. Going home with her is icing on the cake. Unfortunately, this sexy cabaret dancer has made it crystal-clear that she's just doing him a favor by letting him sleep on her sofa, but perhaps, there's more to her offer than meets the eye.

After saying goodnight to Valerie's friends, the two of them walk toward the door. Valerie deliberately doesn't take Guy's arm to walk beside him. Instead, she takes the lead, and he follows.

Maybe, this has all been a ploy from the beginning? I guess I will have to wait and see what happens.

"Voila, ma moto, – Here you are, my motorcycle," says Valerie, as they walk outside the café.

"Je suis désolé - I'm sorry, but I have no helmet for you Guy. You'll have to get on the back and put your arms around me. I'm sure you won't mind - just hold on tight," Valerie cautions.

"Haven't you had a little too much to drink?" asks Guy.

"I'm fine, Guy. Either get on or walk home!" Valerie commands.

Guy doesn't hesitate any further. He obeys Valerie's demand and mounts the back of her crimson Peugeot. He places his arms around her waist and locks his hands together firmly. He's not especially comfortable, but never-the-less, he feels electrified with excitement.

Valerie pumps the kick-starter and the engine comes alive with a roar. Exhaust streams from the tailpipes, as she releases the handbrakes and pops the clutch.

"Better hold on tight, Guy - I don't stop for redlights!" Valerie warns.

Guy obeys and holds Valerie more firmly. She pulls down the clear visor on her fire-red metallic helmet, flanked by two golden dragon decals on both sides. The back wheel of the bike begins to spin on the wet pavement, as Valerie engages the throttle. They speed off together into the night, as a chilling wind streams fiercely through Guy's finely groomed hair. After only a few seconds, the bike's tail-light fades into the darkness, as they disappear around the corner and out of sight, into the misty fog. The Dragon Princess has captured her prey.

III. The Dragon's Lair

Valerie lives on the third floor in an apartment building, along la rue Boudin, which is actually the fourth level from the street. She prefers the top flat because it's less noisy and has a better view of the town. The area of the city where she lives is in the old district, where there is a belltower in the center of the village. It still rings every hour, reminding the residents of the time. There's nothing modern about this little village, compared to La Défense, which is a contemporary business district, not more than six miles away.

In this village, there is a boulangerie just across the street from her apartment, where Valerie buys her baguettes and croissants to have with her morning coffee. She knows all the local business owners by name, and often receives a free drink from the bartender at a brasserie called Le Café Niagara, whenever she stops in. Valerie won't allow any of the men there to buy her drinks because she knows they will expect to be sexually compensated. Their clumsy advances are annoying to her, but difficult to avoid since she often enters the pub alone.

There's a supermarket within walking distance, where Valerie can buy her meat and produce. She usually does her shopping on Sunday mornings when families go to church, so it's less crowded in the store. The train station is also within walking distance. It's convenient for when she wants to leave Paris on vacation or to visit friends in other regions, without needing to take her motorbike to the station.

After what feels like a time trial for Le Tour de France through the streets of Paris, Valerie squeezes the hand brakes on her motorcycle and brings it to an abrupt halt.

"Voilà, nous sommes arrivés – Here you are, we have arrived. You can let go of me now," says Valerie.

"Must I? That didn't take very long. I thought for a moment that I was riding on the back of a Formula 1 car, instead of a motorbike," Guy replies with a smile.

"The trip goes faster when I don't have to stop for red lights or slow down in traffic. There aren't many cars on the road this early in the morning, while it's still dark."

"My legs feel a little weak. That was one Hell of a ride."

"Sorry to disappoint you, but I'm afraid that's probably the biggest thrill you'll have for what's left of twilight," Valerie teases.

"I think I've probably had sufficient excitement for one night, anyway." Guy replies.

Valerie looks at Guy with a measured amount of distrust in his response. She's aware that he's not being completely honest. She knows he wants to sleep with her.

Men aren't often what they seem with their polite manners. When they can't get their minds off sex, they can become aggressive and belligerent. Maybe this man is different, but I doubt it. I need to be careful. He does appear to have class, however. Let's see how much I can provoke him, without pushing him too far.

Valerie still hasn't decided what she'll do when she takes Guy upstairs. She deliberately put him off for the moment, but she isn't done teasing Guy yet. As they climb the steps together, Valerie searches for her house key in her jacket pocket and feels around for her little bottle of pepper spray at the same time – just in case.

"I neglected to tell you that I have a ferocious attack dog at home, and he might not like you," Valerie proclaims.

"Really! What breed is it?" asks Guy.

"He is a Bouledogue Français – French Bulldog,"

Guy laughs, feeling relieved.

"Those little dogs are gentle and harmless. You deliberately got me worked up for nothing!"

"Since I live alone, it's necessary for me to find ways not only to protect myself, but also to amuse myself, every now and then."

"N'inquiète pas - Don't worry. I have a sense of humor," says Guy.

Valerie turns the key and opens the door. At the same time, a little black and white Frenchie comes scurrying across the room to greet his master. She kneels to pet him, as he jumps up to lick her face.

"Bonjour Fafa," says Valerie, affectionately.

Guy reaches down to pet Valerie's little companion, but he's met with a protective growl.

"I warned you; mon petit chien est dangereux – my little dog is dangerous. He may warm up to you eventually, as long as you don't touch me," Valerie teases again.

"You're going to keep milking this aren't you?"

"Only as long as it continues to amuse me."

"Go ahead and hang your coat and hat here," says Valerie, pointing to the hook by the door, as she switches on the light in the hallway.

Guy removes his hat and coat and begins to look around the apartment. It has a small eat-in kitchen, a spacious living room, no dining room, one bedroom, and one bathroom. Instinctively, his mind shifts to thinking about its resale value.

Next to the door, there is an ornate, gold-plated mirror above a matching console table, and several handcrafted, antique furniture pieces, sprinkled about the flat. There is a particularly beautiful aqua-marine, chenille sofa in the center of the room, and a silver, Arabella display case against the wall. Instead of having photographs or awards inside, it's filled with drink glasses and liquor of all varieties - particularly several expensive brands of whisky and gin.

Additionally, there are a couple of apricot-colored barrel chairs on the opposite side of the sofa, a peach and turquoise colored Persian rug, and an antique-silver coffee table, resting above it. There is no television anywhere to be found. Instead, there is an easel with a white cloth covering the canvas in the corner of the room by the window. Additionally, there are copies of Monet, Picasso, Renoir, Degas, and

Matisse paintings, which Valerie painted herself. In the bedroom, hangs what appears to be a copy of a Rembrandt – named 'Storm on the Sea of Galilee,' above her headboard. Guy is not an art expert, but he does recognize works by some well-known European painters.

By chance, Guy remembers reading in the newspaper about several paintings which had been stolen from the Isabella Stewart Gardner Museum in Boston in October 1990. The value of these paintings is worth around $200 million U.S. dollars. However, they won't receive their true value on the black market.

"Have you been out of the country lately – say to America?" asks Guy.

Valerie stalls for a moment, realizing Guy must have noticed the Rembrandt hanging in her bedroom, and may have recognized it.

"Uh, no, why do you ask?" Valerie replies, untruthfully.

"Oh, no reason," says Guy, and dismisses the notion he is forming in his head.

"Would you like a nightcap, while I take a shower?"

"Oui, merci – Yes, thank you."

"I'm sorry I don't have any clothes for you to change into, so you'll have to sleep in your underwear. However, fortunately for you, I have an extra blanket and pillow."

"So, I guess you were serious about making me sleep on the couch."

"You're lucky that I don't make you sleep on the floor with Fafa. Although, Fafa does have bed privileges in my room at night, and he becomes very nasty if he's disturbed," Valerie teases once more, as she gives Guy a facetious look.

Valerie opens her display case and removes a bottle of vintage Courvoisier.

"Would you like ice with your drink?"

"Non, merci. I prefer to drink cognac neat."

"As you wish. I'm sorry I can't join you now since I'm going to clean myself up. Just relax and listen to some music, while I wash up."

Valerie puts on a song called 'Rêve Orange' – 'Orange Dream' by

Liane Foly – a very romantic love song.

Valerie hands Guy his drink, while making seductive eye contact. Her look suggests that she expects him to make a play for her, as she removes her jacket and hangs it on a hook by the door. Then, she deliberately removes her T-shirt in front of him and tosses it on a chair, revealing a black-lace bra underneath. She is deliberately playing with his mind and putting on another striptease act for him, but this time – in private.

Guy stares at Valerie's body with burning desire.

"It's nothing you haven't already seen at the club - isn't that right Guy?" says Valerie, continuing to taunt him.

"I can't say that I've seen that particular bra on you until now, only what's underneath," Guy replies.

"And, how much did that cost you?"

"Quite a lot, actually. However, it was worth every penny."

"You better believe it! Unfortunately for you, the show is over for tonight," exclaims Valerie, as she opens the door to the bathroom, not meaning a word she's saying.

Despite her announcement, Valerie deliberately leaves the door cracked open, so that Guy can continue to watch her undress.

Fafa toddles over to his bed on the floor and curls up, showing little interest in the new guest in the house. Guy sits comfortably on the sofa with his drink in his hand, gazing in the direction of the bathroom. He is unable to take his eyes off the opening in the door, as Valerie begins to unclasp her bra and unzip her jeans. She turns the hot water on in the shower, and steam begins to fill the room. It reminds Guy for a moment of the fog from the machine on the stage at Le Théâtre Coquette.

Valerie removes her gold rings, one by one, and places them in a small jewelry box on a shelf above the sink. Guy begins to unbutton his collar, as he senses his temperature rising. Valerie steps out of her Calvins and slowly removes her panties, before disappearing behind the shower curtain, fully aware that Guy has witnessed her every move she's made.

As she rinses her hair under the warm waterfall, and reaches for her strawberry-scented herbal shampoo, a smile forms across her face. She's pleased with herself and how the events of the evening have unfolded in her favor, knowing that Guy is the one who feels lucky.

Guy does feel very satisfied, and still has expectations about sharing Valerie's bed tonight. He understands that she's been deliberately teasing him and suspects that she's been stringing him along ever since they first met - but to what end, he wonders.

Is this just foreplay for her? How long will she keep this up, I wonder?

Guy still can't guess what will happen when Valerie comes out of the bathroom. He's not getting his hopes up too high because he doesn't want to be disappointed. Valerie is still a dark mystery to him, and he's unable to read between the lines of her metaphors and innuendos. He decides that he'd better be prepared to get comfortable on the sofa.

Suddenly, Guy hears the faucet squeak shut and the curtain being pulled back. He can see Valerie's bare arm reaching for the lilac towel on the wall, then witnesses one of her smoothly shaven legs stepping out of the clawfoot, porcelain tub. Finally, her fully naked body is in clear view. She lifts her eyes for just a moment so that Guy can see that she's aware he's watching her.

After slowly drying herself off, she bends over and slips on a new pair of lacey, lemon-colored panties. Then, she puts her arms through an emerald color satin robe, embroidered with her trademark - a golden Chinese dragon. The Dragon Princess opens the bathroom door gently and Fafa perks his little head up, knowing that his master has returned.

"I hope you've made yourself comfortable," says Valerie.

"As much as possible," Guy replies.

"You don't like my sofa?"

"It's beautiful, but not as lovely as you."

Valerie laughs, then smiles at Guy.

"Flattery will get you nowhere my dear. J'ai besoin pour une cigarette - I need a cigarette."

"May I have a kiss first?" asks Guy, boldly.

"Didn't I kiss you twice already tonight?" Valerie replies.

"I'm not sure if I remember."

"You wouldn't forget if I kissed you – trust me."

Valerie initially ignores Guy's request and walks over to her purse and removes her cigarette case, along with her lighter. Guy is curious to see if she will light it right away or kiss him first. Instead of doing either, she circles the room lighting numerous candles, which make the room glow. The flickering flames cast moving shadows on the walls and set the ambiance. Once again, it makes Guy feel like he's back in the cabaret lounge, especially with the romantic French music playing softly in the background, in dim light.

Valerie hovers over the music player and switches the disc to a familiar song by a popular Italian artist named Zucchero, 'Senza Una Donna' – 'Without a Woman.' It further enriches the intimate atmosphere Valerie is intentionally creating.

Guy rests his drink on the coffee table, as Valerie moves closer to him and rests her cigarette case next to his drink. She places her left knee on one side of him and her right knee across his other leg. She loosens the belt on her robe and allows it to fall open. She stares at Guy with her piercing viridescent green eyes, which shine brightly in the candlelight. This handsome real estate investor finds himself captivated by her glare and intimidated by the power she seems to have over him.

Valerie begins to wrap her soft hands with long, sharp nails around Guy's throat, as if she will squeeze the breath from his lungs. The dragon tattoo which twists around her breast is clearly visible at this close distance. In that moment, Guy senses both fear and arousal. The Dragon Princess suddenly leans in seemingly to kiss him on the mouth, but instead creates tremendous suction around his tongue. Guy closes his eyes and allows her to take control, even though he's becoming more anxious by the minute.

Valerie is attempting to penetrate his psyche and expose his emotional vulnerabilities. Guy struggles to defend himself from what feels like an assault, but he knows he's losing the battle. This isn't just a sexual game Valerie is playing – it's a mind-fuck, designed to mentally subdue her victims. The Dragon Princess is attempting to drain his spirit, while feeding on his energy, as she glides her lips down below Guy's chin. He feels her hot breath burn his neck, as her razor-sharp teeth begin to pierce his skin, as she bites his Adam's Apple.

Guy's instincts tell him to push her away, but instead, he surrenders to her advances. Then, she reaches down to unbutton his shirt, slowly and deliberately, one button at a time. Grabbing Guy's right hand, she pulls it to her chest, inviting him to tighten his grip around her breast, so he can feel her soft flesh and body heat, inside his hand. Valerie shoves Guy on his back, against one of the pillows on the couch, and methodically removes the remainder of his clothing. Then, she takes the belt from her robe and carefully ties his hands above his head.

Guy has never had sex like this ever before. Even though he's intimidated, he allows Valerie to continue her ritual. Every inch of his body is tingling with excitement at this moment. She makes sure that he continues to watch her, as she slides her panties over her legs and tosses them on the floor.

Valerie presses her fingernails across Guy's chest, cutting deep into his flesh, until he cries out in pain. She's getting a rush from his reaction and relishes the energy she's absorbing from him. She gradually lowers her body over him until she makes contact. Then, she begins to move in a wavelike rhythm, as Guy quickly loses himself to Valerie's seductive charms and pleasures of her flesh.

Minutes later, Fafa is startled by his master's screams. He dashes away from his sanctuary on the floor and into the bedroom, hiding under the covers, as the song 'Devil in Me' competes with Valerie's cries of ecstasy. Guy has been holding his breath until he finally exhales, just as Valerie reaches her second climax. Guy opens his eyes to look at her, as she grabs his face to kiss him. The Dragon Princess has penetrated his soul.

"Do you mind if I smoke now?" asks Valerie, feeling thoroughly satisfied.

"Not at all, but can you untie me first, please?" Guy pleads.

"Oh, je suis désolé, tout de suite – I'm sorry, right away!"

Valerie first puts her panties and robe back on, then begins to untie Guy's hands, replacing the belt back around her waist.

"I hope you didn't mind me putting on a second spectacle for you," says Valerie.

"Pas de tout – Not at all. However, you may have left scars on my chest with your nails. I don't suppose you have any antiseptic?"

"Oui - Yes, it's in the bathroom. I hope you can look for it yourself, while I smoke my cigarette."

"Oui, bien sûr, merci – Yes, of course, thanks."

"Whatever happened to you insisting that I sleep on the sofa?"

"Oh, I was serious about that. I wasn't joking when I told you that you're sleeping alone. I just didn't say anything about not having sex with you."

Guy laughs, not knowing what to think.

"I'm glad you cleared that up," Guy replies, still a little confused.

He suddenly flinches, as the antiseptic begins to burn his skin.

"Je vais au lit, Guy. Je suis très fatigué - I'm going to bed, Guy. I'm very tired. You can take a shower now or in the morning, as you wish. I'm putting your blanket and pillow on the canopy for you. I'll see you in the morning - sleep well."

Valerie smiles fiendishly, feeling extremely pleased with herself and their love making.

Guy was not only a good sport, but also a damn good lay!

"Bonne nuit – Good night. Thanks for the nightcap – it was the best I've ever had," says Guy.

"You mean the Courvoisier?" Valerie replies, knowing that's not what he's referring to.

"Is that what you call it? I thought it seemed more like a Fireball."

"Well, something did explode inside of me. Fortunately, I believe I absorbed the impact."

Guy laughs, before flinching again from the sting of the antiseptic.

31

"I'll see you when you wake up," says Valerie.

"Attends! - Wait!" Guy replies frantically. "Would you like to spend some time together tomorrow – It's Sunday. You're not working, are you?"

"No, I'm not working. Peut-être, nous verrons – Perhaps, we'll see, but don't get your hopes up too high. You'll be lucky if I make breakfast for you. Normally, Sunday is my time for myself. Beaux rêves – Sweet dreams."

I feel like I've been dreaming already, Guy says to himself, feeling overwhelmed.

Valerie gently closes her bedroom door, as Guy tries to get comfortable on the sofa. He wants to let his wounds heal a little while longer before taking a shower. He will have plenty of time to clean himself up in a few hours, after the sun comes up.

Unfortunately, Guy can't relax, despite being exhausted. He never expected that this evening would turn out quite like this. He's aware that he's crossed over into a world he's never known in the past - one with endless possibilities and timeless passion. Guy is now intoxicated with sexual fantasies about the Dragon Princess. He has fallen victim to her magnetic allure, sensuality, and charms, which have become a potent elixir.

Just before dawn, Guy finally closes his eyes and allows his unconscious mind to awaken, as he drifts off to sleep, dreaming about a land colored by medieval adventures of knights, dragons, and damsels in distress.

IV.   Courbevoie Ville

By the time Guy and Valerie closed their eyes to sleep, daybreak had already pieced twilight's veil. The clock on the village center tower counts the hours, until it's time for the church bells to ring. Sunday is a day for the residents of Courbevoie to give thanks for the fruits of their labor and to relax from the pressures and problems of the week. Shop windows and doors mostly remain shut on Sunday mornings until after noon, except for stores like the supermarket and boulangerie, which provides fresh bread and pastries to customers serving brunch at home after mass.

Some residents can be seen hanging their laundry out to dry from their terraces, since it had been raining on Saturday. Others walk their pets down the street, stopping to chat with their neighbors, while their four-legged companions water the maple trees next to the sidewalk.

Valerie and Guy are still mostly unconscious, despite Fafa's persistent scratching on the bedroom door to go out. After 10 minutes of being ignored, the furry little Oreo cookie returns to Valerie's bed, licking his master's face, hoping that will do the trick.

"Go away Fafa!" Valerie scolds, while still half asleep. "Je dors encore – I'm still sleeping."

Fafa finally gives up in frustration and curls up into a ball on the duvet. It was close to five o'clock in the morning by the time the two lovers went to sleep. It will be at least 10:00 am before either of them opens their eyes completely and becomes vertical.

The curtains in Valerie's apartment are dense, allowing her to rest without the sun disturbing her slumber after working a tiring late shift at the club. Her bedroom window is a good distance from the road, so she's not bothered by her neighbors who might be making noise, as they start their day. The belltower is the only significant annoyance, but Valerie has become immune to its clamor. Unfortunately for Guy, the constant hourly reminder causes him to toss and turn, interrupting his dreams during the early morning hours, after dawn.

By 10:15 am, Guy decides to peel himself away from the sofa to clean himself up. He manages to find his way to the bathroom in the dark and switches on the light. He is feeling a slight sense of guilt this morning, after a night of debauchery, as he listens to the church bells chiming in the square. He contemplates how he will pay penance for indulging his hedonistic desires with a stranger. More importantly, he wonders what will happen when Valerie wakes up.

Valerie did mention something about breakfast, didn't she?

After turning the shower faucets counterclockwise, Guy steps into the antique bathtub, still feeling a bit ashamed. He prays for absolution, as he lowers his head under the cascade. He's reminded of the gashes he sustained on his chest and side during his night of passion, thanks to Valerie's spear-like talons, as the hot water begins to burn his flesh — punishment for breaking God's commandments. He removes the circular white soap from its tabernacle and attempts to cleanse his wounds as well as his soul, in an attempt to wash away his sins.

Valerie may just want me to leave this morning before breakfast. She didn't even want to sleep with me. She said repeatedly that she doesn't want a boyfriend. What was I thinking? I must be out of my mind!

Guy continues to berate himself, as the scalding water continues to assault his skin, until he abruptly interrupts the flow by quickly closing the faucets. Looking down at his torn muscular body, he steps out onto the floor mat and removes a fresh towel from the second hook. He gently dries himself off, then wraps the towel around his waist.

I wonder how many men have used this same towel before me.

Just then, Guy hears Valerie's voice from her bedroom.

"Guy, can you take Fafa outside for his walk and buy a baguette at the boulangerie for me, s'il te plaît? His leash is on the hook by the door."

Guy is somewhat startled by this unexpected request.

"Oui, d'accord – Yes, okay. Just give me a few minutes to get dressed."

"Merci, mon amour. Je t'adore – Thank you, my love. I adore you."

Valerie closes her eyes again and tries to drift back to sleep. After Guys slips his clothes back on from the night before, he opens the bedroom door just enough to let Fafa through. Guy peers over to see Valerie holding her pillow.

She almost looks sweet, he thinks to himself, as she lies there peacefully.

He grabs Fafa's leash and fastens it to his collar, without resistance. Fafa is anxious to go outside, so he's not being very picky about who takes him.

"Come on little guy. We need to buy your mistress some bread and take you out for your morning walk," says Guy.

Guy loves dogs, but he doesn't have one of his own because he's not home very much. He takes the house key from the ashtray on the console table and escorts Fafa down the stairs to the street. Guy decides to stroll down the lane for a bit before circling back to the bakery. He says hello to several people along the way, who are also walking their furry family members.

"Bonjour," says Guy, to one of Valerie's neighbors.

"Bonjour," says an older woman walking her West Highland White terrier.

"Isn't that Valerie's little dog?" the woman asks.

"Oui, madame. I am simply doing Valerie a favor by taking her dog out for his morning walk."

"Vous êtes très gentil, monsieur - You are very kind, sir. Be sure to tell Valerie that I said hello."

"Comment vous appelez-vous - How do you call yourself?"

"Madame Leffler," she replies. "Et vous – And you?"

"Guy Martin."

"Enchanté, Guy - It's nice to meet you."

"Eh bien, bonne journée – Well, have a pleasant day," Guy replies.

Guy tips his beret to the old woman and begins to head in the direction of the bakery. As he enters the shop, he asks if it's okay to bring Fafa into the store.

"Bonjour, monsieur – Good morning, sir," says Guy.

"Puis-je vous aider - Can I help you?" asks the baker.

"Is it okay to bring this little dog inside here with me?"

"Isn't that Fafa, Valerie's little dog?" asks the baker.

"Oui, in fact - it is. I'm walking him this morning for her."

"Alors, bien sûr – Then, of course."

"Merci, monsieur – Thank you, sir."

"Qu'est-ce que vous voulez, monsieur – What would you like, sir?"

"Une baguette, s'il vous plaît – One baguette, please."

"C'est tout – Is that all?" asks the baker.

"Oui, merci. Combien – Yes, thank you. How much?"

"Dix francs – Ten francs."

Guy pays the man the money and the baker gives him a baguette, as well as a treat for Fafa.

"Voila, monsieur – Here you are, sir."

"Merci," Guy replies.

Guy and Fafa leave the store and return to Valerie's apartment – mission accomplished. The Dragon Princess has finally awakened and risen from her bed, wearing only her robe, a matching pair of satin pajama shorts, no top, and open toe house sandals. Guy removes Fafa's leash and places it back on the hook.

"Merci Guy," says Valerie, as she takes the baguette from him, kissing him on the cheek.

"I walk your dog and bring you fresh bread, and all I receive is a peck on the cheek," Guy teases.

"Oh Guy, don't pout. You got more than you deserved last night," Valerie scolds.

"That's true, but don't ask me to help make breakfast too. I'm not a very good cook."

"I will make some eggs for us, but you're going to help make the coffee."

"Oui, d'accord – Yes, agreed. However, I like it strong with no sugar or cream."

"I wouldn't drink it any other way," Valerie replies.

"The only caveat is that Fafa must be fed first, so go ahead and start the coffee, while I feed my munchkin."

Valerie opens her cabinet, retrieves a bag of dog food, and puts some in Fafa's bowl. Her little pup wastes no time scarfing down his breakfast before returning to his bed on the floor in the salon.

"How do you like your eggs, Guy?"

"Poached."

"Of course, how else would a bourgeois man like you take them," Valerie says, laughing.

"Are you trying to suggest that I'm pretentious?"

"Aren't you?"

"I've never really thought about it. How do you take yours?"

"Over-hard, with hot sauce."

"Why am I not surprised? What else would a dragon eat for breakfast? Perhaps people's choices in food, does say a lot about their character and personality."

"I agree with you Guy, and I appreciate that you know what you like."

"If I'm being honest with you Valerie, I thought I knew what I wanted. However, now I'm not so sure anymore."

"Well, don't change your mind about your eggs, because I've already started cooking them. I would give them to Fafa, but he's already had his breakfast. Plus, his taste is simple like mine, so he wouldn't like his eggs poached, anyway."

"Don't worry, I haven't changed my mind about how I would like my breakfast, but perhaps my taste in women is evolving."

Valerie looks at Guy and smiles, fully aware he's referring to her.

"Well, I'm sure I can't help you figure that out. I'm not a psychotherapist. I'm just a simple nightclub dancer – that's all."

"Perhaps not, however last night was unforgettable."

Valerie smiles again, as she glances over at Guy once more. She knows he's already falling for her. However, she has no desire to be loved or to be in love and would rather be in control of Guy's emotions and actions.

"Voila, - Here are your poached eggs on two slices of fresh bread. I hope the coffee is ready."

"Oui, le café est prêt – Yes, the coffee is ready."

"There are a couple of mugs in the cabinet over there. Please take them out and pour the coffee."

Guy obeys.

"Oui, d'accord – Yes, agreed."

"So, Valerie, can you tell me the significance of the dragon symbols you wear? I'm curious as to why they've become your trademark."

"The dragon is my Chinese Zodiac – the year of my birth."

"So, do you believe that this dragon is a reflection of your character?" asks Guy, as he begins to eat his eggs.

"Oui, je le crois - Yes, I believe it."

"What does the Chinese Zodiac say about dragons?"

"Well, dragons are strong willed and intelligent. They are perfectionists, set high standards for themselves and others, and they are demanding and inspire confidence and trust in others."

"That does seem like the impression I have of you. However, I'm still getting to know you, so I need to withhold judgment."

"What year were you born, Guy?" asks Valerie, while sipping her coffee.

"1962," Guy replies.

"Ho, the year of the Tiger!"

"C'est mal - is that bad?" asks Guy.

"Pas vraiment, non - Not really, no."

"What is the significance of the tiger?"

"Tigers are noble and fearless, as well as generous and stand up for what they believe in."

"Oh, that sounds good. Do you know what the compatibility is between tigers and dragons, while we're on the subject?"

"It's the worst," Valerie teases.

"Pas vrai – It's not true! Are you certain?"

"I'm teasing you, Guy. Dragons and Tigers are actually highly compatible when it comes to passion, but outside of the bedroom, sometimes they clash because they both have strong characters."

"Je te comprends – I understand you. You love your freedom and independence."

"Oui, c'est ça! – Yes, that's it," Valerie replies, as she swishes her eggs in the hot sauce and takes another bite.

"The eggs are very good, Val - merci."

"Don't get used to me cooking for you. This is a one-time deal."

"You don't want to eat together again?"

"I didn't say that. Next time, you can take me out to a nice restaurant."

"So, you're saying there will be a next time – formidable – great!" says Guy, smiling and looking at Valerie from the corners of his eyes.

"Well, I wouldn't refuse if you were to offer to bring me someplace nice to eat – your treat of course."

"It would be my pleasure - anytime."

"Now, finish your breakfast, so you can catch your train to go home."

"So, you've ruled out spending the day together?"

"Do you want to help me do laundry, fold clothing, and my food shopping? I usually do most of my washing by hand. I also spend Sunday evenings painting, after I'm finished with my responsibilities. I can't change my weekend routine just because you're bored and want to stay with me longer."

Guy knew that it would be a struggle trying to convince Valerie to spend more time with him, so soon after just meeting. He's even a little surprised that she still agreed to have breakfast together. Guy assumes that it's compensation for taking her little dog Fafa for a walk, so she could sleep in longer. However, Guy didn't become successful by giving up after his first attempt.

"How about this Val? What if I pay to have your laundry washed at the laundromat down the street, while we go food shopping together. On our way back, we can pick up your clean, folded laundry. Then, we can take the train together to my house where I can get changed. Afterwards, we can go visit Versailles or the Louvre and have dinner at a nice restaurant. Then, I'll drive you back home in my car. What do you say?"

"Well Guy, that's an attractive offer. However, places like Versailles are for bourgeois tourists. I would love to go to Le Louvre with you, but it's an all-day affair. I can't leave Fafa alone for that long without asking my neighbor to look after him. Usually, I must make prior arrangements for something like that. This also sounds very relationship oriented and I told you several times that I don't want a boyfriend."

"My life is complicated enough, and I don't wish to become distracted. So, I must decline your generous invitation. Don't get me wrong, you're an exceptional man, and any woman would be lucky to have you. You're handsome, you have good manners, and you're considerate. However, as you're aware, I value my independence and I have a routine that I would like to stick to. I think it's best if you go home. Je suis désolé – I'm sorry. I need to relax today. If you want to see me again, why don't you come to the club next Friday night. I may have a little surprise for you. I'll walk you to the train station, so you'll be sure not to get lost - okay?"

"Okay Valerie, if that's what you prefer - I respect your decision. I appreciate you rescuing me last night and for making me breakfast. The entire experience has been incredible."

Guy places his dishes in the sink and walks over to put on his beret and raincoat. Fafa runs over to him to say goodbye, putting his front paws on Guy's legs. He is touched by Fafa's affectionate gesture and reaches down to pet his new little buddy.

"Wow, you've made a new friend," says Valerie.

"At least someone appears to want me to stay," Guy teases.

"Laisse tomber, allons-y – Drop it, let's go! The train will arrive soon."

Valerie takes the lead once again, as they descend the steps to the street. The belltower begins to ring again as the clock strikes noon, exactly twelve hours after Guy first walked down the rue de Clichy, toward Le Théâtre Coquette.

A strange feeling comes over Guy, as he begins to realize how little control he has in this bizarre and unpredictable association. For a moment, he has the illusion that he can still charm his way through to Valerie's heart, but he's beginning to realize that Valerie's mind is like a steel trap. One that no one can penetrate and one where he could be imprisoned indefinitely if he's caught in it.

Many townspeople appear along their route, as they make their way to the SNCF station, on le rue de Sébastopol. Guy is reminded that everyone seems to know Valerie by name and says good afternoon to her.

It's a clear day in late April, with few clouds in the sky. Suddenly, Guy feels a chill and senses that this encounter could be an ending, rather than a new beginning.

The thrill that Guy had experienced during the early morning hours has now faded in the face of reality. His mind is consumed with tormented thoughts about what he's doing and why. Valerie observes Guy's displeasure and uncharacteristically takes his arm and walks beside him, glancing up at him with a reassuring smile. It has the effect of putting him at ease. Guy looks at Valerie with fortuitous approval and smiles. She is very taken with him, despite turning down his proposal. Otherwise, the Dragon Princess would not have invited Guy to come see her again. In the distance, they can hear the train whistle blowing, as the metro cars roll thunderously into the station.

"I'm going to say goodbye to you here Guy. It's been a pleasure making your acquaintance. Please come to see me next Friday and ask

41

for me at the reception desk. Leave a note with the coat-check girl, and if I'm not performing when you arrive, I will come to see you in the lobby. If I'm on stage, she will tell you to come inside to watch me. Then, leave a message with your waitress to give to me, so I know you're there. She will deliver it after I'm finished dancing. Then, I will come sit with you again for a little while. Now, kiss me quickly so you don't miss your train."

Guy kisses Valerie goodbye, but her embrace feels different this time. It's sweeter and more romantic. He opens his eyes as their lips part, to witness her smiling at him.

"Now go!" Valerie commands.

"Okay, don't rush me - I'm going. I'll try to come to see you on Friday night. What about your phone number – can I call you?" asks Guy, desperately.

"Don't worry about that now. If you come to the club at the end of the week, I will give it to you then. Now, get out of here; the next train won't arrive for another hour."

"Okay, au revoir – goodbye," says Guy.

"Jusqu'à la prochaine fois – Until the next time," Valerie replies.

The unlikely pair wave goodbye to each other. Then, Guy hurries to purchase his ticket and boards the train when the doors open. He is of two minds this afternoon. One side of him feels a sense of satisfaction and relief, but the other side feels tormented and ashamed. He had an amazing night which he'll not soon forget, but he's frustrated by Valerie's determination not to engage him in a relationship beyond a one-night stand.

As the train pulls away from the Courbevoie station, Guy's mind starts to wander. He doesn't live too far from Valerie's home, but the ride is already starting to seem like an eternity. Station after station passes and each stop is a reminder of his failure to break through Valerie's defenses. He knows she has a firm grip on the wheel and he's holding onto this ride for dear life. Being just a passenger on someone else's train is not the position he is used to being in. For the first time in his life, Guy feels that he's not in control and that bothers him. At the same time, not knowing what's going to happen is thrilling.

Guy's life up until now has been meticulously choreographed. However, this mysterious Dragon Princess may be just the medicine he needs to cure his disease of routine boredom. For a moment, he thinks about his ex-girlfriend Gabrielle, and contemplates what she's doing and whether she still thinks about him.

I wonder what Gabrielle would think of my weekend escapade. She probably would say it's out of character for me and wouldn't be too impressed. Perhaps, she would even be jealous.

Guy is starting to feel better about the events of the weekend, as the train finally pulls into the Aubervilliers station. At this point, he hasn't decided whether to take Valerie up on her invitation to visit her. He still has doubts in his mind about whether this relationship could ever go anywhere. Still, he finds the Dragon Princess to be an exceptionally alluring woman, and he doesn't want to give up on her just yet. Right now, he can't decide what to do, but he still has several days to think about it.

"Aubervilliers!" shouts the conductor.

V.   The Lucky Coin

Friday finally arrives after what feels like a very long work week. Guy hasn't had any contact at all with Valerie, and it feels somewhat disconcerting. He wonders whether he should leave his decision to see her again up to fate by flipping his lucky coin.

Today, Guy happens to be in Saint Michel on business by chance. It's a section of Paris in the Latin Quarter on the Left Bank of the river Seine, across from Ile de la Cité. Many fine restaurants can be found in this neighborhood, which makes it a wonderful place to meet and share a meal or a drink with friends.

Guy's mind is distracted by the fact that his ex-girlfriend is likely working nearby at a chocolate shop called La Maison Jeff de Bruges. He's conflicted about whether he should go to see her while Valerie is still firmly on his mind. The store where Gabrielle works is just down the street, along the rue de Sucre – Sugar Street. Guy is tempted to drop in on her but will let fate decide. So, he takes his lucky coin from his pocket.

Heads I go see Gabrielle; tails, I don't.

Guy flips his coin – it lands on heads.

Merde!

He returns the coin to his pocket and reluctantly begins to walk in the direction of the chocolate shop. It's now close to 6 pm and Gabrielle's normal shift is until 7 pm, usually.

If she's working today, she should still be there, Guy thinks to himself.

44

As he enters the shop, the familiar aroma of rich dark chocolate reaches his nostrils. Ironically, it has the effect of reminding him of the chocolate and honey covered strawberries he shared with Valerie at Le Théâtre Coquette.

The store is not only filled with a wide variety of dark and white French chocolates, but it also has a section to taste some samples. Customers can also sit down at a table and enjoy a slice of chocolate cake or a cup of hot cocoa. Nothing in the store is pre-wrapped, so each of the candies must be individually selected and freshly boxed. Chocolate liqueur can also be purchased at a premium price.

Guy glances over at the display case where he sees Gabrielle assisting other customers. Suddenly he tenses up and starts to panic.

What am I doing here? Guy asks himself.

In the next moment, Gabrielle looks up and sees Guy standing across from her in the store. A look of surprise comes over her face before it turns pink. She abruptly excuses herself from the customers she's been assisting and walks over toward him.

Oh no, what am I going to say to her? What should I tell her about why I'm here? Guy asks himself as he starts to panic.

His anxiety is building. He quickly tries to think of something clever to say.

"What are you doing here?" demands Gabrielle, as she stands in front of him.

"Uhm, well, I was in the neighborhood on business, and I thought I would stop in to buy some chocolates."

"Well, I'm currently helping someone. I can't really talk to you right now. S'il te plaît – Please, give me time to finish taking care of my other customers – then I can assist you. Who are you buying chocolates for, anyway?" asks Gabrielle.

"Oh, Je suis désolé – I'm sorry; I can wait until you're finished taking care of them. I want to buy some sweets for my mother's birthday," Guy replies.

"Well, I have several customers ahead of you, so you'll have to be patient if you want me to help you. Isn't your mother's birthday next month?"

Guy becomes a little frazzled trying to think of how to reply. He knows he's been caught in a lie.

"Uh, it is, but I didn't know if I would have the chance to stop by such a nice shop in the future. You know how busy I am. I just happened to be working down the street, and I remembered your store was close by, so it seemed like a good idea to drop in while I'm here. I'm sorry if I've inconvenienced you. I don't want to be a bother."

"Never mind. Why don't you look around and write down what you want to buy and then leave it at the register, along with your credit card. I will ring it up and bring them to you when my shift is over at seven, d'accord - agreed."

"Oui, merci. C'est très gentil – Yes, thank you. That's very kind. Where do you want to rendezvous?"

"There's a little place called Le Café Fénelon; le connais-tu – do you know it?"

"Oui."

"Bon - Good, I'll meet you there around 7:30 pm, d'accord - agreed? I must get back to my other customers now. A tout à l'heure - I'll see you later."

"Okay, à bientôt – I'll see you soon."

What am I doing? I feel like I just made a date with my ex-girlfriend! This doesn't feel right, but now I must go through with it - I'm stuck. What's wrong with me? Guy asks himself, utterly conflicted.

Guy looks around the store and writes down which chocolates he wants to purchase. He puts his order and his credit card on the counter for Gabrielle before leaving the shop, unsure of why he's there. He's supposed to go see Valerie tonight at the club, but now he's made a dinner date with his ex-girlfriend, in the meantime.

There is time to kill, so Guy stops to watch a woman who is painting by the Left Bank. She also reminds him of Valerie, whose hobby is painting. He begins to think to himself that everything reminds him of her. Valerie is in his head, and he wonders again why he agreed to have dinner with Gabrielle. Guy is in a state of confusion, and he struggles to make sense of his decision.

This wasn't really my choice. It was the coin that decided, right?

Guy walks along the river trying to think before heading toward the café. It's a bit of a bold move to ask Gabrielle to put together a present for another woman he's courting, even though he said it was for his mother. If Gabrielle finds out, despite their current relationship status, she will still be hurt. However, that isn't what's bothering him at the moment.

It's now 7:20 pm, and Guy reluctantly begins his trek toward Le Café Fénelon, talking to himself along the route. As he approaches the café, he sees Gabrielle coming around the corner. He instantly begins to feel apprehensive again.

I'm going to need a strong drink during dinner.

Gabrielle is an intelligent, attractive 29-year-old woman, who lives in Montreuil-sous-Bois. She attended the Paris School of Business and worked in a bookstore for a few years, after she graduated. Then, she found another sales position at La Maison Jeff de Bruges and was promoted last year to Assistant Manager. She is a dedicated businesswoman, but also family oriented, and always willing to help others. Gabrielle is the oldest of four siblings, and desires to have a family of her own someday. She was counting on marrying Guy to achieve that goal.

Guy is beginning to realize that dropping in on Gabrielle unexpectedly, may have been just one more mistake that he can add to his list of blunders concerning women.

I really should stop leaving my decisions to chance, Guy tells himself, knowing that he won't be able to change this habit anytime soon. However, he feels that his lucky coin helps him move forward when faced with tough decisions. Occasionally, he finds himself in an uncomfortable position, like the one he's in now, after losing a toss.

"Bonsoir Guy, voila, tes chocolats et ta carte de crédit – Good evening, Guy, here are your chocolates and your credit card," says

Gabrielle.

"Merci – Thank you," Guy replies, as he opens the door to the restaurant for her.

"De rien – It's nothing."

"Table for two?" asks the hostess.

"Oui, s'il vous plaît – yes, please," Guy replies.

"Right this way."

The hostess finds them a table by a window and hands the former lovers two menus.

"Your waiter will be with you shortly," says the hostess.

"Merci," Gabrielle replies.

"Maintenant – Now then, Guy, what's going on with you? What's this all about? Why did you come to my shop this evening?" asks Gabrielle, feeling a little annoyed.

"No reason, other than what I mentioned to you. I was just in the neighborhood to investigate a property. I needed to buy a gift for my mother, so I thought I'd stop in to buy some chocolates and to say hello. That's all there is to it," Guy replies, innocently.

"Guy, you may have been in the neighborhood on business, but you could have gone anywhere to buy a gift for your mother. It's not even her birthday until next month! You didn't need to come to my shop to buy her chocolates today. Do you think I'm stupid? We were together for three years. Do you really think I don't know when you're trying to hide your motives from me?"

Guy is really beginning to regret his decision.

"Je suis désolé, peut-être ce n'étais pas une bonne idée venir te voir - I'm sorry, perhaps it wasn't a good idea to come to see you."

"Peut-être pas - Perhaps not, but we're here now and I'm hungry, so let's make the best of it, d'accord - agreed."

"Oui – Yes," Guy replies.

Gabrielle and Guy look at the menu in silence for a few moments, trying to decide what to order. They're both distracted by their thoughts, until the waiter comes to their table to take their order and breaks the ice that has begun to form a wall between them.

"Bonsoir, mademoiselle et monsieur," says the waiter.

"Je m'appelle Claude – My name is Claude. Have you decided what you would like for dinner this evening?"

"Oui, I will have some onion soup and the chicken cordon-bleu," Gabrielle replies.

"Et, pour vous, monsieur - And, for you, sir?"

"I will take the garden salad and the beef bourguignon."

"Très bien – Very good. May I offer you a bottle of wine with your meals?"

"Oui, we will take a bottle of your best Burgandy, s'il vous plaît – please."

"Très bien, monsieur – Very good, sir," Claude replies.

"Guy, now that we have ordered, are you going to tell me what this is all about?"

"Well, if you insist. Perhaps, I'm trying to figure out whether I made the right decision to stop seeing you."

Gabrielle rolls her eyes in disgust.

"What motivated you to start thinking about that, suddenly?"

"Nothing really."

Gabrielle scoffs.

"Well, if you don't want to tell me, then maybe you can explain what you thought was wrong with our relationship?"

Guy doesn't want to get into this conversation right now. He's beginning to feel more uncomfortable by the minute. He begins to curse at himself for losing the coin toss. He simply wanted to know how he would feel when he saw Gabrielle again – nothing more. He wasn't planning on having dinner and revisiting their former relationship in detail.

This was definitely a mistake, Guy thinks.

Despite how uncomfortable Gabrielle sees Guy becoming, she isn't about to let him off the hook easily. She was hurt and blind-sided by their break-up. Just when she expected Guy to propose marriage, he dropped her flat, without warning. Bitter feelings of resentment begin to rise within her. Guy notices tears forming in her eyes, which causes them both to feel increasingly disconcerted.

At that moment, Claude returns with a bottle of Louis Jadot. He retracts the cork and allows Guy to smell and taste its bouquet. Guy swirls the wine in his glass, inhales the aroma, while closing his eyes, then tastes the sample, trying to ignore how badly dinner is going.

"C'est bon, merci – It's good, thank you," says Guy, as Claude begins to carefully pour more wine into their glasses. Guy announces a toast to change the mood.

"Santé – To good health," says Guy, as they hold up their glasses, and begin to share a bottle of wine together for the first time in a while. Several minutes later, Claude returns with their appetizers.

"Voila, bon appétit."

"Merci," Gabrielle replies.

"Well Gabby, I'm sorry that things didn't turn out the way we both expected. I just felt that our relationship had become stale and predictable. I thought that we had reached a plateau. I'm sure it was all my fault."

"I didn't realize that you felt our relationship had become boring. I thought you were happy and interested in having a family, but perhaps that was what I wanted and not what you desired. I had hoped and expected that you wanted to build a future together, but I see now that I was wrong. I was blind and foolish."

"No Gabby. I thought that was what I wanted too, but now I'm not sure anymore. I began to feel that I wasn't ready for a lifetime commitment. Perhaps that wasn't even what I really wanted after all - I don't know. At that time, I felt like I was losing control of my life and who I am. Things just seemed like they were changing too fast and I couldn't catch my breath. Je suis désolé - I'm sorry."

"You felt like things were moving too fast! Vraiment - Really! We were dating for three years! How is that too fast? Je ne te comprends pas, pas de tout – I don't understand you, not at all!" Gabrielle shouts, feeling agitated.

"I'm sorry if I can't make you understand how I was feeling. I think that's one of the reasons why I wanted to break it off. I noticed that our communication had become disconnected, and that you didn't understand how I was feeling anymore because you were so focused on getting married. You couldn't hear me anymore – you just heard wedding bells. My identity became our identity. I didn't feel like I existed outside of our relationship."

"So, you're saying it was my fault that we broke up?"

"No, that's not what I meant! Why are you twisting my words? You just don't seem to understand me or what I'm trying to say to you anymore."

"Perhaps, I don't comprehend you anymore, Guy. Maybe it's because you've changed. None of this makes any sense to me."

"Je suis désolé; Je ne voulais pas te blesser - I'm sorry; I didn't want to hurt you," says Guy.

"I'm sorry too," Gabrielle replies, beginning to tear up again.

As they finish their soup and salad, the waiter comes to remove their dishes.

"Was the soup not satisfying, mademoiselle?" asks Claude.

"Non, ça va – No, it's fine; ce n'est pas la soupe - It's not the soup," Gabrielle replies.

Claude peers over at Guy, disapprovingly.

"Well, if it's your companion, I can have him thrown out?" says Claude, winking at Gabrielle in a joking manner.

"Non, ça va – No, it's okay," Gabrielle replies, trying to hold back a laugh, wiping away her tears at the same time.

"Gabrielle, you know I love you, right?" says Guy.

"I used to think so, but it's like you said - now, I'm not sure about anything."

Twenty minutes later, Claude returns with their main courses.

"Voila – Here you are!" says the waiter.

"Merci," Guy replies.

For several minutes, they eat their meals in silence, until Gabrielle finally speaks.

"Guy, I'm sorry for being so emotional, but you must understand that it was a massive shock to me when we broke-up. I didn't see it coming, honestly. It's just going to take a little more time for me to adjust. What's worse is that you just showed up out of the blue today, wondering if you had made a mistake by breaking up with me. It's just a lot for me to process right now. I wasn't prepared for this; I hope you understand."

"Oui, je te comprends - pardonne-moi – Yes, I understand you - forgive me."

"So, what do you want to do? What do you want from me?"

"Well, I haven't exactly thought anything through yet. To be honest, I didn't plan on discussing our relationship tonight. I did want to see you to see how you are doing and how I would feel when I saw you again. Since we are on the subject, I suppose I'm trying to tell you that I need more time to discover what's important to me, and what I really want.

Breaking up doesn't mean that I don't love you. It just means that I recognize that I may be a little lost and unsure of myself. You know Gabby, this has been difficult for me as well, especially discussing our relationship with you this evening. Communication is not my strong point. Most of the time, I try to ignore my feelings and focus my attention on my work because that's what I'm good at. I'm not good at personal relationships."

Gabrielle takes another sip of her wine while spending a moment considering what Guy has just confessed.

"Guy, I'm pleased you finally shared your feelings with me." Honestly, our discussion put a lot of thoughts to rest that I've been having. I felt for a long time that I had done something wrong or that I wasn't good enough for you. I even thought you were seeing another woman, while we were still together. However, now I see that it's really your issue. I don't pretend to understand what you're going through, but it helps me to get on with my life and settle my self-doubts."

"I'm glad that you're feeling better about everything, Gabby. I hope we can remain friends for now."

"I guess we'll have to wait and see; I can't promise you anything right now."

Guy attempts to change the subject.

"How is your chicken?"

"It tastes fine. Do you like your beef bourguignon?"

"C'est bon, merci - It's good, thank you."

"How is everything now?" asks Claude, referring to both the meal and their conversation.

"Ça va mieux, merci – It's going better, thank you," Gabrielle replies.

"I'm glad to hear it. Will you be having dessert?"

"Pas pour moi, merci – Not for me, thank you," Guy replies.

"How about you, mademoiselle?"

"Non, merci," Gabrielle replies, not wanting to prolong her agony or increase her waistline. It's hard enough resisting sweets working in a chocolate shop every day. The day after their break up, she devoured an entire box, guilt free.

"Bon, voilà l'addition - Fine, here is your bill. I will take your credit card when you are ready, monsieur."

"Merci," says Guy.

"Je vous en prie – You're welcome."

"Please come visit us again, perhaps on a more joyous occasion."

Gabrielle smiles sheepishly, feeling embarrassed by the drama she created. Guy takes his chocolates, after signing the receipt and collects his credit card. The wounded former lovers both walk out of the restaurant feeling somewhat battered and exhausted.

"Well Guy, I guess this is goodbye again - bonne courage - good luck."

"Et, toi aussi, Gabby – And, you also, Gabby," Guy replies.

They kiss each other goodbye and go their separate ways. They both feel strange after seeing his ex-lover again. However, something about their impromptu supper felt surprisingly comforting by the time their main course arrived.

However, Gabrielle still feels confused and upset by everything that's happened. She still doesn't know why Guy stopped by today. If she did, she would have thrown him out of her shop, and she definitely would not have agreed to have dinner with him.

As Gabrielle descends the stairs to the metro to return home, she tries to make sense of it all in her mind. Guy walks back to where he parked his navy-blue Renault, understanding a little more about how he feels, and whether he made the right decision, splitting up with Gabrielle. For a moment, he starts to feel guilty about seeing Valerie tonight. So, he decides to leave destiny to chance once more and pulls out his lucky coin from his pocket, hoping for a more favorable outcome this time.

Heads I go to Le Théâtre Coquette tonight to see Valerie; tails I stay home and give these chocolates to my mother.

Guy flips the coin in the air and catches it with both hands. He closes his eyes and holds his breath in anticipation of the result. He gradually lifts his left hand and opens one eye to peek at the coin.

Then, Guy gets into his car, turns on the ignition, and drives toward home, feeling some sense of satisfaction and closure. He is beginning to realize that he has genuine feelings for both women, but he is also aware that his sentiments are very different in nature. Gabrielle is a reliable, familiar friend, whereas Valerie is an unpredictable and exciting temptress. Guy secretly wishes he could have both women in his life because together, they complete his needs.

As Guy downshifts and pulls up to a redlight, he sees a woman with long strawberry-blonde hair on a motorcycle next to him. She's wearing tight blue jeans, black leather boots, a metallic-white helmet, and a black leather jacket with a human skull embroidered on the back. The young lady instantly reminds Guy of his night ride with Valerie, through the streets of Paris.

The woman on the bike turns her head to look over at him, while resting her boots on the pavement. Her visor is up, so he can see her piercing yellowish-green eyes, flanked by coral-white colored eyeshadow. She winks at him and smiles. Guy's heart begins to beat faster as the traffic light changes. The biker opens the throttle and then speeds away, just as Guy steps on the clutch and shifts into first gear.

Guy is becoming increasingly aware that he must have an addictive obsession for the Dragon Princess. He cannot stop thinking about her. Everyone and everything reminds him of her charismatic persona and sensuality. His mind is so distracted and consumed with her image that he drives straight through a stop sign and almost causes an accident.

When Guy finally arrives home, he's drenched in sweat. Fortunately, he has plenty of time to get cleaned up before driving to the club. His lucky coin landed on heads for the second time this evening. If it had come up tails, he would have ended up giving the chocolates he bought to his mother. This time when he leaves for the club, he will take his car, so he won't be stranded again. He's glad that events turned out the way they did the last time, because it gave him the opportunity to go home with an enchanting young woman, who turned his world upside down.

When Guy finally arrives home, he parks his car in the driveway and opens the front door to his two-story luxury home. He hasn't completely given up on the idea of him and Valerie becoming some sort of odd couple, even though he knows that their relationship will never be a traditional one. However, that's what intrigues him about the whole idea of being with her. Guy relishes the idea of having a steamy love affair but wishes it will last more than just a couple of weeks.

This is really going to be a challenge. Valerie has tried her best not to allow me to get too close to her, so far. What I need is a good plan that entices her to slowly change her mind and stay with me.

After climbing the stairs to his bedroom, Guy gets undressed and prepares to take a shower. He notices the scars which are still prominent on his chest and side, from the night when he and Valerie had passionate sex. It makes him wonder for a moment how much more physical discomfort he must endure to keep Valerie interested. Just as Guy is about to step into the shower, he suddenly hears his doorbell ring.

Merde! What terrible timing. I wonder who that could be.

VI.   Return to Paradise

"Who is it?" Guy yells, as he hurriedly ties his robe around his waist and rushes to see who's ringing the bell.

He opens the door and sees a delivery boy standing on his porch with a small package under his arm.

"Delivery for Monsieur Guy Martin," the boy says.

Now what the hell could this be, I wonder?

"Merci."

Guy signs for the package, tips the delivery boy, and then takes it inside. He looks for the name of the sender on the box, which reads…

Sender: Valerie Fontaine

So, that's her last name, but how did she find my address? I suppose she could have looked it up in the book. I told her the area where I live and my last name. Still, this is a surprise.

Guy looks for some scissors to cut through the tape to open the box. He removes the lid and pulls back some hot pink tissue paper to discover its contents. Inside, lies a pair of yellow laced panties, scented with Grand Amour perfume, a pink rose, and a greeting card with his name on it. Guy opens the card and reads the hand-written note that's inside.

Guy, you are cordially invited to join me as my guest at Le Théâtre Coquette for another thrilling evening at midnight. Regards, Valerie

This is the first message Guy has received from Valerie since they parted ways at the train station in Courbevoie.

Wow! I never expected anything like this! I wonder if she thought that I might not go to the club tonight. She probably expects that I can't refuse her now. She's not wrong, but I already planned on going anyway, especially since my lucky coin came up in her favor. I guess this little gesture was just an insurance ploy on her part. Frankly, I didn't think she cared one way or the other, but now I can see she's still interested in me. I better finish getting ready. I still have plenty of time.

Guy picks up the rose and smells its fragrance. Then, he lifts Valerie's panties and brings them close to his face and inhales the tantalizing perfume, which has been strategically sprayed on the fabric. The two scents mixed have an intoxicating effect on his subconscious mind. Closing his eyes, Guy envisions Valerie and him having sex, which caused him to become excited. This is exactly the reaction Valerie wanted Guy to experience with her invitation. At this moment, all thoughts of Gabrielle have vanished from his conscious mind.

Guy heads to his bedroom closet to choose some clothes for the evening. He doesn't want to wear a tie this time, but he still needs to dress nicely. Guy chooses a white, button-down, monogrammed shirt, sans cufflinks, a pair of grey Pierre Cardin dress pants and a pair of black, wingtip shoes. Next, he pulls a black velvet sport coat out of his closet to finish the ensemble. Before getting dressed, Guy splashes his face with a little Christian Dior 'Sauvage' cologne.

That should do it, Guy thinks, as he prepares for his next adventure.

He feels invigorated, but at the same time, he's also still a bit nervous about seeing Valerie again. As he dresses, his thoughts are squarely centered around this provocative nightclub dancer he recently met. He can't imagine what she has in store for him tonight, but he can't wait to find out and watch her perform. He's beginning to feel like a young man on a first date, but he knows that Valerie is not a naive teenager. She's a master manipulator – a seductress of the first order, as well as a bit of a control freak, with emphasis on both the words control and freak. He believes that her nickname 'Dragon Princess,' suits her perfectly because she has an aura of danger about her, and commands attention with her sex appeal and charismatic personality.

Guy leaves his present, along with the note in full display on his bed. He finds his car keys, grabs the box of chocolates, and walks outside to his car. He uses his remote start to warm up the Renault before sliding into the bone-colored leather seat behind the steering wheel. In the next minute, he speeds away with great anticipation, on his way to Le Théâtre Coquette. Twenty minutes later, Guy arrives in front of the club, close to midnight. He leaves the engine running and opens his car door, handing his keys to the valet.

"Merci, monsieur," says Guy.

"Je vous en prie – You're welcome," the valet replies.

Guy ascends the steps toward the red steel doors and enters the nightclub, where Valerie awaits his arrival.

"Bonsoir, monsieur. Welcome back to Le Théâtre Coquette, says Madame Blanche, in greeting."

"Merci, madame. It's nice to be back."

Guy walks over to the coat-check girl and asks if she has a message from Valerie for him.

"Your name, monsieur?" asks the girl.

"Guy Martin," he replies.

"Oui, voila – Yes, here you are," she says.

The coat-check girl hands Guy an envelope with his name on it. He opens it and reads the contents.

Guy, if you are reading this note, it means that you have received my present and have arrived for our date at the club. Please enter the stage door and ask the hostess to seat you at the table that I have reserved for you. I should be on stage at approximately 12:15 am. Valerie

Guy finds the hostess after entering the entertainment lounge. She's an enchanting young Chinese woman with long black licorice-colored hair, which hangs past her waistline. She's wearing a red and gold silk dress, pearl earrings, a circular jade necklace, and a plethora of gold bracelets on her wrists. Guy whispers in her ear and asks to be seated. She smiles and escorts him to his table, situated in the center of the room.

"Enjoy the show," says the hostess.

"Merci, mademoiselle," Guy replies.

The stage is dark for the moment with only the candlelight on the tables illuminating the room. In the corner of the theatre, there is a female musician playing 'Claire de lune' on an ivory grand piano, in spotlight. She's wearing a long white tuxedo jacket, garnished with a red carnation, a black lace bustier, white matching pants, and black stilettos. She has fire-red, frizzy hair, which nests inside a black bowler chapeau. Her face is painted with an excessive amount of makeup. Silver, spiral-shaped earrings shimmer and sparkle, as they catch the light and draw attention to her devilish smile.

A second spotlight projects onto a silver disco ball, spinning above her head. It surrounds the piano player in a whirlwind of tiny illuminations, dancing in the air. Her lips, coated with rouge, make contact with the microphone, as she begins to sing - 'Sous le Soleil,' by Serge Gainsbourg.

An extremely attractive black waitress in her mid-twenties now appears at Guy's table.

"Bonsoir, monsieur. What can I offer you to drink – champagne perhaps?"

"Non, merci. I'll have a glass of chardonnay and some crackers with brie, s'il vous plaît," Guy replies.

"Tout de suite, monsieur - Right away, sir. Je m'appelle Desirée – My name is Desirée, in case you need anything else this evening."

"Merci," Guy replies.

In just a few minutes, the waitress returns with some wine and cheese, just as the entertainer at the piano finishes her set.

"Voilà – Here you are, monsieur."

"Merci."

"Je vous en prie – You're welcome," Desirée replies.

Another array of light encircles a male violin player in a black tuxedo, standing at the opposite side of the stage. He begins to play a Tango-Romantica, accompanied by the rhythm of the Steinway. As this happens, another spotlight hits center stage, revealing two dancers facing one another. A woman in a red ruby dress, cut very low in front and clinging tightly around her hips, stands with her arms raised, ready to dance. She's young and beautiful with dark hair, done up with a sparkling gold hair clip, which matches her high-heel shoes.

The other figure, dressed as a man, is wearing a black eye-mask, a double-breasted grey suit with a red cravat and black wing-tipped shoes. A vermeil Fedora conceals a plethora of blonde hair beneath the rim. It's not easy to make out the person's identity, however, there is no mistaking who's behind the disguise.

The young lady in red extends her bare leg over her shoulder, as Valerie turns her around like a figurine in a music box, until the two dancers are now hip to hip and cheek to cheek. Their arms extend together toward the audience, as they promenade forward toward the front of the stage. The pair walk together in staccato rhythm, timed perfectly with the brisk strokes of the violin.

At midpoint during their dance, Valerie stands behind her partner, lets down her hair, unzips her dress, and allows it to fall to the floor. The young woman now stands in front of the audience topless, with only a red satin G-string strung around the curves of her hips.

Valerie places the back of her hand on her partner's face, and caresses her cheek delicately, slowly moving it down her neck to her breasts. The brunette reactively places her hand over her partner's and twirls away, until their eyes meet again, standing across from one another. Then, Valerie draws her back in and dips her, holding one hand underneath the crescent of her back. As the brunette returns to an upright position, the couple begins to move sharply, twisting and turning across the stage to the rhythm of the tango.

The Dragon Princess is in full command of the dance, as the adoring crowd looks on with enthusiasm. Guy is in a state of shock, as he continues to follow the duet's forceful movements. He sips his wine with cautious trepidation, as if he knew it was laced with poison.

Valerie and her partner now bring their movements to a halt, centerstage. The dark-haired woman raises her knee and leans into Valerie's body, placing her hands around her neck. They embrace, just as the violin and piano go silent and the spotlights go dark.

Roars of applause ensue as club patrons spring to their feet, clapping enthusiastically as the house lights come back up. Valerie and her dance partner strut forward, hand in hand to take a bow. Roses become airborne, filling the stage with a myriad of fragrant flowers. Valerie removes her Fedora and allows her silvery blonde hair to cascade from its hiding place, revealing her gender and identity. The applause only grows louder.

Before leaving the stage, Valerie and her partner kiss each other once again, as the audience continues to cheer in approval. Gradually, the applause subsides as the lights fade to black, and the pair disappear in darkness behind the curtain.

The spotlights come alive again, returning their attention to the piano and violin players. They begin to play 'Ne Me Quitté Pas' – 'Don't leave Me' by Edith Piaf before the next act takes the stage.

Guy feels a little off balance after seeing the object of his desire dressed in men's clothing. He wasn't mentally prepared for this type of Avant Garde exhibition. He begins to question his attraction to Valerie, even though he knows this was just a show deliberately designed to be provocative.

During the dance, Guy was more confused than aroused. His curiosity had still been tweaked. Even though Valerie was dressed as a man, he still knew that it was her behind the mask and under the Fedora. What he didn't expect was to find the two women dancing together - stimulating. The audience clearly loved it, so he feels a little ridiculous for not having the same level of enthusiasm.

Guy's sexual instincts initially lured his attention to the brunette on stage in the scarlet dress. However, because he recognized Valerie in her new role, he felt compelled to keep his eyes on her, instead of her nearly naked partner. It presented Guy with an intriguing dichotomy - one which he doesn't feel comfortable with. He sips his wine and tries to make sense of what he has just seen.

Minutes later, Valerie appears from the side stage door in the dark. She's dressed in a low-cut pearl white jumper encircled by a Greek-style belt. She has on a matching gold choker and a bracelet in the shape of a serpent with emeralds for eyes. The outfit is finished with a shiny pair of gold platform shoes with straps that wind around her calves, just below her knees.

Guy rises as Valerie approaches his table. She greets him by kissing him on both cheeks before sitting down.

"Bonsoir Guy, c'est bien te voir – Hello Guy, it's good to see you! I'm delighted that you made it on time for my performance!" says Valerie.

"C'était mon plaisir - It's been my pleasure. Apparently, you had doubts that I would come tonight because I received a little reminder from you," Guy replies.

"Un petit cadeau, oui. J'espère que tu l'as aimée? A little gift, yes. I hope you liked it. Well then, how did you enjoy my second surprise?"

"Honestly, it was equally unexpected."

"Is that a compliment?"

"I'm still trying to decide. Don't get me wrong Valerie, your skill is unparalleled. You were brilliant, truly mesmerizing. I've never seen a better entertainer at a nightclub before in my life. However, I must admit, the fact that you were dressed as a man was a little unsettling."

"That was the most fun part! I knew it would catch you off your guard, which is why I did it. Usually, my colleague plays the role of the man, but I asked her to switch with me for your benefit. I anticipated you having this reaction, so I deliberately set it up just to tease you. I had so much fun tonight playing a different role. I was hoping that you would be open-minded and enjoy my little trick. I'm sorry if you didn't appreciate my little trick."

Valerie reaches inside her purse and pulls out her cigarette case. She puts one of the fags in her mouth and signals Guy to light it for her. Once again, he fumbles clumsily around in his pockets, searching for his lighter, but ultimately gets the job done.

"Merci," says Valerie, as she blows her first puff of smoke in the air.

"Honestly, Valerie, I don't know how I'm supposed to feel or respond. If you were trying to mess with my head again, then you succeeded. On the other hand, if you're asking me if I was entertained, I would have to say - yes. Your role in this performance was just unexpected, that's all."

"Oh Guy, don't be such a prude! Would you rather have me standing completely naked in front of all those men drooling in their seats, wishing they could have sex with me? Instead, all their eyes were on Bianca tonight. Most men other than you, barely noticed me tonight. I thought I was doing you a little favor."

"Well, most nights, you are the center of attention, aren't you?"

"Oui, but this was one less time because I knew you'd be here watching. To be honest, even though I decided to tease you, I wanted you to feel more comfortable. So, I left my clothes on, knowing that you could always have a private dance some other time."

Guy laughs.

"Is that what you were doing – making me feel more comfortable? To be honest, I'm not sure how I would have felt if you had played the role of the female and stripped naked again in front of a room full of horny men and women. However, that's what I was expecting. That's what made it all so confusing."

"Je t'ai compris – I understand. However, as long as you and the other guests were entertained, that's all that matters. I'm just glad you came tonight to see me. How did you like my partner, Bianca? She's hot, right? I bet you wish you could have both of us in bed, don't you?"

"If you want my honest opinion, I didn't pay too much attention to her, because I was too busy watching you. If you are still fishing for compliments, here's one you can take to the bank. I can't imagine being capable of handling both you and her at the same time because you are more than a handful, all by yourself. Do I think your partner is attractive? Oui, I suppose she is of course. Elle est très belle - She's very beautiful."

"Ha! Merci, mon chéri – Thank you, my dear. However, I think you are just trying to dig yourself out of the hole you've been making for yourself. Well, if you change your mind, I'm sure I can arrange a ménage à trois. If that happens, I promise that you will play the role of the man and I will play the role of the woman. You can have Bianca play whatever role you'd like her to," Valerie says, smiling devilishly.

"You know Valerie, sometimes I wonder if I'm not the one entertaining you, instead of the other way around."

"That's the fun part, Guy - figuring it out - isn't it?"

"Well, I do think that you are the one having most of the fun between the two of us."

"Do you really believe so?" asks Valerie, facetiously, looking at Guy out of the corners of her eyes.

"Well, I haven't completely decided yet. However, I have a strange feeling that I'm going to find out sooner than later," Guy replies, playfully.

Valerie laughs.

"I can guarantee only one thing, mon chéri – my dear."

"What's that?"

"That you won't be bored when you are with me, unlike how you were with your former girlfriend."

Guy grimaces and looks at Valerie disapprovingly. He wasn't prepared for that jab at his relationship with Gabrielle.

Hmm, the dragon's talons are showing. Do I detect a little jealousy?

"Forgive me Valerie; I still haven't offered you something to drink. Waitress! What would you like?"

"I'll take a whisky on the rocks."

"What, no champagne?"

"Don't be cute, Guy."

"I can't help it."

Valerie smiles, as the waitress returns to their table.

"What can I offer you?" asks Desirée.

"Bourbon, avec glaçons, s'il vous plaît – Bourbon with ice please," Valerie replies.

"Tout de suite, mademoiselle – Right away, miss."

"Merci," Valerie replies.

As Desirée leaves their table, the next act takes the stage. Guy is undistracted by the presence of six women in top hats, canes, and fishnet stockings, dancing to 'Life is a Cabaret.' Clearly, a number for American and British tourists. His attention remains focused entirely on Valerie.

"Alors, Guy, dis moi – So, Guy, tell me - Did you really like my initial surprise for you?"

"You mean your creative invitation?"

"Oui, bien sûr – Yes, of course."

"I found it to be quite provocative and compelling. Did you really think that I might not have come to see you tonight?"

"Peut-être – Maybe. I thought that there was a slight chance that you wouldn't come, so I just wanted to provide you with a spicy enticement."

"Well, it worked. However, I can't honestly tell you that I didn't have trouble deciding whether to come tonight, so I flipped my lucky coin and let fate make the choice. The toss turned up in your favor, however, I admit that I was still debating the question in my mind, until I received your unique invitation. I must give you a lot of credit for your ingenuity."

Valerie smiles with great satisfaction.

"From my point of view, I'd say the coin toss turned out in your favor, as well," Valerie replies, as she gives him a suggestive wink.

"Voila – Here you are," says Desirée, as she returns to their table with Valerie's drink.

"Merci," Valerie replies.

"Santé – To your health," says Guy.

"A la bonne fortune," Valerie replies, as the two lovers touch their glasses together.

Valerie stares into Guy's eyes, in an attempt to read what's on his mind, as they both take sips of their drinks.

"Speaking of gifts, I almost forgot, I have one for you too!" exclaims Guy.

"Vraiment, c'est très gentil – Really, that's very kind!" Valerie replies, excitedly. "Qu'est-ce que c'est - What is it?"

"Tu verras; ouvrez-le - You'll see; open it."

Valerie unties the crimson bow, wrapped around the little snow-white box, and removes the lid. She carefully pulls back the turquoise tissue paper and sees the fine dark chocolates inside.

"Guy, tu es si doux. Merci, mon chéri - you are so sweet! Thank you, my dear."

"C'est rien - It's nothing."

Valerie gives Guy a sensuous kiss on his lips, then whispers something provocative in his ear.

"You like what you see?" asks Valerie, as she changes her gaze to the performers onstage.

Valerie is tempting Guy to take his eyes off her for even just a moment, but he doesn't dare take the bait.

"I love what I see right in front of me," says Guy, as he stares into her eyes.

This is exactly the reaction Valerie is hoping for.

Suddenly, the side door to the stage opens again and the 23-year-old bombshell, who danced with Valerie, walks gracefully toward Guy's table. She's dressed in a sheer black top, a short, clingy black leather skirt, and knee-high boots. She kisses Valerie on both cheeks before greeting Guy with the same display of affection. He can't help but inhale her intoxicating Black Opium perfume she's wearing. It causes him to pause for a moment to take in the aroma.

"Bonsoir, à tous – Good evening, everyone. May I join you?"

"Oui, bien sûr – Yes, of course, Guy replies," as Valerie carefully watches his reaction to her colleague.

She deliberately sits down opposite Valerie, so that Guy is sandwiched in between the two of them.

"Guy, Je te présente ma belle amie … Bianca Dubois - May I introduce to you my beautiful friend..."

"Enchanté – It's nice to meet you," says Guy.

"Toi aussi – You also," Bianca replies.

"May I offer you a drink?" asks Guy.

"Oui, merci – Yes, thank you."

"Serveuse - Waitress!" says Guy.

Desirée quickly returns to the trio's table, once again.

"Oui, may I get something else for you?"

"A Gin Martini and make it dirty, s'il vous plaît – please," says Bianca.

"Tout de suite, mademoiselle – Right away, miss."

Bianca looks at Guy and smiles, then glances at Valerie. She turns her head toward Guy and looks him square in the eyes, as Valerie continues to monitor his involuntary reactions.

"So, Guy, Valerie tells me so many good things about you."

Guy didn't expect anyone else to be joining them this evening. So once again, he feels a little off balance with Bianca sitting next to him. He wonders if this is just another one of Valerie's pre-conceived escapades for her own amusement. Guy is beginning to realize that he's out of his league when it comes to the art of manipulation.

"What kind of things has she said about me?" asks Guy.

"Oh, that you are a perfect gentleman, thoughtful, generous, as well as an exceptional lover," Bianca replies, displaying a suggestive grin.

"She said that, did she?" Guy says, knowing that he's probably being played.

He glances over at Valerie suspiciously. She smiles back at him with a guilty expression, rubbing his calf with her bare foot under the table to reassure him.

"Oui, bien sûr – Yes, of course. Is it not a compliment?" asks Bianca, innocently.

"Oui, but I just didn't expect that Valerie and my after-hours tryst last weekend would become the subject of a discussion," Guy replies, blushing with embarrassment.

"N'inquiète pas - Don't worry, I will keep your secret," says Bianca, winking at Valerie. "I'm just trying to figure out whether my good friend here has been honest with me about how sexy a man you are."

Guy is now very embarrassed by Bianca's comment. He's feeling more uncomfortable by the minute. His face is visibly flushed. He looks over at Valerie to try to solicit another supportive gesture from her. However, he already realizes that whatever is going on, must be a bit of mischief of her own design.

Desirée returns with Bianca's drink and sets it in front of her.

"Merci," says Bianca.

"Valerie, what have you been telling this poor, innocent woman about me?"

"Seulement, la verité, mon amour – Only, the truth, my love - and Bianca is neither poor nor innocent."

"Somehow, I doubt that what you've been telling her about me has anything to do with the truth," says Guy, as both women look at each other and smile, fiendishly.

"Here's to fun, and adventure," Bianca says, as she makes a toast, and the three of them lift their glasses. Bianca rubs her free hand along Guy's knee up to his inner thigh, being deliberately provocative, smiling and winking at him, flirtatiously.

Valerie, in fact, did make previous arrangements with Bianca to come to their table with instructions as to how to behave. She is deliberately using her friend to continue to play with Guy's mind and emotions. Bianca understands Valerie's intentions very well. She is all too willing to play along and participate in her game of cat and mouse.

Underneath it all, Valerie does like Guy very much, but she doesn't know how to behave in a normal adult relationship. She's used to playing games and not getting involved emotionally. Her talents lie in being manipulative and seductive. She uses these gifts and sexual allure whenever she's bored with daily life. Men to her are merely pawns on a chess board to be used for her pleasure and discarded whenever necessary.

At least half an hour passes, as more acts come and go on stage. A saxophone player accompanies the piano, as the stage lights go dark once again for another brief intermission.

The newly formed trio share a cheese and charcuterie plate while they sip their drinks. Bianca continues to beguile and tease Guy, until Valerie interrupts.

"Guy, I have something to show you upstairs. Why don't you come with Bianca and I, and we will give you a private tour of our establishment."

Guy stares Valerie in the eyes and tries to read her poker face.

What mischief can she be up to now? Guy wonders.

The three of them quickly finish their drinks before leaving the entertainment lounge together, in haste. Outside the lounge, just before the entrance, there is an elevator which can only be accessed by a special keycard. Valerie removes a gold metallic card from her purse and inserts it into a slot next to the elevator door. The doors open and Valerie, Bianca, and Guy step inside. She inserts the card into another slot inside the elevator and presses a red button, which takes them to the top floor.

As the elevator doors close, Valerie glances over at Bianca and smiles, sinfully. Bianca raises her eyes and smiles back. Guy catches the exchange and begins to feel his level of anxiety building again. Not knowing what's going to happen next is exciting, but also a little disconcerting.

A minute later, they arrive on the third floor. The doors begin to open slowly, as Valerie leads the way onto the landing, followed by Bianca and the Guy. They walk down the corridor to the end of the hallway where Valerie, once again, uses her passkey to open one of the locked doors. As Guy enters the room, Bianca switches on the lights to another large entertainment lounge, meant for private celebrations. It's also used for important parties for influential businessmen, famous entertainers, and politicians.

A shiny black grand piano sits in the corner of the room, flanked by large bay windows, accented by a black and white Italian marble floor. There's a bar off to the side with a stereo system on the shelf behind it. Several comfortable chairs and tables are scattered throughout the space for relaxation and conversation. There's also a large dance floor in front of an oval-shaped stage, which supports a live band - far grander than the stage Valerie and Bianca perform on, downstairs.

"Wow, this is quite impressive!" says Guy.

"It's our own little secret hiding place away from our audience. We come up here when we want to relax and escape the prying eyes of the public. Sometimes we entertain important guests here, but it's also for us to entertain ourselves and our friends."

"Very nice!" Guy replies. "What's in the other rooms along the hallway?"

"Be patient, Guy. I'll show you the other rooms in just a few minutes. How about we do a few shots of tequila first?" says Valerie.

"I'm up for that!" Bianca replies.

"Guy, how about you?"

"I have my car here tonight, so maybe just one."

"Don't be silly! Bianca and I will take good care of you. You'll have nothing to worry about."

Bianca pops behind the bar and pours the shots, while Valerie pulls out a few limes from the mini-fridge and begins to slice them. She also finds a saltshaker and an empty bottle from one of the cabinets on the wall. The game is just getting started.

"Alors, here's how we're going to do this," Valerie announces. "We're going to spin this bottle, one at a time, and the person it points to will drink the first shot. The spinner must then put a little salt on their neck, and the drinker must lick the salt from the spinner's neck. Then, the person who takes the shot must suck the lime from the teeth of the last person. Comprenez – Do you understand?"

"Oui," says Guy, looking a little uncomfortable again.

"Guy, since you're our guest, you can spin the bottle first," says Valerie.

Guy gives the bottle a twirl on the counter. As its momentum begins to dissipate, it points to Bianca, who turns her head toward Valerie and smiles. Bianca picks up the shot glass to drink, just as Guy shakes a little salt on his neck. The moment Bianca throws back the tequila in her throat, Valerie places one of the lime slices in her mouth.

71

Bianca leans in towards Guy and proceeds to lick the salt off his neck, just after she places the shot glass on the table.

Guy picks up the scent of her perfume again, as she caresses his neckline with her tongue. He tilts his head back a little more, fully engaged in the game, as he feels Bianca's tongue sliding up and down against his flesh.

Guy is noticeably aroused. Valerie watches the two of them anxiously with a keen, penetrating stare. Next, Bianca turns toward Valerie to suck the lime from her mouth. Valerie's lips open wider, as Bianca sinks her teeth into the fruit. The game continues to unfold, as the two female dancers embrace for Guy's and their pleasure.

This is nothing like what I experienced before at college parties, Guy thinks to himself.

"It's your turn," Valerie says to Bianca.

Bianca grips and spins the glass bottle, until it gradually slows down and points toward Valerie. The Dragon Princess pours another shot of tequila, as Bianca shakes the salt underneath her chin. Guy plucks another lime from the cutting board and places it in his mouth, waiting for Valeri's kiss.

"Bottoms up," says Valerie, as she swallows the contents in the shot glass, then gently grabs Bianca behind her hair and plants her rouge-colored lips against her neck. Valerie moves her wet tongue over the salt, tickling Bianca's soft white skin to a point where she flinches with delight.

Valerie can't wait to see Guy's reaction, after she's done tasting Bianca's flesh. She stares at him for just a moment, then with lightning speed, she bites the lime in his mouth. When Guy finally opens his eyes, he sees Bianca licking her upper lip. She can't help but notice there is more than anticipation growing in the room.

It's Valerie's turn to spin the bottle. After she lets it whirl, it ends up pointing to Guy, who by now is extremely turned on. He pours another shot and snaps his head back, letting the alcohol burn in his throat. Valerie awaits his open mouth over her neck, while Bianca shoves a lime between her teeth. When Guy approaches Bianca, she encircles his neck with her right arms and pulls his lips toward hers until the lime disappears entirely.

Just to make the game more interesting, Bianca slides her left hand below Guy's belt. Valerie's eyes widen with desire, as she watches her friend seduce her new playmate. Guy feels the heat from the fire burning in the room. He's now ready for almost anything conjured up by Valerie's devious scheme.

Guy can no longer resist the temptation at the table. This luscious dinner Valerie has planned for the evening is only just beginning to be served. This nouveau threesome has already had their appetizers downstairs, and now it's time for the soup du jour. Soon, the main course will be served, along with a mouthwatering dessert. Valerie has spared no expense setting the table for what she hopes will be a delicious ménage à trois. All three of them are extremely aroused and ready to act on their carnal proclivities.

Guy is just beginning to understand that he is the main character in a three-act play, produced, directed, and acted by the Dragon Princess herself. He is now in the mood to tear off both these women's clothing. Valerie has successfully enticed Guy into a sexual frenzy. However, she deliberately interrupts the mood to prolong Guy's tension and to continue to screw with his mind first.

"Okay, that's enough for now," Valerie announces.

Guy glances over at Bianca, as if to lodge a protest. She shrugs her shoulders and lifts her eyebrows, as if to say – *Don't look at me, this isn't my game we're playing.*

Valerie holds open the door and escorts her lover and her partner in crime out of the room, before turning off the lights. Guy and Bianca are both noticeably frustrated and perplexed, as they look at each other in bewilderment. The Dragon Princess leads her victims to another door and unlocks it with her gold passkey, then flips on the lights.

"This is our costume room Guy, where all our outfits are made. We have our own in-house staff, who design, create, and repair everything we wear onstage. Many of our guests are regulars and we simply can't be seen in the same costumes, week after week. Our routines must change frequently or else our regular guests will become bored."

Guy peeks his head inside to witness a room filled with many colorful and sexy outfits and accessories: hats, costume jewelry, garter belts, stockings, bustiers, corsets, elegant gowns, tuxedos, as well as various types of beads, rhinestones, and glitter. There are at least six tables with sewing machines and thread, where seamstresses work on the showgirls' and male performers' outfits.

"I know that it's not particularly exciting, however, this is what's behind door number two. Door number three is Madame Blanche's office, door number four is just a bathroom and door number five is just a room full of cleaning supplies, so I won't bother opening those doors. However, I think you might like what's behind door number six. It's at the opposite end of the hallway. Come I'll show you," says Valerie.

Guy glances over at Bianca, who gives him a suggestive smile. He is a little wary of what Valerie has in store for them next, but he's willing to continue playing along for now. Despite the premature ending to Valerie's game of foreplay, Guy and Bianca are still in a state of heightened arousal. As the trio approaches the last door, Valerie gets ready to insert her keycard, and gives Guy a tantalizing look.

"Are you ready for this? Close your eyes!" Valerie demands.

Guy obeys, but just at that moment, the elevator doors open. He opens his eyes to see who's coming. Valerie pauses for a moment, as an older woman steps out of the elevator and enters the corridor.

"Valerie! I have been looking all over for you!" shouts Madame Blanche.

"Je suis désolé, madame – I'm sorry, madam. Bianca and I have just been giving Guy a little private tour of the club."

"I know exactly what you and Bianca have been giving our guest. We don't give away our services at Le Théâtre Coquette for free, you know. Anyway, Valerie, I need you for the final act. The performer who was supposed to be in the finalé has fallen ill. You will have to take her place. Monsieur Martin can return with Bianca to his table where they can enjoy one last drink - comprenez - understood?"

"Oui, madame," Valerie replies.

"Maintenant, allez – y, tout de suite – Now, get going, immediately!" Blanche demands.

The three of them scurry into the elevator and descend to the stage floor. Valerie hurries to change for the final performance of the night, while Guy and Bianca take their seats. Desirée returns to take their final drink orders, as the piano player keys one last melody between acts – New York, New York, by Frank Sinatra. After the song ends, the audience begins to applaud, until the spotlight closes over the pianist, and the theatre goes black and silent once more.

While waiting in the dark, Bianca returns her hand to Guy's knee and asks him a provocative question.

"So, Guy, how did you like playing Valerie's little game of shots? Did you have a good time?"

Guy squirms in his chair, fearful of how far up Bianca's hand will travel.

"Well, I have played drinking games before in college, but nothing quite like that one. It was unexpected, like everything else with Valerie, however I must confess – I enjoyed playing with both of you."

"I'm only sorry that we didn't get to finish. Valerie had a big surprise planned for you in the last room. I guarantee you would have enjoyed it. She wanted to take us around the world and back again."

"So, you're saying this wasn't an impromptu tour, after all. Valerie had set that all up in advance?" says Guy.

"Oui, I must confess," Bianca replies, apologetically.

Guy is still aware of Bianca's hand movements, which are reaching further up his thigh, under the table. Suddenly, he feels a little squeeze in his crotch area and flinches. He looks Bianca in her eyes, as if to ask... *Are we still playing Valerie's game with me?*

"What was in that last room that Valerie was about to show me?" asks Guy, trying to distract Bianca's attention from her target for a moment.

"It's not my place to tell you. Anyway, the finalé is about to start, so pay attention. You won't want to miss it!"

VII.   Fire & Ice

Viridescent laser lights flash from multiple points on the stage, as psychedelic music starts to emanate from the speakers around the theatre. Water from fountains surrounding the stage springs to life with rainbow colors and begins to bounce with jubilation. A beam of amber light projects down from the ceiling forming a cone, encircling center stage and mist from fog machines blankets the floor. A figure dressed in purple satin with wavy blonde hair and fuchsia knee-high boots rises from below the surface, until she is encased in the neon beam of light.

As Valerie turns to face the audience, the cone vanishes, and she is hit with a spotlight. Lasers and fountains continue to produce special effects all around her. More lights spring to life, revealing a live band, which begins to play the introduction to 'Les Cris de L'âme – 'The Crisis of the Soul,' by Jeanne Mas.

The silver ball creates a whirlwind of lights which fly in circles around the room, producing a tornado effect. Valerie struts forward through the fog and laser lights and grasps the microphone, which is standing at the front of the stage.

"She's going to sing?" Guy asks, astonished.

"Regards! – Watch!" Bianca replies, as Valerie begins to belt out the lyrics with intensity.

"Wow! I didn't know she could sing like that."

"There are many things you still don't know about Valerie."

Six chorus girls dressed in rhinestone laced bodysuits appear from the sides of the stage and join in the chorus. Valerie lifts the microphone off its stand and begins to move around the stage. She reaches out with one hand to the predominantly male audience, inviting them to stand up and clap along with the beat.

"She is amazing!" Guy exclaims.

"You have only scratched the surface. And, if you ever hurt her – I'll kill you!" says Bianca, staring at Guy with daggers in her eyes.

She abruptly removes her hand from Guy's thigh. Her warm flirtatious nature suddenly turns cold and takes on an aggressive posture.

"I think you have it backwards. It's Valerie who is the dangerous one - not me," Guy says.

Bianca looks up at Guy with some measure of distrust. He takes a large sip from his drink, feeling suddenly threatened.

I wonder if she meant what she said, literally?

At the end of the song, Valerie returns the microphone to its stand and saunters back to center stage, as the instrumental music gradually grows fainter. The moment the spotlight closes, the cone of laser light reappears, and Valerie reenters the beam. Mist fills the stage and engulfs her body once again. The water fountains begin to dissipate and a blast of pyrotechnics fires through the air with a loud bang and bright light. At that same moment, the floor gives way and Valerie descends out of sight, leaving laser lights in a smoke-filled room behind.

The audience springs to their feet applauding wildly, as the house lights come back up. Roses once again, are hurled through the air and cover the stage floor. Whistles from the audience pierce the background noise, as the fog dissipates. As the air clears, Valerie returns to the stage from behind the curtain to take her final bow.

"Incroyable - Unbelievable!" Guy exclaims, as he rises to his feet, looking at Bianca, who is now smiling with pride.

"Oui, Valerie is exceptionally talented, and Madame Blanche knows it, which is why she cuts her a lot of slack around here."

"I can see why."

"You know Guy, Valerie is not just some showgirl floozie and this is not some sleazy strip club. This is a very classy establishment, and it attracts the richest and most important clients in Paris. Valerie is an extremely gifted performer and a very intelligent woman. She likes to live her life in a simple manner. But, make no mistake – she is not an ordinary woman. Elle est exceptionnelle - She is exceptional! So, don't underestimate her and don't take her for granted. If you don't show her that you're worthy, she will eat you alive and pick her teeth with your bones."

Guy looks at Bianca, even more intimidated than ever.

"Je te comprends – I understand you," Guy replies, nervously.

"Ask for the bill. I'm going to go talk to Valerie in the dressing room, while she gets changed. I will tell her to meet you out in the lobby. I won't be joining you later, but it was enchanting meeting you, Guy. I'm sure our paths will cross again."

Bianca kisses Guy on both cheeks, just to reassure him that he's not her enemy.

"Le plaisir était pour moi - The pleasure was all mine," Guy replies. "Jusqu'a la prochaine fois; bonne soirée - Until the next time; have a good evening."

As Bianca rises and heads to the dressing room, Guy signals Desirée to bring the bill. After paying, he heads to the lobby to wait for Valerie. Bianca is greeting her friend in the dressing room and tells her how much she enjoyed her performance.

"That was really wonderful!" says Bianca, as she kisses Valerie.

"Merci, ma belle amie – Thank you, my beautiful friend," Valerie replies, as she changes her outfit. She slips into a tight-fitting, green satin cocktail dress with gold, open-toe heels.

"I told Guy to wait for you in the lobby."

"You won't be joining us?" asks Valerie, a little disappointed.

"No dear, I think you should spend time with Guy alone tonight. I think we gave him enough to absorb for one evening – don't you think?"

"Perhaps you're right."

"Allez, au revoir, bonne soirée – goodbye, goodnight," says Bianca, as she kisses Valerie again.

"Ciao, mon amie; à la prochaine fois – Goodbye, my friend; until next time."

When Valerie finishes dressing, she walks toward the entrance to meet Guy. As she passes through the lobby doors, she sees several guests still making their way to the exit and Guy, who is waiting patiently for her. He smiles as she approaches. She feels slightly embarrassed by Guy's expression and blushes. He gives her a look of admiration and pride. It makes her feel similar to when she used to come home from school with a good grade and her father gushed over her success.

Valerie kisses Guy and motions for him to escort her to the door.

"You were really spectacular tonight," says Guy.

Valerie smiles.

"Merci," I'm glad you enjoyed my performance more this time."

"I had no idea that you could sing like that. You are full of surprises."

"Guy, I'm a little hungry, will you take me to my favorite after-hours restaurant?"

"Sure, which one is that?"

"Maxim's! It's near la Place de la Concorde on le rue Royal.

"Oui, Je le connais – Yes, I'm familiar with it, but it's quite impossible to get a reservation at this time."

"N'inquiète pas – Don't worry. I already called ahead. I know the manager."

"Why doesn't that surprise me? Can you leave your motorbike here for tonight so we can drive together?"

"Oui - Yes, it's in a safe place. I can take the train to work tomorrow evening. I guessed that you would come tonight, but just in case, I rode my bike to be sure I wouldn't get stranded. I didn't want to be stuck here needing to catch a ride off some stranger, like some kind of loser," says Valerie, grinning, as she glances at Guy, reminding him of his mistake.

"Yeah, who would do such a thing, I wonder?" Guy replies laughing.

"Allons-y, alors. Es-tu prêt? – Let's go then, are you ready?" asks Valerie.

"Oui," Guy replies.

Guy gives his valet ticket to the attendant who brings his car around for him. He holds the door open for Valerie, who makes herself comfortable in the passenger seat. Guy tips the valet, slides behind the wheel and heads toward Maxim's, still excited by the events of the evening.

"So, Guy, did you miss me this past week?" asks Valerie.

"Oui, but I couldn't call you because you still haven't given me your phone number."

"Oui, je sais; Je suis désolé – Yes, I know; I'm sorry. I will keep my promise since you kept yours. You will have it at the restaurant - n'inquiète pas – don't worry."

"So, where did you learn to sing like that?"

"J'ai participé à L'Ecole de Beaux-Arts de Paris – I attended the School of Fine Arts in Paris, where I learned to develop all of my artistic talents."

"Intéressant – Interesting."

"That's an expensive institution."

"Oui, but I earned a scholarship."

"Formidable - Fantastic!"

"Aren't you going to comment on how I'm choosing to utilize my talents?" asks Valerie, suspicious that Guy doesn't approve of what she's doing for work.

"No, you're an excellent performer. I suppose if you weren't working at that nightclub, I might not have met you. So, I'm grateful for that."

"Ah, oui, c'est vrai – yes, that's true."

"What about painting? What are you doing with that, exactly?"

"If you must know, I work for some people on a private basis. I do some illustrations for myself, but mostly I do contract work for clients by special request. I'm a member of the local artists guild here in Paris and I have sold several of my paintings over the years for a good price. I actually make more money doing that than dancing at the club, but I really enjoy performing more because it's thrilling."

"Is there anything you can't do?"

"Eh bien – Well, I'm not very good at fixing things. In fact, I have a leaky faucet in my bathroom – perhaps you noticed it when you were in there?"

"As a matter of fact - I did, but unfortunately, plumbing and carpentry are not my strengths either."

"Tant pis – Too bad. So, you're just good for sex then."

Guy smiles, while glancing at Valerie.

"Voila - here we are. I'm going to let you out in front of the restaurant and then park the car. I'll meet you inside. Let your friend know we've arrived, okay?"

"Oui, bien sûr – Yes, of course. Antoine will have found us a good table by now."

"What are you waiting for?"

"I'm waiting for you to open the door for me."

"Oh, Je suis désolé – I'm sorry. I just thought since I...Never mind. Un moment, s'il te plaît – one moment, please."

Guy hurries around to the other side to open Valerie's door for her, then offers her his hand. Valerie grabs her purse and steps gracefully onto the pavement with Guy's assistance.

"Merci," says Valerie, smiling.

Having learned his lesson, Guy escorts Valerie to the restaurant entrance, then opens the door for her.

"Merci," says Valerie.

"I'll meet you inside in just a few minutes."

"I will be seated by the time you arrive. Ask the hostess to escort you to our table."

"Okay."

Guy hurries back to the car, which is still running, then looks for a place to park around the corner. Fortunately for Guy, he has a dinner jacket and tie in his trunk for emergencies. He quickly changes his jacket and slips on one of his silk ties. He knows he would never be allowed into a restaurant like this wearing only a sport coat.

"Bonsoir, Antoine - Good evening, Antoine," says Valerie, as she greets her friend, affectionately.

"Ah, bonsoir Valerie; ça va – Good evening, Valerie; how are you doing?" Antoine replies.

"Ça va – I'm doing well."

"You're not here by yourself. Where is your companion?"

"My friend is parking his car. Il s'appelle Guy – His name is Guy. Can you make sure the hostess directs him to our table when he arrives, s'il te plaît – please?"

"Oui, tout à fait – Yes, absolutely!"

Antoine snaps his fingers, and a well-dressed hostess with short light brown hair walks over to escort Valerie to a private table in the corner of the room. After she is seated, the young lady hands her two menus, along with a wine list.

"Merci," says Valerie.

Despite the late hour, the restaurant is filled with regular patrons, politicians, celebrities, and aristocrats, some of whom have been waiting in line for over an hour. They are there to soak in the ambiance at one of the most famous Art-Nouveau staples in Paris.

Maxim's isn't just a place to have a five-star meal - it's the place to be seen by the most influential, upper-class citizens and foreigners, anywhere in Europe. Dignitaries, wealthy businessmen, and movie stars all have come to Maxim's over the years to rub shoulders and to make deals. Very few people can get into Maxim's without a reservation well in advance. The President of France, descendants of Charles de Gaulle, Gérard Depardieu, and Valerie are among those exceptional people, who can arrive at a moment's notice to Maxim's and still be seated promptly.

The origin of Maxim's began when a simple waiter by the name of

Maxime Gaillard, started this venture back in 1893, with the help of a young aristocratic woman by the name of Irma de Montigny. She enticed the most influential names in Europe to come to dine at Paris' latest trendy tavern. It quickly became one of the most famous restaurants in France and became known as "the place to take beautiful dames, but never one's spouse."

Since Maxime's strength was not accounting, he was eventually forced to sell his restaurant to a businessman named Eugene Cornuché, who transformed this modest establishment into an 'Art Nouveau' dining destination.

Maxim's was renovated just in time for the 1900 World's Fair in Paris, during 'La Belle Epoch' - The Golden Age. Later, during WWII, the French bistro fell on hard times once again and the Vaudable family took it under their wing. Ultimately, Maxim's was bought by the fashion icon Pierre Cardin, who transformed the toast of Paris from "a poor man's dream, into a rich man's reality."

At this time, the dinner tables at Maxim's were cloaked in white silk, and the chairs were upholstered with red velvet. The walls, adorned with magnificent 18th and 19th century French and Italian art, created by some of the most famous painters in history. The ceiling is stained glass, the woodwork is solid mahogany, and the floors are made of beautiful black and white Italian marble.

The waiters all wear ivory-colored jackets, bowties, white gloves, and patent leather shoes. Only the finest and freshest ingredients are prepared and served by some of the most renowned chefs in France. There's nothing on the menu that isn't prix-fixe – a set price, nor is there a main course which costs under 500 francs. Also, very few women work at Maxim's, and the ones who do are exceptionally beautiful and highly intelligent.

Nothing is too good or too expensive for Valerie's taste. She demands the best of everything, and if her new love interest couldn't afford her lifestyle, she wouldn't be with him. Guy finally enters the restaurant after a short while and is escorted to Valerie's table.

"I see you are clever enough to have brought a change of clothes with you. At least you are prepared tonight versus the last time," says Valerie.

"Well, I like to be ready for anything, usually. I never know, in my line of work, when I might need a clean shirt, fresh tie or if I'm going to be dragged to some formal dinner party."

"See what you want for supper Guy, because it's getting late and the kitchen will be closed soon," Valerie cautions.

"Okay, since you've already had a chance to look at the menu, why don't you peruse the wine list and choose something for us to drink, while I decide what I want to eat," Guy replies.

"I always order champagne when I come to Maxim's."

"Of course; what was I thinking?"

"It's way past the dinner hour, so as you can see, they only have a late supper menu to choose from."

"Oui, je vois - Yes, and there are only three courses, instead of five. Go ahead and order some champagne, while I finish looking over the menu."

"Garçon – Waiter!" Valerie shouts, to rise above the myriad of voices in the room.

A waiter arrives at their table a moment later.

"How may I be of service, mademoiselle?" asks the waiter.

"I will have a glass of champagne and my companion will have a glass of burgundy, s'il vous plaît – if you please."

"Je vous en prie - My pleasure," says the waiter. "Je m'appelle François – My name is François. I will be back to take your dinner order as soon as I bring your drinks."

"Merci," Valerie replies.

"So, Val, are you going to tell me what you have in mind after we finish eating?"

"What do you mean? You're going to take me home like you promised, right?"

"Oui, bien sûr – Yes, of course, but I want to know if you're planning on having me spend what's left of this night with you?"

"Well, that depends, I guess."

"It depends on what?"

"It depends on Fafa, of course. He was a little traumatized the last time I brought you home," Valerie teases.

"You're joking, right? Fafa and I got on magnificently. I think we've already established a solid, amicable rapport between us."

"Hmm, well, he may have given you that impression, but I know he doesn't trust most men that I bring to my apartment. He sees them as a threat to his position in the house."

Guy laughs.

At the same moment, the waiter returns with their drinks.

"Voila – Here you are," says François, as he pops the cork on the champagne. He pours Guy's wine after filling Valerie's glass.

"What shall we toast to this time?" asks Guy.

"I always toast to good fortune," Valerie replies.

"À la bonne fortune, alors – To good fortune, then."

The couple clink glasses and drink to the future.

"What can I offer you for supper?" asks François.

"I will take the escargots along with some seafood pasta," Valerie replies.

"For the gentleman, what will you take?"

"I will take the onion soup, along with the steak tartare, s'il vous plaît - please," Guy replies.

"Excellent choices, monsieur et mademoiselle. I will return with your appetizers in just a moment."

Valerie smiles as she looks Guy in the eyes and sips her champagne. Both Guy and Valerie know that in any fine French restaurant in Paris, nothing is served in a prompt manner, despite the late hour. It will be at least 15-20 minutes before their appetizers arrive and 30-40 minutes before they will have their main course. If the time was closer to 8:00 pm, it would be at least four hours before anyone would have the chance to ask for the bill. However, since it's so late, service is expedited to some degree.

Guy is in no hurry, and he's not looking forward to sleeping on

Valerie's couch again if that is to be his fate at the end of the day. His back is still a little sore from the first time he slept in her salon.

"Valerie, I'm still curious as to what you had planned to show me inside that last room at your club tonight."

"If I told you, that would spoil the surprise that I had in store for you. It will have to be kept for another time. In any case, the moment is gone for now. You may not experience that little segment of my tour for a while now, unless the opportunity presents itself again sooner than I imagine. You shouldn't worry about it. I will keep you sufficiently entertained in the meantime. Speaking of my unique little tour, how did you enjoy my drinking game?"

Guy blushes.

"Uh…It was amusing, but somehow I think you enjoyed it more because you seem to love putting me in uncomfortable situations."

"Why do you say that?"

"I don't know; maybe because you seem to relish watching people's reactions by shocking them."

"I confess that I enjoy certain types of mind games. People's reactions to provocative situations do amuse me. You must understand that my work is artistic in nature, designed to elicit vibrant responses from my audience. I think it's only fair that when I'm not working, it's other people's turn to entertain me – don't you think?"

"When you put it that way, I can see your point from your perspective."

François returns with their appetizers.

"Voilà, bon appétit!"

"Merci."

"Mmm - This is delicious soup. How do your snails taste?"

"Délicieux, merci – Delicious, thank you."

"So, how do you find Bianca – do you like her?"

"She's very young and beautiful, but she has a sharp tongue, not unlike yours. However, it's you who I'm interested in, especially."

"Oui, bien – Yes, well, I guess that it all depends on what you're looking for exactly – doesn't it? Do you know what that is in your case, Guy?"

"If I'm being honest - not exactly, no. However, I believe that I'm in the process of discovering that very thing for myself, thanks to you."

"Well Guy, I wish you good luck with your search and discovery mission. As for me, I know who I am, what I want, and I know how to get it. I'm perfectly comfortable in my own skin and I don't need anyone to validate me or what I'm doing. If you're looking for validation from me – you can forget it. I don't judge people, nor do I blow smoke up their ass. I either like you or I don't. I'm a very simple woman, who leads a complex life."

"What is it that you want from life, exactly?"

"Well, I want passion, independence, and adventure. I'm not looking for anyone to offer it to me. It's something I want to experience for myself, without obligation. I have told you many times that I am not looking for a romantic relationship, but I like you Guy – that's all. Be glad you're on my good side. I have a bad temper when I'm angry. You don't want to ever see that side of me."

"Oui, Je te comprends – Yes, I understand you. You continue to beat the independence drum and remind me that you have a fierce temper and a free spirit. I hear your message loud and clear. However, I'm curious. Why did you invite me to see you again if you don't want to develop a close relationship with anyone?"

"Tout simplement - Quite simply, I enjoy your company and you're good in bed. C'est tout – That's all."

Guy tries to absorb that statement. He's not quite sure how he feels about it yet.

"I have never been to this restaurant before now. It's quite elegant. I'm aware that it has a rich history and an aristocratic following. To be honest, if I may be impertinent - it's not the kind of place I expected you to be frequenting. C'est très Bourgeois, n'est ce pas – It's very sophisticated, is that not true?"

"Oui, c'est vrai; tu as raison – Yes, that's true; you are right. You say this because you see me as just a lowly artist who dances in a cabaret –

c'est ça - is that it?" asks Valerie.

"Je ne sais pas - I don't know. I don't mean any offense. It's just that you seem to be more of a woman of the people - not an upper-class snob, like most of these people here. To be frank, I don't feel that I relate to most of these people here either. I have money, it's true, but I don't come from money. I had to work hard for it. I don't usually attend fancy dinner parties, unless I'm obligated to for work. I don't enjoy rubbing elbows with politicians or celebrities unless I need to acquire a zoning permit or sell some property. I feel comfortable with you because you are down to earth, and I appreciate that very much."

"Ah, Je te comprends mieux, maintenant - I understand you better, now. Alors – So, to answer your question the best I can, I would say that I come here sometimes to show these stuffed shirts that they are no better than me. In full disclosure, there is no better cuisine in all of France, and I love a good meal and fine champagne. I'm also very interested in the art and the history of this place. I feel a strong connection to La Belle Époque – the Golden Age, which this restaurant exemplifies!"

"Je comprends - I understand; that makes sense to me."

"Additionally, I'm good friends with the manager - he adores me. He is a frequent customer of Le Théâtre Coquette, which is how I came to know him."

"Have you slept with him too?" asks Guy.

"Don't be jealous, Guy and don't ask questions about who I may or may not have slept with again."

"Je suis désolé - I'm sorry; I'm only teasing you," says Guy, trying to cover his tracks.

François returns at just the right moment to remove their first course plates.

"How did you enjoy your appetizers?"

"They were delicious," Valerie replies.

"Bon - Good," says François. "Your main course is still being prepared, but it won't be much longer - I assure you."

"Merci," Valerie replies.

"So, Guy, did you really enjoy my encore performance more than my first act tonight?"

"Oui, I told you that already. I have to say what struck me the most was how versatile a performer you are. Most people are only good at doing one thing. You seem to be exceptional at several things when it comes to art and entertainment. To answer your question – I enjoyed both your acts but in different ways."

"Merci encore, mon chéri – Thank you again, my dear. You say you dislike politicians, yet you answer questions like one. Anyway, I'm happy you enjoyed yourself tonight. Now, getting back to my earlier question - how are you planning to reciprocate?"

Guy smiles, as he looks Valerie in her eyes.

"I'll tell you what Val - how about when you decide to take some time off, I'll take you to the Riviera. We can go and enjoy the sea and the art museums together. How does that sound?"

"Vraiment, formidable – Really, terrific! Now, there's an offer that I might not be able to refuse. We can take the Blue Train to Nice and stay at Hôtel Le Negresco. What do you think? You see Guy, this is why I like spending time with you. You can almost read my mind."

Valerie gives Guy a kiss.

I think I just hit the jackpot, Guy says to himself.

François returns once again with their main course.

"That looks absolutely delicious," says Guy.

"Merci, monsieur. Bon appétit," François replies.

"I must admit Val, you have superb tastes. I don't mind spending this kind of money when the quality matches the price – along with the company."

"I hope you feel the same about your experiences at the club."

"Oui, bien sûr – Yes, of course. Your nightclub is very classy, and you are unparalleled on the stage."

Valerie smiles.

"Tu es trop gentil – You are too kind."

Valerie and Guy continue to enjoy their late supper among the all-night crowd, which has not diminished since the pair arrived.

In fact, the boisterous atmosphere inside Maxim's only seems to be growing livelier, as the clock ticks closer to 3:30 am.

Guy is a little surprised that Valerie accepted his getaway invitation to the south of France so easily, because going away on a trip together is very relationship oriented.

Perhaps, she has an ulterior motive? Guy wonders.

And, in fact, she does.

Valerie and Guy finish their main course, while continuing to banter about love, lust and life.

"How did you enjoy your seafood pasta?" asks Guy.

"It was wonderful! May I recommend a dessert for both of us to share?"

"What do you have in mind?"

"Mousse au chocolat. It's the best of its type in Paris."

"That sounds perfect."

"I knew you'd agree."

François returns to collect their dinner plates.

"Will you be having dessert with us?" asks François.

"Oui. Nous partagerons le mousse au chocolat - We'll share the chocolate mousse," Valerie replies.

"An excellent selection, mademoiselle."

"I have had chocolate on my mind, ever since you brought me that fine present this evening. I can't wait to savor that sweet taste in my mouth, along with a little Grand Marnier. The chocolates you bought for me are a very good brand. I admit that I have a weakness for fine things. This is also why I like you, Guy – you appreciate things that I like. I believe that you're a man of exceptional quality – a rare breed indeed."

"Merci," says Guy, feeling flattered.

It is an unexpected compliment, but Guy still doesn't know quite where he stands with the Dragon Princess. However, it's becoming clearer that she does appreciate him on some level and enjoys his company.

He's still uncertain whether Valerie will expose her vulnerabilities and allow him to enter her inner chamber of well-kept secrets. She seems to protect her feelings and her past, as if they were the crown jewels of England. Guy is determined to try and break down her barrier and penetrate Valerie's more sensitive side, but he needs to find out where she keeps that hidden.

Guy is aware that Valerie's family is a sore spot with her, so he knows that he needs to tread lightly when it comes to that subject. She may not want to have a close relationship with anyone right now, but he's still curious enough to want to peek into her soul, in order to reach her heart.

Guy's only reservation is that he may not like what he finds if he opens Pandora's Box. He may wish he had kept his distance in the end. On some level, Guy doesn't truly understand what he's getting into with Valerie. He has no idea what's in store for the two of them in the future, but he will soon find out.

François returns with their dessert.

"Merci," says Valerie.

"Je vous en prie, mademoiselle – You're welcome, miss," François replies.

Valerie slips off one of her shoes and runs her finely painted toes along Guy's leg. She looks up at him to watch for his reaction. Guy stares into her eyes and smiles. For the first time in years, Guy feels totally alive.

It's currently 3:45 am and Maxim's will be closing shortly. After finishing their desserts and paying the bill, Valerie pulls out a cigarette from her case and waits for Guy to fetch his car. Antoine returns to her table to chat for a while and to say goodbye before she leaves.

"It's so wonderful seeing you again, Valerie. How was your supper this evening?" asks Antoine.

"Superbe, mon ami, merci – Excellent my friend, thank you. Et toi, ça va – And you, are you doing well?" asks Valerie.

"Oui, ça va - everything is good with me," Antoine replies.

"Je suis heureux de l'entendre. Jusqu'à la prochaine fois, alors – I am glad to hear it. Until the next time, then."

"Oui, but allow me to walk you to the door."

"Merci, tu es très gentil – Thank you, you are very sweet."

"Je t'en prie – It's my pleasure."

Antoine escorts Valerie to the front door and they both say a final good night to one another, just as Guy pulls up in his car.

"Bonne soirée – Good night," says Antoine.

"Au revoir – Goodbye," Valerie replies.

Antoine has long given up introducing himself to Valerie's dates because she comes to Maxim's with a different gentleman almost every time. He believes there is little chance he will meet the same man with Valerie more than once or twice, so he doesn't bother to make a point of getting to know any of them anymore.

Guy opens the passenger side door, then proudly takes Valerie's arm and escorts her to his car. Valerie feels fulfilled during the time she spends with Guy and thinks he might even be growing on her. He opens the car door for her and she slithers comfortably into the form fitting leather seat.

"Merci," says Valerie.

As Guy gently closes the car door, many thoughts begin to sift through his mind.

I wonder if Valerie might be too tired to make love to me tonight – it's very late now. Will I still end up on the couch again? Maybe she's exhausted after a long night and will want me to just go home.

As Guy pulls away from Maxim's, the words *"I don't want a relationship"* resurfaces from his subconscious mind. Suddenly, he begins to feel nervous and uneasy again.

"So, Val, did you enjoy yourself tonight?"

"Oui, immensely!" Valerie replies, enthusiastically.

"You must be very tired."

"A bit, yes, but I'm nocturnal – a creature of the night."

"Do you want me to stay with you tonight or just drop you home?"

Guy asks politely.

"You don't want to stay with me?" asks Valerie, surprised.

"No, I mean yes, I do, but I didn't want to presume or pressure you."

"Guy, my darling, you need to learn to stop being so polite and say what's on your mind. How did you become so successful in your business when you act so timid most of the time?"

"I suppose I act differently when it comes to work versus when I'm with a woman. I find that talking to men is much easier for me."

"What do you mean?"

"Well, men are more predictable. If men in my business reject an offer, it doesn't seem personal. It stings a little to lose a deal, but I know there will always be other opportunities, even with the same person."

"That's true with women too Guy, don't you know that?" If one woman turns you down, either she or another woman will likely be more receptive in the future."

"I suppose that's true, but it's not quite the same. Women are a lot more complex to negotiate with when it comes to propositions. In business, emotions aren't typically involved in whether a deal goes north or south. Men like me who buy and sell properties are only concerned about profit, and there's usually nothing personal about the deals we make. When dealing with women on a personal level, their reactions seem to change from day to day or even hour by hour, depending on their mood. You can't always please women simply by throwing money around. Women have a heart and a soul, and it takes a lot of work to understand what will satisfy their emotional needs and desires."

"Ha! Oui, c'est vrai. Tu as raison – Yes, that's true. You are right. However, sometimes the reverse is also true. Some women think like men. I am a good example. Also, some women you can please by spending a lot of money on them. However, I think you are halfway to the point of discovering some of our secrets. Just remember, all women are not alike and don't think or react the same way. Unlike most men, at least you know what to look for, even if you don't know where to look concerning the female sex. I can give you a small hint. Don't ever try to guess what a woman is thinking or tell her how to feel because you will fail miserably. Understanding women is much simpler than you might imagine. You just need to ask the right questions."

"Oui, but that's the trick - isn't it? Knowing what questions to ask. I have tried my best in the past to ask women what they want, but I have found that they don't often want to give me straight answers. Sometimes, I think women enjoy making men squirm, while we try to guess what's on their minds. It's like a power game to many of them, I think."

"That may be true for some women, Guy. However, I'm usually clear about what I like and what I don't like – what I want and what I don't want. I enjoy playing games, but not guessing games. Most of the time, I'm straight forward. People know where they stand with me. Speaking to that matter, I will cut to the chase concerning your previous question. Yes Guy, I want you to stay with me tonight, okay. Are you satisfied now?"

Guy looks at Valerie and smiles.

"Oui, I'm glad we got that settled finally."

"Bon."

Guy and Valerie arrive in front of her apartment building a few minutes later.

"You can park in the back, off the street."

Guy glides smoothly into Valerie's parking space, then circles around to open her door.

"Merci," says Valerie, as she steps down with her hand extended for Guy to hold.

By this time, it's nearly dawn – just over an hour before twilight in Paris comes to a close. This is around the time when Valerie often returns home, and most town folks are just awakening.

Valerie and Guy climb the stairs to her flat where Fafa eagerly awaits his master's return. As she turns the key to her apartment, the

95

faint sound of scratching by her little companion can be heard behind the door. As Valerie opens the door, Fafa springs up enthusiastically to greet his master with wet kisses.

"It's a good thing I can depend on my neighbor to look after my little baby while I'm working. She has a spare key and lets herself in while I'm out. She's a very sweet lady and takes good care of Fafa."

Valerie picks up her little dog to kiss him before setting him back down on the floor again. Fafa begins to sniff Guy's leg as he reaches down to pet him and licks Guy's hand in a gesture of affection.

"Wow, he seems to remember you. It's a good sign when he doesn't try to tear your pant leg off right away," Valerie says, teasing again.

"You see Val, he does like me."

"You may be the very first. I know it's a bit late for you to have another drink, but perhaps you would like some tea before going to bed?"

"Oui, that would be very nice, merci."

"I'm going to put a little whisky in mine, but I'm sure you don't want any - correct?

"Oui, c'est vrai – Yes, that's true."

"I'm going to change first, if you don't mind," says Valerie.

"Be my guest," Guy replies.

"It's you who is my guest," says Valerie, winking at Guy.

Valerie leaves her bedroom door open again, just enough so that Guy can watch her changing. She knows Guy won't be able to resist watching her, as she undresses. This is another one of her games she loves to play. If her house guest looks away, she doesn't make love to him or her. However, no one ever does. Guy gazes upon Valerie with intense desire, as she unzips her dress and slips into her satin robe, leaving only her stockings and underclothes on.

Only when Valerie makes her way to the kitchen does Guy look away and begins playing with Fafa. He grabs one of his toys for a Tug-of-War, while Valerie brews the tea. She notices the two of them interacting and smiles.

"I think you're trying to get on my good side by playing with my puppy, Guy. You might be trying to use him just to gain my trust or manipulating him to gain his."

"Oui, I'm hoping he will give up his side of the bed tonight, if he likes me well enough."

"Oh, I doubt that will ever happen. He's very attached to me and it's his habit to sleep on my bed with me. He believes that's his space. It's also his job to be on guard in case any intruders enter my chamber. If that happens, he will leap into attack mode and defend my virtue with his life."

"Your virtue? You must be joking, right?"

Valerie smiles facetiously, as she brings the tea into the salon. Fafa takes his cue and returns to his basket on the floor.

"You never told me what you've been painting," says Guy.

"Oh, it's just a portrait of Bianca. It's not finished, so you can't look at it just yet."

"I wasn't aware that you did portraits, but I suppose I shouldn't be surprised at anything you do anymore."

"I paint whatever inspires me. It doesn't matter what the subject is."

"You're truly a woman of many talents and many secrets."

"Oh, I don't know, Guy. My work is nothing particularly spectacular, and keeping secrets is how I maintain my allure."

"Au contraire – I beg to disagree. What I've seen so far of your work is exceptional. As for your allure, you don't need to keep secrets for that."

"Merci, mon amour. Tu es trop gentil – Thank you, my love. You are too kind. I find that porting a veil of mystery around me keeps seekers of adventure on the hunt, and I relish being the object of the chase and their desire."

Valerie takes Guy's teacup from his grip and sets it on the coffee table. She takes his hand and leads him to her bedroom.

"What about Fafa?" Guy asks.

"Don't worry about him; he will come when I am finished with you," Valerie replies.

Valerie gives Guy a suggestive look, as she leads him to her bed. Then she unfastens her robe and closes the door.

VIII. Montmartre

A few hours later, Guy finds himself waking up on Valerie's sofa, once again. His back is sore, but not only because of the couch. Valerie has left him branded for the second time. It's as if his newfound lover doesn't want him to forget their night of passion. It's nearly 10 am and Guy has barely had four hours of uninterrupted sleep. Valerie's door is open just a crack, but it's enough for little Fafa to push it open and venture into the salon where Guy has just begun to open his eyes.

Fafa waddles over to the couch and begins tugging at Guy's blanket. The little Oreo cookie is trying to tell him that it's past time to go outside for his walk. Fafa's agitated growling and persistence soon alerts Guy, as he struggles to see the living room in focus.

Today is Saturday, so there are no church bells or town folks dressed in their Sunday best clothing. All the village shops have opened and daily life in Courbevoie has sprung into action. The aroma of fresh fish, baguettes and buttered croissants permeates the air, penetrating Valerie's open windows and arousing Guy's senses of smell and taste.

"I suppose you want me to take you out for your walk this morning, don't you? I'll bet that your mistress is also expecting me to buy fresh bread for when she wakes up and peeks her head out from her cave – isn't that right little one?"

"Ruff!" Fafa replies.

"That's what I thought. Well, you will have to wait a moment until I get dressed. I can't be seen in public without clothing, the same way you are able to get away with it. So, you'll just have to be patient."

"Ruff!" Fafa barks again, in protest.

Guy rubs his eyes and slowly elevates himself from the sofa and searches for his clothes. Valerie cannot be seen or heard. It will likely not be until at least 11 am before The Dragon Princess makes an appearance. Once he's dressed, Guy finds Fafa's leash and grabs the house keys from the ashtray on the console table. He heads out the door with his new best friend, who proudly accompanies him down the staircase to the street.

Guy repeats the same path he took the week before, but this time he's slightly more aware of the townspeople who are noticing him walk Valerie's pup for the second time in a week. It's as if the Dragon Princess has spies all around the village, watching every move he makes during their promenade. To an extent, it makes Guy feel a bit vulnerable. However, he thinks it's something he must get used to if he wants to continue seeing this queen of the stage.

Guy stops at a market to buy cheese and eggs before heading to the bakery, in case Valerie has none left in her refrigerator.

Perhaps she'll make an omelet for me this morning, he wonders.

Suddenly, it occurs to him that he's becoming this woman's 'gofer,' and he's even footing the bill. This title is an addition to his new role as 'dog walker.' With that thought firmly in the front of his mind, Guy leads Fafa to the bakery next. He continues to overhear people whispering around him as he and Fafa walk by.

"Bonjour, monsieur le boulangère – Hello, mister baker," says Guy.

"Well, good morning. I see you're back again with Fafa," replies the baker.

"Oui?" Guy replies.

"What can I get for you today?"

"Une baguette et deux croissants chocolat, s'il vous plaît – One baguette and two chocolate crescent rolls, please."

"Tout de suite, monsieur - Right away, sir. Will that be all?"

"Oui, merci – yes, thank you."

"Je vous en prie, monsieur – My pleasure, sir."

The baker puts the bread in a bag, after completing the sale. Then, he offers Fafa a little treat, which the little French bulldog hungrily scarfs down in seconds.

"Merci beaucoup - Thanks a lot," says Guy, as he leaves the store with his happy companion.

As Guy ascends the staircase to Valerie's flat with little Fafa in tow, she can be seen peeking her head out of her bedroom window, watching the two adventurers approach. Guy unlocks and opens the door and announces that he has bought some things from the market for breakfast.

Valerie puts on her robe and greets them as they enter her flat.

"Bonjour, Guy. Thank you for taking Fafa out for his walk and for bringing breakfast."

"De rien – It's nothing. I bought some eggs and cheese to make an omelet if you're interested."

"Oh, are you cooking breakfast for me this morning? C'est très gentil – That's very nice," Valerie says, playfully.

"Well, we can cook together if you like. I see you have already made the coffee."

"Oui, would you like some?"

"Oui, merci – yes, thank you."

"How did you sleep?" asks Valerie.

"I slept okay, under the circumstances."

"Don't be too upset, mon chéri – my dear. You know, I adore you. I just have my habits, c'est tout - that's all."

"Sometimes, I wonder about that."

"Well, let's get cracking, the eggs, I mean," says Valerie.

Guy smiles at Valerie's bad joke.

"I still haven't taken a shower yet," Guy protests. "I got dressed right away because your munchkin was bugging me to go out."

"I'll tell you what Guy, since you have been a sweetheart and walked Fafa and brought breakfast, I will cook while you take a shower, d'accord – okay?"

"Vraiment – Really!" Guy replies, excitedly. "Now, I feel special - merci."

"Laisses tomber - Never mind. Just go get cleaned up and I will start breakfast. First, I need to feed my baby boy."

Valerie takes out Fafa's food bowl, while Guy happily heads to the bathroom to take a shower. He's thinking that he should have been more prepared by bringing an overnight bag with him - at least one with clean underwear and his toothbrush. He may have been ready for a night out at Maxim's, but he still needs to be prepared to sleep over at Valerie's place whenever he sees her. He never really knows what to expect when he's with her.

Perhaps I can stop by a clothing store after breakfast? In the future, I may need to leave an overnight case in the trunk of my car. Maybe Valerie will allow me to leave some things here, but I doubt it. That would be too much like a relationship.

As Guy turns on the water in the shower, he's reminded of his first night with Valerie. Once again, the hot water burns the flesh on his back. He won't complain because it's the best sex he's ever had in his life. Guy tries to clear his mind of the previous evening, but the steam from the shower reminds him of Valerie's last performance at the club, and how things got hot at the club and in Valerie's bedroom last night.

Guy had never been with two women at once. The drinking game at the club was a bit overwhelming. He allows his mind to wander and daydreams about what happened upstairs in the lounge while he's in the shower. He can't help but feel aroused all over again. He turns the faucet to stream colder water so that it shakes his mind from his thoughts about sex. Guy finally turns off the faucet and takes his time drying himself, knowing it will still be a few minutes before he can comfortably get dressed. The sudden silence allows him to hear the beat of his heart, which is still pounding rapidly.

In the meantime, Fafa is hungrily cleaning his bowl of the remnants of food his master has prepared for him. Then, he toddles off to his basket in the salon, curls up in a ball and closes his eyes.

"Breakfast is ready, Guy!" Valerie shouts.

"J'arrive – I'm coming."

Guy quickly finishes getting dressed and arrives in the kitchen within the next two minutes.

"Voila, Guy, le petit déjeuner. Here you are Guy, your breakfast. I have a special surprise for you afterwards."

"I can't imagine what that could be."

"Tu verras - You will see."

"You don't take cream or sugar in your coffee - isn't that right Guy?"

"Oui."

"I like mine - Irish style."

"Don't you ever get tired of drinking?"

"Jamais - Never! Guy, don't get the idea that because you're here with me, you can start lecturing me on how to live my life – tu comprends – You understand?"

"Je suis désolé – I'm sorry. I'm not trying to tell you what to do. I'm just concerned about your well-being, c'est tout – that's all."

"Well, don't be - I'm fine. Bon appétit."

"Wow, this is really delicious!" exclaims Guy.

"You're surprised? I'm glad you like it. I added some jambon et champignons avec fromage – ham and mushrooms with cheese, and fresh herbs with just a dash of hot sauce, which I call – 'Dragon's Breath.'"

"How appropriately named. C'est délicieux - It's delicious! Among all your other talents, you can cook well too.

"C'est rien - It's nothing. You see Guy, when you do me favors, you are rewarded. It's kind of like when Fafa obeys me, he gets a treat."

Valerie gives Guy a mischievous glance, then resumes eating her meal.

"So, you're saying that you're training me to do things that please you – just like your little sidekick - is that it?"

"Oui," Valerie replies, smiling again playfully.

"I'm not so sure I want to be treated like your pet."

"Oh Guy, don't misunderstand – you should know by now that I treat my little Fafa like a little prince and I love him dearly. Now, stop your pouting and eat your breakfast. I have plans for us today before going to work."

"Oh really, what do you have in mind?"

"I would like to head over to Montmartre today to pick up some paint supplies and visit with some fellow artist friends of mine. Normally, I like to do this alone, but since my motorbike is still at work, I thought I would ask you to drive me. You can tag along with me while I'm there if you like. This way, I won't need to take the train to work. You can just drop me afterwards. Does that work for you?"

"So, are you saying you don't necessarily want to spend the day with me, but you need a ride - is that it?"

"Relax Guy! Stop being such a needy ninny. Of course, I want to spend time with you today, but keep in mind, it's not my usual habit to have male company during the day, aside from my friends. I'm making an exception for you, so don't make a fuss. Instead of complaining, you should be grateful."

"That's fine, I'm happy to oblige because it's not far from where I live. I can change my clothes at my house beforehand and then take you to Montmartre."

"Bon – Good. Let me just take my shower and get dressed. Then, I'll knock on my neighbor's door to make arrangements for Fafa – d'accord - agreed.

"That sounds fine to me."

After washing up, Valerie quickly throws on a pair of tight jeans, a sleeveless black T-shirt, her red leather jacket, and black knee-high boots, so that she will be dressed to ride her motorbike when she goes home later that evening. After they leave the apartment, they're off to Guy's place and then to the art district.

Montmartre never used to be part of the city of Paris in the past. It was a separate village where some of the most famous painters in history lived. Artists like Picasso, Renoir, Van Gough, Degas, etc. It was also a writer's haven for authors like F. Scott Fitzgerald, Gertrude Stein, T. S. Elliot, Mark Twain, and Ernest Hemingway. For many of these artists and writers, it was a generation after 'La Belle Epoch,' but the 1920s could certainly be considered as another Golden Age.

Montmartre also has the distinct honor of being the highest natural location in Paris, exhibiting a panoramic view of the city. Le Sacré Coeur – The Sacred Heart Cathedral is perched at the summit and is only eclipsed in height by Le Tour d' Eiffel.

"Arêtes ici - Stop here," demands Valerie. "That's Henri there painting at La Place du Tertre. Let me out here and then go park the car, while I greet my friend. Then, come and meet us."

Valerie pops out of the passenger seat like a jack in the box and scurries over to greet her longtime friend Henri.

"Salut Valerie, ça va – Hi Valerie, how's it going!" exclaims Henri, excited to see her.

"Ça va bien, mon ami, merci – It's going well, my friend, thank you," Valerie replies.

Henri and Valerie greet each other with kisses on both cheeks.

"So, Valerie, are you still painting? You don't grace us with your presence much around here in the square these days."

"Oui - Yes. I find it's easier to paint at home nowadays. I'm at the club very late most nights, so I sleep late and then I just feel like working alone at home, and spending time with Fafa."

"How is your little furball doing?"

"Oh, he's doing well. He's happy, especially when I'm home with him. He's not much of a guard dog or retriever, but he keeps me company and my neighbors love him because he's cute and quiet."

Guy finally approaches, after spending time trying to find an empty space to park his Renault.

"Merveilleux - Marvelous! Who do we have here now - a new boyfriend, perhaps?" asks Henri.

"Uh, not exactly - this is Guy, a new acquaintance of mine. We met at my club about a week ago. He's a real estate investor. Guy, may I present to you my very good friend and mentor, Henri Richard."

"Enchanté, monsieur – Nice to meet you," says Henri.

Guy and Henri shake hands.

"Is this your painting?" asks Guy.

"Oui, do you like it?" Henri replies.

"C'est formidable - It's fantastic!" exclaims Guy. "You are an exceptionally talented artist."

"Merci, monsieur, mais c'est rien, vraiment – Thank you sir, but it's nothing, really."

"Don't be modest. Henri is one of the most renowned painters in Paris, currently. He has taught me much of what I know how to do on canvas," says Valerie.

"Tu es trop gentille, Valerie - You are too kind, Valerie," Henri replies.

"So, if you haven't come to paint with us - why are you two kids here today?"

"I have come to buy more painting supplies, and to say hello to you and some other friends. I know I don't stop by often enough, but I wanted to take some time today to say hello. Guy was good enough to bring me before I have to go to work. Perhaps you will join us for an early supper, since I don't need to be at the club until around 9:30 pm. Shall we say around 7:00 pm? There are a few places around here that open before eight. I'm going to ask Céline to join us as well, if I can find her. Have you seen her today?"

"I think she said she was going to meet Pauline for lunch at La Maison Rose. I'd be delighted to catch up with you later, after I'm finished painting. Where would you like to meet?"

"How about we meet at L'Artist? That place has a wonderful wine selection."

"Oui, d'accord, - Yes, agreed. I will see you both later at seven. Bonne journée – Good day."

"Okay, à plus tard – see you later," Valerie replies, as she kisses Henri goodbye.

"Guy, let's try to find Céline to tell her about meeting later for an early supper. Then, I need to go buy some paint supplies."

"Okay."

Guy and Valerie walk together toward La Maison Rose where Pauline and Céline are enjoying a light lunch on the patio, in front of the restaurant. To her surprise, Céline notices Valerie and her companion approaching, and stands to greet them. The four of them exchange kisses and say hello.

"Ça va, Valerie – How are you, Valerie!" exclaims Céline. "Tu m'as manqué - I have missed you."

"Ça va bien, merci, ma belle amie – I am well, thank you, my beautiful friend," Valerie replies.

"Je vous présente mon ami - I present to you my friend... Guy Martin, and this is Céline and her girlfriend Pauline."

"Enchanté – Pleased to meet you," says Guy.

"We are almost finished with lunch Valerie, but won't you join us for a coffee?"

"Oui, delighted."

Céline is young and beautiful, about Valerie's age with long-flowing, scarlet hair and verdant green colored eyes. She's athletic, so she keeps her body in fine shape. Her girlfriend Pauline is attractive as well, but she's in her mid-40s. Her greying hair is disguised by frost-color hair dye, which brings out her cobalt blue eyes. The crevices in her cheeks are covered-up by generous portions of foundation, which she thinks helps to hide her crow's feet. She's a bit concerned that Céline will eventually lose interest in her and considers Valerie to be a threat to her girlfriend's attention. Both women are artists, which is how they met in the square.

"What brings you back to Montmartre today?" asks Céline.

"I needed to pick up some more supplies to finish my portrait of Bianca. Also, I wanted to say hello to you and Henri."

"Ah, genial! So, when are you going to paint my portrait?" asks Céline, flirtatiously.

Pauline gives Céline an annoyed look and kicks her gently under the table.

"Perhaps, someday when you aren't too busy or when Pauline will

107

give you the opportunity." Valerie replies.

Just then, the waiter comes to their table to take Guy and Valerie's drink order.

"Deux espressos, s'il vous plaît – Two espressos please," Guy demands.

The waiter nods and turns to fetch their coffees.

"So, how are things at the club Valerie?" asks Céline.

"Routine - another night, another customer, another dollar."

"Is that where you met this nice looking fellow?" asks Pauline.

"Oui, he was foolish enough to miss his train home when he came to see me perform. So, I offered him a ride on my motorcycle. Guy is returning the favor by bringing me here and dropping me at the club tonight."

"How generous," says Céline, winking at Valerie, as she catches Guy looking at her poking fun at him.

"We came looking for you to invite you both to have an early supper with us tonight, along with Henri."

Pauline reacts in an alarmed manner. She knows Valerie is a temptress, and that she and Céline have slept together before they met. She doesn't want her girlfriend provoked into repeating any of her past indiscretions with the Dragon Princess. Céline gives Pauline a look which suggests that she wants to go, but Pauline gives her a disapproving stare, and gently kicks her again, under the table.

"Oh, well, I'd like to, Valerie, but I'm not sure we can – Je suis désolé – I'm sorry," Céline finally blurts out, reluctantly.

"I was planning on cooking at home tonight," says Pauline, interrupting.

Valerie looks at Pauline in an annoyed manner because Pauline has just deliberately interfered with her plans.

"Oh, okay, perhaps another time," Valerie replies, clearly disappointed.

Céline gives Pauline a look of disgust but tries to put on a happy face for the remainder of their visit. This is one thing Céline doesn't appreciate about her relationship with Pauline. She is a free spirit, like

Valerie, and doesn't like her girlfriend's insecure jealous behavior and controlling nature.

"So, Guy, what do you do for a living?" asks Pauline, trying to distract Céline and Valerie's discontentment.

"I'm a real estate investor."

"Oh, that sounds interesting."

"It's one way to make money. It's not especially creative compared to the way you all spend your time, but it pays the bills."

"Well, we artists need successful patrons like yourself, to spend money on our work. Otherwise, we'd all be poorer than we already are," says Céline.

Everyone laughs.

"I suppose you could look at it that way," Guy replies.

As he speaks, Valerie gives Céline a provocative look, which implies that she'd like a call from her soon. Pauline catches the exchange and becomes visibly agitated. Valerie notices Pauline's disgust and takes it as her cue to leave.

"Well ladies, I guess it's time for Guy and I to go look for my painting supplies."

"It's been very nice meeting you both," says Guy, as he finishes his coffee quickly.

"You as well – it's been a pleasure," Céline and Pauline reply.

The four of them kiss goodbye. The exchange between Pauline and Valerie is noticeably awkward. Valerie and Guy then head to the paint supply store, after leaving some cash on the table for their drinks.

"So, Guy, what did you think of my friend Céline?"

"She seems nice. However, I have a feeling that her girlfriend Pauline is the jealous type."

Guy doesn't realize that he's just opened a can of worms.

"She's jealous and possessive all right, especially of me. She often spoils my ability to spend time with Céline, like she just did a few minutes ago. She's feeling her age and she thinks she'll lose Céline to someone younger. However, she shouldn't be too concerned about me because I don't hold committed relationships. So, she's really wasting her energy focusing her attention on me."

"Her concern may not be just about her girlfriend leaving her to pursue a new relationship. She's also probably worried about her lover having a one-night stand with someone else. In the end, it's Céline's choice what she wants to do about it. It's probably best not to interfere in a love triangle involving one of your friends. It wouldn't end well, I think." Guy replies.

"Perhaps you're right, but I feel sorry for Céline losing her freedom because of that witch. Anyway, here we are at the store. Let's go inside and look for the things I need."

Valerie spends almost a half an hour in the store, looking at and scrutinizing each brush and brand of paint.

"I didn't realize that choosing art supplies would be so complicated," says Guy.

"Well, you have to understand that every artist has different criteria, based on their unique needs, tastes, styles, and preferences."

"That makes sense, but you must appreciate that I don't know the first thing about what an artist's needs are. I can recognize a quality painting when I see it, but I'm just not familiar with all the idiosyncrasies that go into creating it. I can recognize famous artists' styles like Picasso, Monet, and Renoir, and even make a good guess at their value. However, since I'm not a painter or any kind of artist, I must confess that I have never stepped foot inside an art supply store, until today. I never imagined how many choices there are."

"The right brush with the right bristles, the best brand of paint and texture of canvas, etc. – it all makes a difference. Every painter wants something different for their work. Some artists want something different each time they create something new, depending on their objective."

"I suppose that's true with musicians and musical instruments as well. I don't suppose you play an instrument too?"

"As a matter of fact – I play the flute."

"You're joking!"

"No, I'm not - I'm quite serious. I told you where I went to school, right?"

"Yes, you did, but I didn't imagine you studied music there as well."

"I went there for all their art program Guy, which includes music, dancing, singing, drawing, creative writing, and painting. You can specialize of course, but everyone has an opportunity to take any number of classes they want, so I took everything. I don't like to limit myself. It's a very exclusive school and you must be invited to apply in the first place, after an interview process."

"How amazing! What a great honor and privilege."

"I know that expression, Guy. You're probably thinking… what am I doing performing in a nightclub, when I have all this ability, right?"

"I wasn't thinking that exactly, but now that you mention it – I can imagine so many other things you could do with your talents."

"You mean, instead of stripping at night in a club? You know Guy, we had this discussion once before, already."

"I know, that's not exactly what I meant to say."

"Well then, tell me Guy, what did you mean, exactly?"

Guy is becoming increasingly uncomfortable with what's inadvertently becoming another confrontation.

"What I meant simply is that since you are clearly extremely talented, you could do anything you want. So, why not just dance on the weekends and spend more time with your artwork? I know you said that dancing is thrilling, but I just think you are neglecting your other gifts. I don't understand why you spent all that time at the University only to take a job using your body."

"Eh bien – Well then, I will tell you. I do it because J'aime faire la spectacle - I love performing. C'est tout – That's all!

"Okay, I think I understand. It's just that I'm not an artist or a performer, so I can't really relate to your experience."

"Anyway, thank you for the compliment, Guy – I think. Don't mind me. I'm simply giving you a hard time. I saw you struggling, trying to find words of praise, after your clumsy first missteps, so I thought

I'd have a little fun with you."

Guy looks at Valerie disapprovingly. No matter what happens, he always seems to feel slightly awkward around her. Previously, he thought it might be just sexual intimidation, but now he knows it's something more than that. It's more like psychological manipulation that's making him feel uncomfortable at times – A mind fuck!

Guy never seems to feel like he's in control whenever he's around Valerie. He is confused about what to do about it, but suddenly he has an idea. This plan could easily backfire however, since Valerie is so unpredictable. His Achilles heel, for the moment, is that he's not ready to take any big risks yet, for fear of losing her. He needs time to think it through before taking any action.

It's getting close to the time when they must rendezvous with Henri at 'L'Artiste,' along la rue Gabrielle, ironically. They hurry so they won't be late. When they arrive, they see that Henri is already sitting down, and he's with a lady friend. As they approach Henri's table, they notice the pair has already begun drinking some wine.

"Bonsoir Valerie, Guy - I hope you don't mind that I brought Estelle along for our early supper. I noticed her aimlessly wandering around the square, so I thought I'd invite her to join us this evening. I hope that's okay. She is an old acquaintance of mine – another former student. In fact, I think you have met her before Valerie – do you remember?"

"Oui, it's nice to see you again, Estelle."

Valerie kisses her and Henri before sitting down at the table.

"Enchanté – It's a pleasure meeting you, Estelle," says Guy.

"Have a seat Guy, and I'll pour you both a glass of wine," says Henri.

"Merci," Guy replies.

"So, did you find Céline – will she be joining us?" asks Henri.

"Oui - Yes, we found her, but unfortunately she won't be coming."

"Oh, pourquoi pas - why not?" asks Estelle.

"Well, because her girlfriend is too insecure to let her out of her sight for five minutes. I didn't mind if Pauline came along with her, but apparently, she had already decided to make dinner at home, and she couldn't possibly change her plans."

Henri laughs and rolls his eyes.

"Well, who can blame her," says Henri. "You would make the President's wife nervous, n'est ce pas – is that not true, Valerie?"

"Oh Henri - don't exaggerate."

"Valerie, you told me you're still painting at home, but I hope you're doing work on the level of your abilities. I'd hate to think that you're neglecting your God given talents."

Guy looks at Valerie and smiles, as if to say... *You see, even Henri thinks like I do."*

"Don't you start on me too, Henri. I am serious about my art, but I have other responsibilities beyond painting. You know, I am not your apprentice anymore."

"Oui, c'est vrai – Yes, that's true! You are now a master artist in your own right, like me.

"What are you working on?" asks Estelle.

Valerie lets out a sigh in frustration. She hates having to repeat herself more than once on the same day.

"I'm working on a portrait of a colleague of mine. It's actually almost finished," Valerie replies politely.

"I'm certain it will be a masterpiece," says Henri.

"It can't compare to any of your work, Henri. However, I think you will be pleased with it when it's finished."

The waiter finally comes to their table to take their order. They choose several plates to share, since this is a casual meal among friends.

"Guy, what do you do?" asks Estelle. "Are you an artist as well?"

"No, not at all. I'm simply an admirer of the arts. I am a real estate investor."

"Oh, well, if you ever buy my building, please don't raise my rent – promise? I can't afford to pay more than I already am."

"Well to be honest, I do have my eye on a few properties in this area, due to its everlasting popularity. However, I will take your case into special consideration if you happen to be one of the tenants of a building I decide to buy."

"Bless your heart young man. Now, don't let this maneater here lead you to ruin. You should know that Valerie has a long list of former lovers that she has left broken-hearted. You certainly wouldn't be the first of her romantic partners to end up being tossed aside."

Everyone at the table freezes in shock at Estelle's brazen outburst.

"Estelle! How can you be so callous!" shouts Valerie.

Valerie glares at Estelle with flames in her eyes, which seemed to change from green to red in an instant. She raises her hand, showing her long fingernails and begins to grind her razor-sharp teeth in anger. Valerie is no longer amused by this woman's clumsy speech and twisted mind.

"Oh, don't get offended Valerie. You might know I have a weakness for levity and a flare for being dramatic. However, I'm basically correct, aren't I? I adore you dear, but everyone knows you're a predator and not interested in having long relationships - n'est ce-pas - isn't that true?"

Estelle seems to be digging herself into an even deeper hole and reducing this friendly dinner gathering into a cat fight.

"If your previous statement was adoration Estelle, I'd hate to hear what you have to say about me behind my back."

"Don't be upset with me dear. I'm only warning this nice young man not to get too attached - that's all. Is that so wrong?"

"N'inquiètes pas, madame - Don't worry, madam, I can take care of myself. Anyway, Valerie and I are only having a bit of fun - right Val?" Guy says, winking at her.

"That's right! We are simply enjoying each other's company."

"Well, that's a relief. I'd hate to think you had fallen in love with the Dragon Princess of Paris. Love is not part of her vocabulary."

Valerie gives Estelle another look that could kill.

"That's enough Estelle!" Henri shouts, regretting that he invited her to dinner. "Perhaps you've had a little too much wine."

"Pardonnez-moi, Valerie - Forgive me, Valerie. I'm just a stupid old fool, who can't stop blabbering on after a few sips of fermented grape juice."

"Laisse tomber – forget it," says Valerie.

Henri changes the subject.

"So, Valerie, what do you plan to do with the portrait you're working on?"

"Well, I was thinking of selling it at an auction or perhaps just giving it to Bianca as a gift."

"Oh, I thought Bianca might have commissioned you to paint her portrait," says Henri.

"Well, she might have, I suppose, but I asked Bianca if I could paint her because she's so beautiful. I'm even thinking of keeping it myself, at least for a little while. Perhaps I'll put it in my bedroom where I can stare at her every night before I go to sleep. Then in the morning, she'll be there smiling at me when I wake up."

Valerie looks at Guy to see his reaction. Guy is slowly learning not to act surprised every time Valerie tries to provoke him. He has decided that giving Valerie the reaction she is looking for will only encourage her to find more ways to get a rise out of him.

Perhaps if I look uninterested, she'll stop trying to manipulate me.

Occasionally, Guy thinks that he should turn the tables on her to see how she reacts, instead.

"Tell me Valerie, will Bianca need to pose for you again so you can finish the painting or is there enough finished that you don't need her again?"

Valerie looks at Guy as if to say… *What are you asking?* Valerie recognizes what he's doing and decides to put on her poker face and anti-up.

"Well, yes Guy. In fact, I think I will need her to come back once more – perhaps on Sunday. Why - would you like to come and watch?" Valerie teases, playing along with Guy's game, knowing that Bianca will be posing nude.

"Sure, as a matter of fact, I would," Guy replies, calling her bluff.

Estelle glances at Valerie and rolls her eyes, while Henri just looks at Valerie and smiles, just as their main courses arrive.

"Bon appétit," says Henri.

"Merci," everyone replies.

For the moment, the four of them take a break from their conversation and begin enjoying the delicious food in front of them. There is still tension in the air between Valerie and Estelle, but the group begins to talk about more pleasant things.

The Dragon Princess is still noticeably quiet. After finishing their food, without the usual amount of conversation, Valerie announces that they need to leave because she must go to work. She's obviously still a little rattled by Estelle's intrusive and inappropriate behavior.

Secretly, Valerie is hoping Guy took what Estelle said as a joke, but she knows deep down that much of it is true. Perhaps, Guy already knows it. Regardless, Valerie hopes that Guy will forget about Estelle's rude comments. Valerie is far from being ready to cast Guy aside at this point.

Suddenly, Valerie is aware that she's starting to care about what Guy thinks and how he feels about her. It's an alarming discovery, and she quickly attempts to put this thought out of her mind. Unfortunately, it's stuck in her head now, like gum on the bottom of her shoe.

Guy generously pays for everyone's dinner, and they all say goodbye. The embrace between Valerie and Estelle is rather cold and awkward, just like it was with Pauline earlier. It's evident to Guy that some women clearly don't like Valerie, despite her enormous popularity among men.

Overall, the dinner was enjoyable for most everyone, but Estelle's words still left a bitter taste in Valerie's mouth – one which even good wine couldn't wash away. Since things had turned a bit sour during dinner and he sees that Valerie is out of sorts, Guy attempts to cheer her up.

"Qu'est-ce qui a, Valerie - What's wrong, Valerie?"

"Oh, c'est rien - it's nothing."

"Estelle's comments are still bothering you, aren't they?" Guy persists.

"Oui, but let's not talk about it now, okay Guy."

"If you prefer, try not to let that woman's inappropriate behavior bother you anymore."

Valerie looks at Guy and smiles.

"You're very sweet, Guy," says Valerie.

Suddenly, a warm, unfamiliar feeling comes over her. She doesn't quite know what to make of it. It's something she hasn't felt in a very long time – not since she was a child. The whole experience feels strange, and it bothers her mind. However, she feels better after Guy's attempt to comfort her.

"You still seem distressed," Guy persists.

"N'inquiète pas – Don't worry; I'll be fine in a little while. Let's just get to the club."

"Okay Val."

When they reach Guy's car, he opens the door for her. The Dragon Princess is clearly rattled, but it's not Estelle's words that's bothering her now. She feels strange and annoyed at how her sentiments for Guy have affected her. She looks at him and wonders if he could be the true source of her torment. In any case, she's still annoyed with her friends' companions and decides that she will try to avoid them in the future. Valerie chooses to ignore what's on her mind and focuses on her upcoming routines. She must be mentally prepared to perform well tonight, but right now, she's not in a good frame of mind.

"Guy, I know we didn't talk about it before, but I would prefer if you just drop me off tonight and not come in with me - okay. You can visit with me at the club another night. You have my number now, so you can call me. Perhaps we can get together again on Sunday when I finish Bianca's portrait. I hope you don't mind. I just want to be alone tonight after work."

Guy is surprised, but he takes Valerie's request in stride. He's beginning to get used to her spontaneous decisions.

"That's fine Val. I'm just happy that you gave me the opportunity to spend the day with you and meet some of your friends. I'm sorry everything didn't turn out the way you expected."

Valerie looks at Guy with an approving smile.

"You're very sweet, Guy. I've never met a man like you before. I think you're exceptional and not like most of the men I've known in my life."

Guy smiles, as he pulls up in front of Le Théâtre Coquette. Valerie gives him a sensuous kiss on the lips before getting out of the car. Then, Guy escorts her to the red doors of the cabaret. As Valerie darts inside, she turns to look at him with her penetrating eyes. Suddenly, that strange warm feeling returns.

Could I be falling in love? Non, a thousand times, non! Valerie scolds herself.

And with that thought, she disappears from Guy's sight, and heads to her dressing room where Bianca is waiting for her.

IX. Game of Hearts

Valerie is beginning to think that she might have made a mistake by bringing Guy to Montmartre with her. Her relationship with Guy was supposed to remain entirely physical, but she's beginning to miss him when he's not around, and she has been daydreaming about their future trip to Le Côte D'Azur – The Blue Coast. Valerie has lived a certain lifestyle for many years – alone and free, and she doesn't want to become attached to anyone, only to be disappointed in the future. Her poor relationship with her father has left permanent scars in her mind and it has affected her relationships with men. She doesn't trust any of them. However, she thinks Guy may be different.

In any case, Valerie decides to make another attempt to refocus his attention, away from her to some degree, which might help to shake things up a little. Her first attempt to bring Bianca into the picture didn't work out as well as she planned, so Valerie is thinking that maybe she should increase the stakes. Her plan would start by not seeing Guy again for several days and then take him to Club Bougie to have a little fun.

Club Bougie is an underground, swingers club, but geared mostly for young single people and not so much for older married couples. Guests are expected to dress well when they arrive, but then to shed most of their clothing by night's end. Instead of the club providing entertainment, the patrons become the spectacle themselves for others to watch and touch.

At one time, this popular hook-up spot used to be a destination for middle-aged men to escape from their wives and boring lives. However, these after-hours clubs have become more of a destination for a much younger and single crowd of enthusiasts. The current club-goers are thrill seekers and risk takers who desire to engage in casual sex in a safe, yet public environment. If you're looking for more privacy, like some brothels offer, this isn't the venue for you.

The atmosphere at this singles spot looks more like a labyrinth than a nightclub, designed for hedonists, nymphomaniacs, and exhibitionists, who find depravity and debauchery to be la soupe du jour. This nightclub is not a cheap, back-alley ballroom in the heart of the ghetto of Paris. The cover-fee at the front door is 1,500 francs for couples and 800 francs for men. Women are not allowed to be admitted unchaperoned – they must come with a male companion of some description. The dress code is very strict and if you don't meet the club's minimum standards for how you look, you will be turned away at the door, no matter how much money you shell out to bribe the bouncers.

In addition to the younger folks on the scene, this is also a destination for the rich, including: musicians, artists, corporate lawyers, stockbrokers, and playboys and girls, who desire to shed their daytime masks and engage in the carnal pleasures of anonymous and guilt-free sex. Champagne, cognac, caviar, raw oysters, and macaroons are just some of the delights served to wet young appetites and put them in the mood to indulge themselves in earthly pleasures.

No one is allowed to charge for sex, and any type of physical abuse, beyond blindfolds, bondage, and horseplay is strictly prohibited. Guests must also sign a ledger when they arrive for insurance purposes, although they are not asked to present identification. So, the names they write down are often inauthentic. The club is very discreet, and the owners go to great lengths to see to it that there are no problems among their guests. If a man is accompanied by his mistress and his wife or fiancée happens to pop-in on the same night, the gentleman will be notified promptly, to avoid any unpleasantness.

Valerie visits this establishment regularly. The propriétaire loves when she arrives because her presence always attracts many single, rich men, so he allows her to enter free of charge. She thinks that taking Guy to this sex club may be a good way to create a little distance between them and broaden his experience a little more.

Maybe if I bring Guy to Club Bougie, he will become so caught up in the lifestyle Paris has to offer after dark, that he will forget about wanting an exclusive relationship with me. There are many desirable young women who come here. It's worth a try. I just don't want Guy to form an attachment to me.

Valerie is in denial about her own feelings. After taking Guy to Club Bougie, she may ultimately regret it. She needs to be careful what she wishes for, because she may end up getting the outcome she desires. Instead of making herself happier, she might end up making herself miserable. For a woman like Valerie, her emotions can sometimes be volatile. She's normally in full control of her environment, but occasionally, she can act like a volcano and explode at any minute.

I wonder now whether it will be better to disinvite Guy to my flat on Sunday, because it will give me more time to relax and focus on finishing my portrait, without distraction. I've already played the Bianca card with Guy, and it fell flat. On the other hand, if he's there, we could all end up sleeping together. Then, I won't get the portrait done. I'm also not certain what effect creating a love triangle might have on my relationship with Bianca. The women Guy and I will encounter at Club Bougie will not likely be close friends of mine, so I won't need to worry about that problem there. I need to play my cards right if I am to win this game of hearts. I must think this through before I make a mess of everything.

For Valerie, love and lust are just games to be played like poker. Gamblers need to read their opponents carefully, without being concerned about the hand they are dealt. The game of hearts can be a lonely one, but it can also be thrilling when the pot is full, and the stakes are high.

Valerie carefully considers all the angles, while she finishes getting dressed for her opening act. She's aware that the men and women in her life can also be like pawns in a game of chess, where she is the queen, and the only objective is to conquer the king.

This is what I think I will do. I will ask Bianca to come alone to my flat tomorrow and I will take Guy to Club Bougie, after he's had some time away from me. That way, I can give both Bianca and Guy my undivided attention.

Valerie imagines that she's in complete control over the situation. In reality, her feelings for Guy are starting to get the best of her, despite her efforts to ignore them. Love is always a dangerous game when you try to manipulate the outcome. Someone's heart is bound to be broken.

In any relationship, there will always be an X-factor – something unforeseen happening. This is why Valerie has tried her best not to mix her feelings with her pleasure games, because the lines of love and lust ultimately become blurred.

As Valerie finishes formulating her plan in her mind, she puts the finishing touches of makeup on her face, and then hurries to find her position in the dark on stage. As the music begins to play, the spotlight illuminates, revealing her presence. The moment she begins to move, the audience begins to feel the heat from the Dragon Princess' flame, and her dance of desire begins again.

*

After Guy drives away from the club, he heads toward his home in Aubervilliers. Overall, he had a nice day, and he's glad Valerie decided to introduce him to some of her friends. He thinks about what Estelle said earlier and what he knows to be true about Valerie. He turns his thoughts about his new lover over in his mind several times, wondering if he should heed Estelle's warning. His emotions are a mélange between caution and desire. He loves the sense of freedom Valerie brings to their relationship. On the other hand, he feels uncomfortable that this love affair will likely never lead anywhere.

Perhaps I should just enjoy this liaison while it lasts and not worry about the future?

Guy begins thinking about what he really wants for himself.

Do I merely want an exciting short-term relationship with no commitment? Is this just my way of sewing my oats before feeling ready to ask Gabrielle to marry me? Perhaps, what I want is to figure out a way for Valerie to fall in love with me? However, that's not something I have control over. Two people falling in love must happen naturally and it's not something that comes easily for either of us. I wonder if Valerie is even capable of it. She doesn't seem to be the type to me. I should probably get used to the idea that she is just every man's fantasy and I'm nobody special to her — just another toy to be played with, until she becomes bored and throws me away.

Guy's thoughts torment him incessantly. So, he decides to stop off for a drink at Le Café Olympia, on the avenue de la République.

Perhaps my friend Étienne will be there to talk things over with me.

His thoughts now drift to imagining Valerie taking her clothes off in front of another crowd of thrill seekers. Even though that's how he met her in the first place, he's becoming increasingly disenchanted with her chosen profession. Guy's mental struggle needs to work itself out before he drives himself crazy.

Perhaps a few drinks with Étienne will help clear my mind.

As Guy enters the café, he looks around for his friend, who he assumes will be there by this time. However, protocol dictates that he must first say hello to everyone in the bar. A ritual Guy wishes didn't exist. Fortunately, there aren't that many people there yet —only about 25 or so, since it's still relatively early. As he's making his rounds, he spots Étienne sitting at the end of the bar drinking alone. He's waiting for an attractive divorcé to come sit by him, so he can offer to buy her a drink, and strike up a conversation. His usual routine often ends in failure, but he never gives up.

Étienne is a colleague of Guy's and a mortgage broker, who he frequently makes deals with when buying properties. Étienne is older than Guy. He's 39 years old, good looking with sandy blonde hair and hazel eyes and recently divorced. His marriage only lasted about three years. He simply wasn't ready for the responsibility or the challenge of getting along with someone who has completely different interests.

Étienne claims his wife was controlling and jealous and found himself bickering with her constantly over trivial matters. She didn't appear to be that way when they were first dating, and he believes that she changed the minute they were married. However, Étienne knows that difficulties in a marriage sometimes have to do with elevated expectations people have once they become committed and dependent on one another, versus simply having fun on dates.

On the flip side, Étienne showed very little empathy toward his wife concerning her point of view on important matters. He often refused to talk to her about the problems they were having and didn't show much interest in doing anything about them. Instead of addressing her frustrations, he ignored her, instead of listening. Occasionally, Étienne would become verbally abusive, which only pushed her away further and caused their physical relationship to dwindle, leading to more resentment and emotional distance.

Now that he's alone, Étienne is even more miserable than he was when he was married. Apparently, he ignored the golden rule – 'Happy wife, happy life.' So, now he drinks to forget how badly he screwed things up for himself and spends his weekend nights with the occasional salope or lonely housewife.

Guy recognizes that Étienne isn't a relationship Guru by any stretch of the imagination, but he understands how challenging they can be. Guy also knows that he will find a sympathetic ear talking about the pitfalls of trying to cultivate a compatible partnership. He believes that if nothing else, his friend can shed some light on his dilemma and perhaps provide him with a little perspective over a drink.

"Bonsoir Étienne," says Guy.

"Guy, ça va – How's it going? May I buy you a drink? I'm not having any luck meeting women tonight, so I might as well drink with you, instead of drinking alone," Étienne replies.

"Oui, bien sûr – Yes, of course."

"Deux bourbons avec coca, s'il vous plaît – Two bourbons with coke please," Étienne demands.

"Merci. I stopped in, hoping to see you."

"Oh really? What's up my friend? Don't tell me, let me guess – you're having second thoughts about breaking up with Gabrielle."

"Not exactly."

"Then what?"

"It's about a new woman, who calls herself Valerie. Her nickname is the 'Dragon Princess.'"

"Oh wow! Where did you meet a woman with such an exotic label?"

"We met at Le Théâtre Coquette. Have you heard of it?"

"Oui. What does she do? Is she a cocktail waitress?"

"Non, she's a dancer."

"You mean she's a stripper."

"Oui, but she's much more than that. She can really dance, she sings and plays the flute, and in her spare time – she paints. Plus, she's very intelligent."

"That doesn't sound anything like Gabrielle, except for the intelligent part."

"Exactly, that's just it. I broke it off with Gabrielle because I found her to be too predictable and she kept pushing for us to get married and have a family."

"It sounds to me like you may have fallen hard for this manslayer, n'est-ce pas – isn't that true?"

"Peut-être, oui. Je ne sais pas - Maybe, yes. I don't know. I just haven't figured out what to do about her yet. She is not someone who I can bring home for family get-togethers, if you know what I mean. Even if I asked her to attend a family function, she would never agree to go anyway. She's not the type of woman to settle down or even be committed to one relationship at a time. She's definitely not family oriented and I know she doesn't want children."

"Perhaps that's her charm. You don't seem to want or care about family matters and commitment, and neither does she. This Dragon Princess sounds like a dream date to me. I'm guessing that despite your reservations, you really like this woman. You've been out with her and had a great time, but she's maybe a bit too elusive for your taste and comfort - is that it? You're loving the excitement of dating a cabaret dancer, but you might be concerned that she won't fit into your lifestyle, nor you into hers. Maybe, you're even worried that she may become bored with you and move on, leaving you out in the cold."

"Oui, I knew you'd understand Étienne - that sums it up nicely. I wasn't sure what was bothering me about her exactly, but I think you hit the nail on the head. If I wanted someone just like Gabrielle, I would still be with her. I'm very attracted to Valerie, perhaps because she's so unpredictable. Maybe, that's what I'm looking for – spontaneity and a little adventure."

"If I asked Valerie how she feels about me, I doubt she would tell me what I want to hear. Perhaps, she doesn't feel anything at all for me. I'm a bit scared to find out how she feels. Let's say that she tells me that she loves me in the future. In her world, that doesn't mean that we would have the kind of relationship I would expect, and she would probably never agree to marry me. I don't even think she understands the concept of sexual fidelity. Loyalty yes – faithfulness – no. I wonder why I am attracted to someone like that. Does that mean I don't really want to be exclusive with anyone and that's why I picked someone like Valerie? Perhaps I don't know what I'm talking about."

"It sounds like you have a tiger by the tail, my friend," says Étienne.

"More like a dragon by the teeth to be more precise. Remember, I told you that she's known as the 'Dragon Princess' among her circle of friends. She has one of those mythical reptiles tattooed around her body." Guy replies.

"Now that sounds exciting! I'd be lucky to find a girl who will even paint her fingernails, much less her body."

"Oh, don't exaggerate. You've gone out with plenty of good-looking women. You were even married to one."

"Oui - Yes, but you're missing my point. I haven't dated anyone quite like your Valerie, in terms of how you describe her character. You've got hold of a tornado, mon ami. You should try to enjoy the ride while it lasts, before it blows up in your face. You're already aware that this isn't a long-term proposition. She is like a woman you meet on vacation – someone you can have fun with for a few weeks. Then reality sets in when it's time to go home."

"You're probably right Étienne. Except…"

"Except what?"

"Except, that…I really like her, and I may be falling in love with her."

"Oh boy, then you're in trouble, mon ami – my friend. However, I'm not surprised to hear it. Anyone would be blown away by a woman like that. Guy, she's an exotic entertainer, and according to you…a very sexy one. It's only natural that you're dazzled by her because she's so titillating. However, you can't allow yourself to fall in love with a woman like that. She will only break your heart."

"Oui – Yes, I know you're probably right."

"Bien sûr, j'ai raison - Of course, I'm right."

Just then, the bartender returns.

"Can I get you gentlemen another drink?"

"Oui, Étienne replies, and keep mine coming."

"You're a good friend Étienne. Perhaps, I just need to shake this feeling I have for Valerie and focus on enjoying her company. A roller coaster is thrilling, but at some point, the ride must end, and one must put one's feet back on the ground."

"The best way to shake your love addiction my friend is to hook-up with another woman and go to bed with her. According to you, it doesn't seem like this dragon lady will mind too much. In fact, she may even want to join you, by the way you describe her. It shouldn't be too hard for a good-looking rich guy like you to find another woman to sleep with."

"I'm not sure I'm ready to do something like that. I'm not really an orgy kind of guy, I think."

"Where is your lady-friend tonight – performing?"

"Oui, and she told me not to stay for the show tonight, after I dropped her off at work."

"You see, she's already putting some distance between you. Trust me, you'll thank me later. I can tell that you're already in too deep with this shark – allowing yourself to tread in dangerous waters. You need some time to screw your head back on straight, mon ami – my friend."

"You make a good case Étienne, but I don't think going to bed with another woman is the answer for me – especially with someone I'm not really interested in. Unfortunately, I don't think anything is going to change my mind or my feelings about Valerie at this point."

"Alors, mon ami - Then my friend, for you, I am most sorry. I'm afraid you may already be lost. Suit yourself. However, it seems to me that you're in over your head with this dragon lady."

"Dragon Princess."

"Oui, that's what I meant. That makes it even worse. Her title suggests that she is a double threat. You know what you're supposed to do with dragons - don't you, Guy?"

"Slay them?"

"Oui, that's exactly right." Do yourself a favor - put an imaginary sword through her heart before she destroys you first."

"I can't do that."

"Then, Heaven help you. All I can say is - I wouldn't want to be in your shoes, unless I had no real feelings for this woman."

"Je t'ai compris – I have understood you. Listen Étienne, it was great catching up with you. Thanks for the drink and the advice, but now I need to go clear my head."

"Just remember what I told you – this Dragon Princess will burn you up, then eat you alive! You don't have the kind of armor you need to play with that beast."

"You may be right, Étienne. Thanks again for being such a good friend. Bonne soirée – Good night."

"Ciao, mona mi – Goodbye, my friend."

Guy exits the bar after leaving a tip. Unfortunately, instead of the conversation with his friend making things better, he feels even more tormented and confused than he was earlier. His little parlé with Étienne didn't go quite the way he imagined it. Perhaps, he was looking for encouragement, instead of advice.

As he heads to his car, he thinks about Valerie performing at the club in front of all those lust-crazed men and feels jealous. He suddenly has a strong desire to go to Le Théâtre Coquette uninvited, but he knows Valerie wouldn't appreciate it. Pulling a stunt like that could ruin everything. He doesn't want to be accused of spying, so he dismisses the idea from his mind.

After sliding into the front seat of his Renault, Guy starts the engine, but then just sits there behind the wheel for a few minutes thinking, before heading home. All kinds of thoughts and feelings explode in his mind and in his heart. His hands begin to shake, and anxiety begins to permeate throughout his body, despite the alcohol still streaming through his system.

Coincidentally, a song called 'Valerie Loves Me' by an American band called Material Issue, is playing on the radio. Guy has studied English, so he comprehends the lyrics to the song. He can't get the words out of his head, which talks about Valerie's lonely future, after all the men she knew have gone. Guy senses he's losing control of his emotions and his direction in life. Unfortunately, there's nothing he can do about it – not right now anyway.

Guy reacts to his emotional state of mind by gripping the steering wheel tighter, as if the wheel is an integrated part of his mind and he's trying to control it. After merging onto the highway, his speedometer surpasses 100 kilometers per hour and is still climbing. He doesn't usually drive this fast, but in this instance, his mind is not focused on his speed.

As he exits the freeway and enters his town, a traffic light ahead turns red, but Guy doesn't acknowledge it. Suddenly, he sees a truck coming across his path and he slams on the brakes, just short of the stoplight, narrowly avoiding impact. His body is thrust forward toward the front windshield, but his seatbelt pulls him back. He's breathing hard, while his heart races and his body is drenched in a cold sweat. The only other sound he hears besides his heart pounding is the engine idling.

What's happening to me? I need to stop thinking about Valerie so intensely!

He tries to relax for the moment, as the light changes from red to green. It takes him several seconds before he puts his car in gear again. He drives more slowly now, on the route to his home, where he will go to bed early and try not to think anymore tonight.

*

The next morning, Valerie is awakened by Guy's call around 11 am.

"Oui," Valerie responds, after searching for the phone with her eyes maladjusted.

"Bonjour Val, c'est Guy – Good morning, Val, it's Guy."

"Ah, bonjour, ça va – good morning, how are you?" Valerie replies.

"Ça va - I'm doing fine."

"I called to see if you still wanted me to come over today."

"Oh, Je suis désolé – I'm sorry Guy, but I think I should just paint alone with Bianca. I will be able to concentrate better if I want to discuss some things privately with her, if you don't mind."

Guy is a bit blindsided and upset by this last-minute change of plans. However, he's polite as usual, and pushes his feelings to the side for now.

"Sure, it's okay. I understand Val. Have you had a chance to think about when you could take a trip with me to the south of France?"

"Oui, I can get away the following week on Monday. Will that work for you?"

"Oui, ça c'est superbe – Yes, that's great!"

"Bon, je t'embrasse pour maintenant, au revoir - Good, I kiss you for now, goodbye."

"Attends - Wait! Will I see you before then?" Guy asks, desperately.

"Oui, I almost forgot to tell you. I have somewhere I want to take you tomorrow night, around 11:30 pm. Is that too late for you?"

"No, it's okay," says Guy, not wanting to admit that it's later than he wants to be out during the work week.

"Bon! Viens me chercher, chez moi - Come look for me, at my house, around 10:30 pm. We can have a drink before we leave at eleven. Is that okay?"

Guy is encouraged, despite being initially disappointed that he wouldn't be seeing Valerie today. He's happy that he will be going out with her tomorrow night instead, despite the late hour. He was awake most of the night before thinking about her anyway, so being out late together instead might be an improvement on losing sleep lying alone in bed. He will just need to be patient. Guy is beginning to realize he's developing an addiction for the Dragon Princess, but he doesn't want to admit it.

I'm in control of this! Guy tells himself, as he goes to the liquor cabinet and pours himself a drink. It's not even close to noon yet, and for the first time since his college days, Guy is drinking in the morning, which is uncharacteristic of him.

*

Valerie can't go back to sleep after Guy's call, so she slowly reopens her eyes to find Fafa sitting on her bed, staring at her in the face.

"Bonjour, mon petit – Good morning, little one. I know, you're waiting to go outside for your stroll, but maman needs to make some coffee first."

"Ruff," Fafa growls, clearly displeased.

Valerie's thoughts shift to the previous night. She had sat down with a customer to chat after her performance and he became a bit too aggressive, trying to put his hands on her. She had to call Bruno the bouncer over to deal with him. After that unpleasant confrontation, she got up from his table and he was thrown out, but the whole incident put Valerie off. She was bothered by the man's advances more than usual, and she didn't know why. She can't quite put her finger on it, but she knows something must have changed with her.

Maybe I was just tired?

Valerie puts the coffee on to brew and tries to put this thought in the back of her mind. She is still feeling strange by the time she pours her first cup and stares out of the window before looking at the clock. It's almost 11:30 am and Bianca will be arriving in just a couple of hours. Valerie knows she still needs to take Fafa out, but she also wants to make breakfast and take a shower before her friend arrives.

"Stop looking at me like that Fafa. We'll go for a walk in just a few minutes. Let me finish my coffee first. Your breakfast is right over there, so eat up."

Instead of eating, Fafa runs out from the kitchen and starts scratching at the front door. He looks back at her with sad eyes and begins to bark.

"Oh, merde," says Valerie, as she buries her head in her hands. "This dog is going to drive me crazy this morning."

Valerie finishes her morning brew quickly, slips on her jeans and a T-shirt, then removes Fafa's leash from the hook near the door.

"Viens bébé – Come baby, maman will take you outside now."

As they promenade along the sidewalk, Madame Dupont interrupts their stroll.

"Bonjour Valerie. I see that you are both without your male companion this morning," says Madame Dupont.

"Oui, because he has family business this morning," Valerie replies, telling a little white lie.

"Oh, Je comprends - I understand. He seems like such a nice young man. You know, you ought to be thinking about getting married soon my dear."

Valerie can't help but laugh at the suggestion.

"Married!" exclaims Valerie. "Oh, mon Dieu, non – my God, no! Guy is a gentleman, and I am very fond of him, but we hardly know each other. However, thank you for the kind advice."

"Well, keep in mind what I said, Valerie. A good man is hard to come by. Anyone who takes such good care of you and your little dog Fafa, the way he does, is a man worth keeping."

"I will take your suggestion into consideration, Madame Dupont - bonne journée – good day."

After stopping off at the boulangerie to buy bread and croissants, Valerie and Fafa return home in a relatively short time, so she can eat breakfast and take a shower before Bianca arrives.

"It's so funny, isn't it Fafa, how people want to run other's lives. People can't even run their own life properly, much less anyone else's. They think they know best when it comes to making decisions for other people. This is how people in government think with their twisted minds. Anyway, eat your breakfast now pumpkin, while maman fixes something for herself."

Valerie whips up some eggs to go with her croissant and pours herself another cup of coffee before jumping into the shower. The time is now close to 12:30 pm, and Bianca will be arriving in a little while. Valerie believes she's made the right move by putting Guy off for a day and meeting with Bianca alone.

After washing her hair, she steps out of the shower and dries herself off before putting on her robe. She walks into her bedroom and looks at herself completely naked in her full-length mirror. Everything seems firm and tight – her breasts and backside look round and smooth. However, she's beginning to become aware that she's getting

133

older and realizes that her career as an exotic dancer won't last forever.

Nothing to worry about, she thinks to herself. *I'm still young and beautiful. I certainly don't need a husband! A man will only slow me down and complicate my life. If that were to happen, I would start looking older from all the stress. The next thing you know, he'll want me to start having children. Non, C'est pas pour moi - that's not for me! A dragon's life is one of solitude and independence. A leopard can't change its spots any more than I can change my scales.*

And, with that thought, Valerie proceeds to get dressed. Moments later, the doorbell rings. Fafa, who has been resting on his bed in the salon, alerts his master to the potential danger. Valerie opens her front door but is surprised when she's greeted by a delivery boy, instead of her friend.

"What's this?" asks Valerie.

"Flowers for Mademoiselle Fontaine," replies the delivery boy.

"Ah, merci."

She hands the boy a tip, closes the door and reads the card.

I noticed since the first time I visited your apartment that you have no flowers anywhere, so I bought you some to brighten your day. Guy

How sweet! Oh no, wait. *Guy is becoming very romantic lately. I think he's becoming too attached to me. I've done so much to discourage that from happening. I'm truly baffled by this gesture. Doesn't he understand that our relationship is only about sex?*

"What do you think Fafa - Is Guy falling in love with me?"

"Ruff."

"I think so too, my sweet boy. Don't worry Fafa, no man will take me away from you. You will always be number one in my life."

Valerie walks into the kitchen to find a vase for the flowers. After filling it with water, she puts them on the coffee table in the center of the room.

Just then, the doorbell rings for the second time, and once again, Fafa alerts his master by barking.

"Salut, mon chérie – Hi, my dear," says Bianca, as Valerie greets her with kisses.

"Ça va, toi – Are you doing okay?" Valerie replies.

Bianca notices the flowers on the table the moment she arrives.

"Oh, someone has sent you roses. Who are they from?"

"Guy sent them."

"Really! He must be taken with you."

"It's beginning to look that way. I haven't encouraged him romantically. I keep reminding him that our relationship is just for pleasure and for the short term, but I'm not sure I've been getting through to him."

"Valerie, I think he's falling for you, which is not hard to imagine. You have a special charisma which attracts the whole of Paris."

Valerie smiles and then quickly changes her expression.

"Anyway, I'm taking Guy to Club Bougie tomorrow night to have a little fun with him. I'm hoping that will sufficiently distract his attention from his romantic fantasies concerning me."

"You're taking that prudish guy to a sex club! Are you sure you want to do that so soon?" asks Bianca.

"Oui, I'm expecting that he will reveal that he is merely looking to spice up his life a little and isn't focused on having a committed relationship. I know what men want. They desire to have passionate sex with hot women, who will take their minds off their dreary and predictable lives. Men are not very complicated."

"I don't know Val, this man seems different from most of the men who come to our club. He is a gentleman with class, beyond money. He's intelligent, sophisticated and most of all - kind. This ploy of yours could end up backfiring on you. You better be careful."

"N'inquiète pas – Don't worry. I know what I'm doing. Now, enough talk about Guy. Remove your clothes in my bedroom, slip on my robe, and let's get your portrait finished, d'accord – agreed."

"Oui, d'accord – Yes, agreed."

When Bianca returns, she stands in the bedroom doorway, as the sunlight from the window shines upon her dark chocolate brown hair, causing it to shimmer and glow. Her eyes sparkle like the stars at night, and her smile lights up the room. At such a ripe young age, Bianca is truly a child of the universe - beautiful and wondrous, full of life and optimism.

Her body is perfectly symmetrical, with curves in all the right places. She looks more like a statue than a real woman, chiseled by the gifted hands of Michael Angelo. Her arms and legs are long, smooth, and delicate. She is truly magnificent. She almost makes Valerie envious, but instead, she feels pride, as though she were her child.

"Sit over on the sofa Bianca and take off your robe. I have everything set up already."

"You mean you're not going to offer me a drink first before you demand to see me naked?" asks Bianca, with an impish grin.

"Normally, I would be happy to oblige you, but you take forever finishing your drinks, so no. Let's get to it!"

"Alright then," Bianca replies, as she minces over to the couch and unties Valerie's robe, allowing it to fall to the floor.

"How much am I being paid for this again?" asks Bianca, facetiously. "You know it's one thing to remove my clothes at the club, but at least I'm compensated handsomely for it."

"Making love to me afterwards isn't enough of a reward?" asks Valerie, playfully.

"It might be, but you've done that without me having to pose for you before, so I think I deserve a little extra reward this time when you're finished."

"You are a greedy little bitch, aren't you? It's a great honor to sit for me. That should be reward enough," says Valerie, as she begins to paint.

"You know, I'm just teasing you, right Val?"

"Oui, je sais – Yes, I know. Now, close your lips and open your legs."

Valerie spends most of the afternoon putting the finishing touches on Bianca's portrait. When she finally puts down her paint brush, the two of them make love, shower together, then go out for a celebration dinner. Bianca spends the night, so they have time to make love again. The next morning, Valerie walks Bianca to the train station and kisses her goodbye before she leaves.

Valerie is pleased with her work and making love to Bianca was icing on the cake. She adores her sultry young colleague and being intimate with her after painting her portrait felt deliciously satisfying. Her young protégé is not only a good dancer and model, but she is also an excellent student in the art of making love. Valerie has groomed Bianca to be her special playmate and she has filled her role perfectly.

After Bianca leaves, Valerie takes Fafa for his late afternoon walk, and thinks about Guy and her plans for the evening.

I wonder how Guy is going to react to my little scheme. He will either love it or hate it. One thing is for certain – I have that boy wrapped up in a blanket. Soon, it will be time to set this man on fire!"

X.   Club Bougie

Guy arrives at Valerie's place on time, as usual. Other than Sunday, this is the only other night of the week Valerie has off from work. She won't need to arrive at Le Théâtre Coquette the next day until after dinner. Guy, on the other hand, needs to work early the next morning, but he has resigned himself to sleeping less, ever since he met the Dragon Princess. It's a small price to pay for a little excitement, but it's still taking some time to get used to this new lifestyle.

"Bonsoir Guy," says Valerie, as she opens the door to greet him. "Ça va?"

Guy kisses Valerie enthusiastically on the lips, as if he hasn't seen her in weeks.

"Ah, so you missed me yesterday. That's good to know," says Valerie.

"Did you receive the flowers I sent you?"

"Oui, merci – Yes, thank you. You're very sweet. They are right over there on the table. Elles sont très belles – They are very beautiful."

"What would you like to drink?"

"How about a whisky-sour?

"Oui, pas de problème – Yes, not a problem!"

"Where is little Fafa?"

"I put him to sleep in my bedroom already. He will stay quiet until we return. My neighbor will check on him later. I hope you brought a change of clothes for tomorrow this time."

"Oui, je l'ai fait – Yes, I did."

"So, how did the painting go yesterday?"

"It's finished."

"May I see it?"

"Oui, si tu veux – Yes, if you want," Valerie replies, as she walks over to uncover the portrait of Bianca.

"Voila – Here you are!"

Guy is startled for a moment by its life-like appearance. The colors and detail are so vivid.

It's quite exquisite – really mesmerizing, Guy thinks to himself.

It almost seems as if Bianca is in the room with them. Her eyes appear to be staring seductively at him, as he gazes upon her naked figure. He feels paralyzed for a moment and can't speak because the image seems so real.

"Well, what do you think - cat got your tongue?"

"It's remarkable - truly magnificent! You have incredible talent!"

"Merci. Does it make you desire her?"

"I don't know if I should answer that question."

"Don't be shy, Guy. It was my intention to make her appear sexually provocative. If you don't want her, then I didn't do a good enough job."

"You did a fine job," says Guy.

"Bon, merci – Good, thank you!"

"Here's your drink Guy – you may need it to calm your nerves," Valerie says smiling. "If you think this portrait is hot, wait until you see what you're in store for later tonight."

"I assumed we were going to some kind of club, since it's so late."

"It's not just any club mon amour – my love. We're going to someplace very special!"

"Should I be worried?"

"No, but you'll need to keep an open mind. Have you finished your drink? Let me know when you are ready to go."

"Oui, je suis fini – Yes, I am finished. We can go now if you like.

"Allons – y alors – Let's go then," says Valerie.

When the pair arrive at the scene of the surprise, Guy is a little confused, because he sees no sign of any club.

"Where is it? I don't see anything."

"Suis-moi, mon chéri - Follow me, my dear."

Valerie and Guy walk for a little while, until they find an alleyway around the corner, which snakes around and leads to a dead end. There is a door on the left, but no sign in front of it. Dozens of people are waiting in a line behind a large man dressed in black.

"Bonsoir Hugo," says Valerie.

"Valerie! It's a pleasure to see you again," says the man in black.

"Who's your friend?" asks Hugo.

"This is Guy – Guy Martin."

"Enchanté, monsieur. Valerie, you know there is no cover for you, but it will be 800 francs for your friend. He can pay Margot inside."

"Oui, d'accord, merci – Yes, agreed, thank you."

"Have a good evening; enjoy yourselves."

Hugo allows Valerie and Guy to enter the club immediately, which annoys the others still waiting in line. Once inside, Guy notices that the only illumination in the room is by candlelight, which reflects the name of the club.

"Valerie, bonsoir!" says Margot. "Who is your handsome friend?"

"Je te présente - May I present to you – Guy Martin."

"Enchanté," says Margot. "Welcome to Club Bougie. I hope you're planning on sharing this fine-looking man tonight, Valerie, because this one will garner a lot of attention from the ladies. Otherwise, you may cause a brawl, and we don't want that to happen."

"We will have to wait and see," says Valerie, as she glances over at Guy suggestively.

"What does she mean by that?" asks Guy, as he whispers in Valerie's ear.

"I will explain it to you in a minute."

"You must leave your belongings in a locker over there, including your wallet. I will give you a debit card for 1000 francs with which you can buy food and drinks. I will charge this amount to your credit card, and you will be refunded any amount that you don't spend."

"Your entrance fee entitles you to one free glass of champagne each. No money may change hands with the other guests to discourage any drug exchange or sex for money. This is not a house of prostitution nor a place to sell drugs. Also, definitely no cameras of any description are allowed! Comprenez–vous, monsieur – Do you understand sir?"

"Oui, Je vous comprends. Yes, I understand you."

"Enjoy yourselves," says Margot, after Guy pays the fee and puts their belongings in a locker.

Guy and Valerie descend the winding staircase toward the interior of the club where dozens of people are gathered. Before they enter, Valerie explains to him exactly what they will encounter on the inside.

"Alors – So Guy, this is not a bordello. This is a club where people come to have sex with one another in public, or they can simply watch, if they wish. It's more than just a swingers' scene. Instead of swapping partners in a foursome, you can experience multiple partners at the same time or individually. It's all on a mutually consensual basis."

"These are people just like us, who come here to have a good time with whoever and whenever they choose. No one is obligated or pressured to do anything they don't want. Everyone is free to engage as they wish, and individuals must agree to participate in any type of tryst or sexual experience, in advance. The people who come here are not only thrill seekers, but exhibitionists, so most don't mind an audience. If people want a more discretionary experience, there are private rooms where people can engage in more extreme sexual encounters. In some of these rooms, guests use props like whips and crops and perform acts of sadomasochism and humiliation."

What Margot was alluding to before was that you will be red meat among a lot of hungry, she-wolves here tonight. Tu comprends – Do you understand?"

Guy nods without saying a word, but his expression is one of shock and confusion. He thought they were just going dancing. The moment

Valerie finishes her sentence, they complete their descent. When Valerie opens the entrance door, the pair encounter a large room full of good looking, well dressed, semi-dressed, and completely nude individuals. Some guests are engaged in conversation, others are eating and drinking, and several people are having sex, out in the open.

Off to the side, Guy notices the private rooms, as well as a large oval-shaped bar. Techno music and flashing lights fill the space but cannot completely distract his attention from the ecstatic cries of pleasure from some of the guests who appear to be having their fill of carnal pleasures.

Guy has never seen anything like this in his life, except maybe at a wild college party. He can't even imagine what's going on behind closed doors in the private rooms. He wonders if this is really what some people are comfortable with doing in public, or if they are just too high to realize what's happening.

"What do you think Guy?" asks Valerie.

"I don't know quite what to tell you. This is all very new to me."

Valerie smiles, as she sees a friend of hers approach them.

She's a tall, elegant, 30 something African woman named Nia, wearing an orange and red Bohemian garment. She kisses Valerie squarely on the lips in an extremely sensual manner.

"Salut Valerie, ça va – Hello Valerie, how are you and who is your luscious companion?" asks Nia, as she eyeballs Guy with great interest.

"This is Guy."

"Enchanté – It's nice to meet you, Guy," says Nia, as she extends her hand to be kissed.

Without hesitation, Nia becomes the first to proposition the new couple.

"There is a room free in the back - would you both like to join me there?"

"We haven't even had anything to drink yet," Guy protests.

"I can see this one's a bit squeamish," says Nia, locking eyes with the Dragon Princess.

"Guy is a newbie to this scene. You'll need to give him a little more time to adjust to the culture," Valerie replies.

"Well then, why don't you two follow me to the bar, so I can help you put a couple of champagne flutes in your hands."

"Oui, d'accord, allons-y – Yes, agreed, let's go," Valerie replies.

The trio make their way over to the bar to ask for some champagne.

"So, Valerie, where did you dig up this precious cargo of yours?" asks Nia.

"Oh, he's not mine, exactly. I'm just taking him on a little Tour de Paris," Valerie replies.

"Bien, alors – Well then, are you his exclusive guide, or can anyone help show Guy the sights?"

"That's up to him," Valerie replies.

"Trois champagnes, s'il vous plaît – Three glasses of champagne, please," Guy demands, as he catches a bartender's eye.

"Tout de suite – right away," the server replies.

Before receiving their drinks, Nia makes her next pitch for Guy's attention.

"Alors – So then, what do you think of these?" asks Nia, as she exposes her perfectly shaped breasts to him.

Taken by surprise, Guy stares at Nia's chest for a moment before glancing over at Valerie to gauge her reaction. Her look is one of approval and encouragement, as if she is goading him once again. Guy grabs one of the champagne flutes from the bar and swallows some before responding.

What is Valerie up to this time, I wonder? She seems to want me to have sex with other women, but I'm not entirely sure why. Is she just baiting me, or does she get-off on watching?

The idea of becoming entangled in a ménage à trois with Valerie might be stimulating in his imagination, but it could also mean that their relationship might take a turn down an unforeseeable path. Guy begins to weigh the risk vs reward scenario in his head. He's turned on because the woman in front of him is incredibly sexy, but at the same time, he's also trying hard to remain in control of his reactions to Valerie's manipulative ploys.

Guy realizes that attempting to navigate any situation Valerie is involved in is a futile endeavor. Despite not coming up with satisfactory answers to his own questions concerning Nia's proposition, Guy attempts to respond to her provocative invitation in a way that allows him to at least seem like he's not just one of Valerie's toys.

"Attendez - Wait! Before you respond, I want you to see everything," says Nia.

She casually unbuttons the rest of her outfit and lets it fall to the floor. She stands in front of Guy, completely naked, except for the red, patent leather high-heels she's wearing, and an 18-karat gold rope chain she wears around her neck. Valerie doesn't flinch. Instead, she gazes upon Nia's beautifully sculpted bronze corps with desire. Guy is noticeably uncomfortable. Despite the sexual atmosphere around him, he wasn't prepared for such a provocative maneuver from a total stranger. Her deep dark eyes are hypnotic and capture Guy's attention.

Nia gently places her right hand across her inner thigh and slides it down her leg, while her other hand caresses one of her breasts. Guy is transfixed by every move she's making. He's aware that his efforts to resist this seductive encounter have now gone out the window.

Initially, Guy thought he had an answer to Nia's proposition, but her enticing display of provocation suddenly causes him to have second thoughts. He doesn't even possess the ability to look at Valerie, who is observing him out of the corners of her eyes. Nia turns around slowly with her arms raised, showing Guy and dozens of onlookers her entire body to admire and covet.

"Eh bien, qu'est-ce que tu penses maintenant - Well, what do you think now?" asks Nia.

Guy is finally able to turn his head to glance over at Valerie, who is smiling at him, devilishly.

"Tu es magnifique, exceptionnel – You are magnificent, truly exceptional!" exclaims Guy.

Nia glances below Guy's beltline to verify that he's telling the truth and truly inspired by her raw display of sexuality. She smiles, pleased that she has made a strong impression, after verifying his natural and undeniable response.

"Perhaps you need just a little more encouragement," says Nia.

She steps forward and puts her arms around Guy's neck and presses her glossy lips against his mouth before thrusting her tongue to the back of his throat. He feels Nia's breasts pressing against his chest, as a warm sensation begins flowing through his body. His heart is beating rapidly, and his palms are beginning to perspire. The room is getting warmer by the minute.

Other than the drinking game that he had at the club with Valerie and Bianca, this is the most enticing experience he has had in his life. Still, it makes him feel uncomfortable because he's not in control of anything. In one respect, Guy craves to lose himself in this surreal fantasy, but at the same time, he pleads with himself to resist this temptation.

Once more, he glances over at Valerie, who appears to be turned on by watching her friend try to seduce her lover. She touches a hand to her cheek and licks the top of her lips, as she glares at the exhibition in front of her with lustful anticipation.

Abruptly, Guy releases himself from Nia's tight grip, grabbing her hands from behind his neck and gently pulls them apart. Valerie and Nia are startled by Guy's action.

"Attendez - Wait," says Guy. "You are incredibly desirable Nia, but I don't think I'm ready for this kind of thing right now. Je suis désolé – I'm sorry. Believe me, I wish I could agree to your request."

Nia turns her head and catches Valerie's eyes which are wide open in disbelief. She shrugs her shoulders, apologetically.

"Suit yourself, monsieur. I'll be around if you change your mind," says Nia, as she pulls her garment back over her shoulders. "Enjoy your evening - both of you. Valerie, it's been good seeing you again."

Nia blows them both a kiss, before disappearing into the crowd.

"Es-tu fou ou quoi - Are you crazy or what! Guy, how can you turn down a woman that hot? You just rejected one of the most beautiful women in all of Paris! You must be out of your mind!" exclaims Valerie.

"Je suis désolé, - I'm sorry, Valerie. Believe me, I was tempted to accept her proposition. You're right – she is extremely beautiful. However, you must understand that I don't live in your world of uninhibited sex and adventure. I'm just a real estate investor from Strasburg. It's a conservative town. I didn't grow up in Paris, like you."

"I've broken many of my rules and habits already, just by being with you. I'm used to dating just one woman at a time. If you want me to be honest with you – I'm not really into this kind of scene. I'm a very straight-laced, traditional kind of guy. As far as sex goes with other women - honestly, I'm not really interested. I only want to be with you and no one else."

Valerie is a little shocked but not completely surprised by Guy's revelation. She's never run into a man quite like Guy before. His reaction to Nia's advances was unexpected, and she feels a little perplexed by his proclamation. Somehow, she also feels pleased and flattered.

"I don't know what to say," says Valerie.

"You don't need to say anything. I'm simply telling you how I feel. That is something that has always been challenging for me to do, but, I feel comfortable telling you. I thought I needed to say something, after what seems to have been a series of orchestrated attempts to distract my attention from being placed solely upon you." Guy replies.

Valerie is embarrassed that her little shell game has been uncovered. *"This man is smarter than I gave him credit for."*

"Pardon-moi, Guy, s'il te plaît – Excuse me, Guy, please. I apologize for bringing you here. I thought that you might like it. Would you like to leave now?"

"Don't apologize Valerie. There's no harm done. It's been an experience that I'll not soon forget, and I don't mean that in a bad way. I'm grateful that you are showing me things that I would never have done on my own. I don't want to discourage you from introducing me to other things in the future. It's just that I'm not ready for this kind of thing yet. Perhaps, I will want to come back again with you in the future, when I feel more comfortable."

"I don't want you to change your lifestyle or who you are for me. All I'm saying is that as far as sex is concerned, you're free to do whatever pleases you, but I would like only to be touched by you for now, if that's okay."

"That's very sweet of you to say, Guy," Valerie replies.

Once again, Valerie is at a loss for words. She's never known a man to be so devoted to her, especially when there are so many desirable women in Paris. Sure, other men have been crazy for her, but it's been all about their lust-filled fantasies. None of it was ever sincere sentiment. Their attention has never been about true love's devotion. For Valerie, this is something completely new and unexpected. She's not sure what to make of it or what to do about it.

"Guy, I… I'm very flattered that you feel that way about me. However, I told you…"

"Oui, je sais – Yes, I know! You're not looking for a boyfriend."

"Oui, mais, s'il te plaît – Yes, but please, give me some time to reflect on what you've confessed, okay."

"Oui, d'accord. Allons–y alors – Yes, agreed. Let's go then."

Guy and the Dragon Princess make their way to the stairs and ascend from the debauchery and hedonistic orgy still happening in the cave. Guy knew that such places existed in Paris but seeing one up close for the first time has been quite a surreal experience.

"Are you two finished with your evening so soon?" asks Margot.

"Oui, however, we enjoyed ourselves," Valerie replies.

Guy collects his and Valerie's things from the locker, has the money he didn't spend returned to his credit card, and heads for the door.

"I hope you both will come again." says Margot.

"Merci, bonne soirée – Thank you, good evening," Guy replies.

"Au revoir - Goodbye," says Margot, winking at Guy, as he and Valerie exit the nightclub.

"That man is in love with her. It's so clear," says Margot to herself.

Valerie is beginning to feel a little peculiar now. She doesn't quite know what to think about what's just transpired. Guy stops for a moment, underneath the moon and the stars, takes Valerie in his arms and kisses her tenderly. Valerie feels her body reacting in an unfamiliar way. Guy's kiss is so passionate, so sincere, so loving that she nearly collapses in his arms.

She's frightened about what's happening to her because deep down, she knows the truth. Tears begin to form in her eyes. She closes them and loses herself in the moment, as one of her teardrops falls discreetly onto the stone pavement. The Dragon Princess, who has praised herself for being self-reliant and emotionless, may have finally opened her heart – at least for this moment.

After walking back to Guy's car, the two lovers drive back to Courbevoie together, without much conversation. Valerie sings quietly along with the radio, attempting to drown out her thoughts, until Guy breaks the ice.

"I'm sorry Valerie for making you feel uncomfortable, if that's how you're feeling."

"N' inquiète pas, mon amour - Don't worry, my love. It's not your fault - it's mine."

"You see, I've always been a one-woman kind of a guy. It's not that I don't find your girlfriends alluring – I do. It's just that I don't find them as interesting as you. I know that you keep saying you don't want a relationship and I can appreciate that. I'm not trying to change your mind. I simply like you very much – I can't help it. I understand that you enjoy attracting attention from other people and it doesn't bother me too much. However, do you really want to live the rest of your life without ever having a long-term relationship or experiencing true love?"

Valerie is floored by the question.

"Je ne sais pas – I don't know, Guy. I don't want to think about it. Right now, I'm debating between going home with you and ripping your clothes off with my teeth or having you drop me off alone, so I have time to think."

"Well, if it's all the same to you - if you choose the first option, I will prefer it if you didn't rip my clothing, because they cost me a bundle."

Valerie looks into Guy's eyes and smiles. She appreciates his sense of humor.

"I'll tell you what Guy…I promise that I won't try to distract you with other women anymore, but I'm not sure if I will ever be ready to have an exclusive relationship with you or anyone else. I find you very pleasant to be around and I like your manner. Perhaps I even have feelings for you, but I can't make any promises to you right now and perhaps not in the future. I'm happy to spend time with you, but only when I wish. I don't want to feel obligated to you when I want to be alone or spend time with others. I'm truly looking forward to traveling to the Riviera together, but I don't want you to be upset with me for living my life the way I'm accustomed to. I also don't want anything to spoil the fun we've been having together. Do you understand me?"

"I appreciate your candor, Valerie. Je crois que je te comprends - I believe I understand you."

"I'm not saying never, Guy — just not now and probably not for a while. I'm just not in a place where I'm ready to change my life drastically. I hope that doesn't change anything between us."

"I understand - really. Well, we've arrived. Do you want me to stay or go?"

Valerie looks at Guy with indecision.

"I don't want to think anymore tonight Guy — so stay, but let's not talk anymore about our relationship - okay. I also need you to leave after breakfast, so I can get some things done and prepare to go to work later. I know you have work tomorrow too, anyway. We can talk about our trip over the phone during the week — okay. I'm free to leave after next weekend."

"Okay, that sounds good, Val."

Valerie puts her arm around Guy's neck and kisses him. They walk the stairs to her flat in silence. Guy is smiling because he feels like

149

Valerie has at least left a window open concerning their future. He's optimistic that there is still hope for a relationship. It may only be false hope, but he's willing to let the ball on the roulette wheel fall where fate dictates.

Guy always has his lucky coin with him to help choose his path. That night Guy and Valerie not only make love, but she even allows him to remain in her bed. After Valerie falls asleep, Guy stays awake a little longer, just watching her.

Somehow, I feel different with Valerie than I did with Gabrielle. I can't quite put my finger on what it is exactly, but I know I don't feel the same. I always wondered what was stopping me from asking Gabrielle to marry me and now I think I know why. I loved Gabrielle, but I wasn't in love with her. I feel something for Valerie that I've never felt before.

Unlike Gabrielle, however, Valerie refuses to be vulnerable and won't commit to anything. That's the main barrier now between us. It's next to impossible trying to get inside her head and penetrate that cold heart of hers, but I think I might have made some progress tonight. I don't quite understand why I'm so attracted to a woman like this, but I am. I wonder what that says about me. All I know is…I think I'm in love with her, regardless of what that means for my future.

Guy turns his head and watches Valerie a little while longer while she sleeps peacefully. He puts his arm around her, touching her shoulder lightly, which surprisingly feels like the coldness of death. He senses danger. It's merely an inclination, but just the same - he has the feeling something terrible will happen in the future.

Don't let your mind play tricks on you Guy, and don't let Valerie get inside your head too far."

Guy watches Valerie's bare chest gently rise and fall, until he closes his eyes before finally drifting off to sleep. Fafa is aware of the silence and leaves his bed on the floor in the salon. He pokes his nose through Valerie's door, then climbs up onto the bed. Fafa is not about to give up his place so easily. He finds a space just big enough to burrow himself in between his master and his new male friend to go to sleep.

Fafa has seen many women and men come and go through Valerie's revolving bedroom door, but he's confident he's the only one who will be staying permanently. However, this is the only time he's ever had to share his master's bed with anyone all night. What this little bulldog doesn't realize yet, is that even though this is the first time, it's likely not going to be the last.

XI. Secrets and Lies

It's Tuesday evening and Valerie is back at work. She's getting dressed for her act to kick off the evening when Bianca walks into the dressing room.

"Salut ma chérie – Hi my dear," says Bianca, as she kisses Valerie.

"Bonsoir, ma belle fille – Good evening, my beautiful girl."

"How did your night out at Club Bougie go with Guy?"

"Well, it was fine, but things didn't turn out quite the way I anticipated."

"What do you mean?"

"Well, at first I thought everything was going smoothly, until Nia introduced herself to Guy."

"Oh," says Bianca. "Ce-qui s'est passé - What happened?"

"As you know, Nia is incredibly striking, so I was thinking since Guy seemed comfortable with you, he would warm up to her as well. Unfortunately, I thought Guy was going to have a panic attack when she propositioned him to have a ménage à trois in one of the private rooms."

"Really!"

"Oui. At first, it seemed like he was turned on and I started to get excited, but then I realized that he was becoming uncomfortable. Nia came on too strongly, I think. Her aggressive approach was just too intimidating for Guy to handle."

"Oh my! So, did he turn her down?"

"Oui. He didn't like the whole scene at Club Bougie. I think he was just too overwhelmed by everything. Apparently, he's never been to a place like that before. It's not really his style."

"I tried to warn you. Does Guy know you go there frequently?"

"Not exactly. He knows I've been there before, but he doesn't know how often I go."

"I see. So, then what happened? Did you end up having sex with anyone there?"

"Non, pas de tout – No, not at all. In fact, he wanted to leave after the fiasco with Nia. You know, she was completely naked in front of him and even stuck her tongue in his mouth and he still didn't bite."

"Pas possible – Not possible! I can't believe it! I wonder what would have happened if I had been in Nia's place, instead?"

"I hate to say it, but I'm certain the results would have been the same. He said he only wants to have a sexual relationship with me, and he was very clear about it."

"Mon Dieu – My God. That can only mean one thing."

"Oui, je sais – yes, I know."

"Guy is in love with you!"

"I'm afraid so."

"Wow, that's big! So, what are you going to do about it?"

"I told Guy that I still want to spend time with him because I like him, but I'm still not interested in having an exclusive relationship. And, honestly, I'm not sure I'm capable of falling in love with anyone. He still wants me to go with him on a trip to Le Côte D'Azur – The Blue Coast."

"What did you say?"

"I said yes of course because you and I have some pressing business there. However, I made it clear that going on vacation together doesn't make us a couple."

"Hmm, that was a little cold. What was his reaction?"

"He seemed to be content with our arrangement for now.

"Does Guy know about our side-hustle yet?"

"Shh, don't talk about that here; someone might be listening," Valerie scolds. "No, I will never tell him, if I can help it. You know, Guy is aware of what happened concerning that little episode in Boston. He recognized the painting on my wall, but I assured him that it was a copy. He hasn't brought it up again, but I'm going to replace it with your portrait so that he forgets about it."

"Looking at your nude body instead might refocus his curiosity in another direction. Guy may be in love with me, but he's still a man and therefore still susceptible to psychological and sexual manipulation. I'm planning to take the Rembrandt with me when we go to the Riviera. I have a clandestine buyer ready to take it off my hands -you're coming too."

"Well, you'd better be cautious just the same. If we ever get caught, we may never see each other again, and that won't be the worst of it."

"N'inquiète pas - Don't worry, I have it under control."

"You'd better hurry and finish putting your makeup on Valerie; your number is next."

"Oui, je sais; arrête de t'en faire – Yes, I know; stop worrying."

As Valerie finishes getting ready, she can't help but think about Guy and the Rembrandt. She doesn't want him to know anything about what she's planning to do during their excursion to Nice – just that she has some business to take care of in Monté Carlo.

Flying to Boston last March and stealing several paintings from the Isabella Stewart Gardner Art Museum was a highly risky, but fruitful endeavor. Smuggling them into France was equally challenging, but Valerie managed to do it. The whole ordeal was thrilling as well as potentially lucrative, if she could sell them successfully, without being caught.

Valerie and Bianca had disguised themselves as policemen. When the time was ripe, they subdued and bound the gallery guards. An accomplice disabled the alarm system, allowing them to get away cleanly with 13 rare paintings valued at over $200 million dollars at the time. These works of art included 'A Horse Leaving the Paddock with its Rider,' by Degas, in addition to the 'Storm on the Sea of Galilee,' by

Rembrandt and 'The Concert,' by Vermeer.

It was a brilliantly planned scheme, masterminded by Valerie herself. She had to hire a securities expert, through her connections in America, to take care of the alarm system. Once he did his job, stealing the paintings and slipping away unnoticed couldn't have been easier. The police, the FBI, and Interpol all have no clues as to the perpetrators' identities. They suspect that the Boston Mafia were involved, but despite several arrests, offers of clemency, and a $10 million-dollar reward, the authorities remain in the dark. There have been no further developments in the case - the trail has gone cold.

As Valerie puts on the final touches to her makeup, she gazes in the mirror and smiles fiendishly, knowing that she got away with one of the biggest art heists in history. It gives her great satisfaction realizing that she had outsmarted everyone. The money she and Bianca will earn from the sale of the stolen merchandise will be enough to buy a new place to retire along the Riviera, while having plenty of money left over - enough for the rest of their lives.

*

After work, Valerie and Bianca stop by Le Café Noir to have a drink and to say hello to their friends.

Bonsoir Jacques," says Valerie.

"Valerie, Biannca, ça va – how are you?" Jacques replies.

"Ça va Jacques – I'm fine Jacques."

"So, what will it be ladies? Your first drink is on the house."

"In that case, how about two shots of Johnny Walker Black."

"Tout de suite – Right away."

"Is everything all right Valerie? You look a bit tired," asks Jacques.

"I'm fine, just a bit stressed, I guess," Valerie replies.

"Is your work becoming too demanding?"

"No, it's not that. I just need a little vacation - that's all."

"So, why don't you get away for a while?"

"I'm actually traveling to the Riviera next week with the man I introduced you to recently."

"So, he's your boyfriend now?"

"Non, pas vraiment - No, not really. I would describe him as my current romantic male interest."

Bianca gives Valerie a look, as if to say… *Guy is a little more than just that.*

"Well, I hope you can catch up on your rest while you're there. Knowing you, I'd say you might come back more exhausted than when you left."

Bianca laughs, while Valerie gives her a disapproving look.

"You ladies enjoy the rest of your evening."

"Merci, Jacques," they reply.

"To good fortune," says Valerie, as they raise their glasses to toast.

The pair toss their whisky back in one gulp.

"Feeling a little better now Val?" asks Bianca.

"Not quite. I need at least two more of those before I'll begin to relax."

Two men approach Valerie and Bianca, hoping they'll be an easy score.

"Bonsoir ladies. Can we buy you gals another drink?" says one of two men, looking for a little action.

Bianca is about to say yes when Valerie speaks up, instead.

"Vas te faire foutre! – Go fuck yourself," Valerie replies.

"Hey, take it easy. No need to bite my head off. We're just trying to be friendly," the man says.

Valerie gives the men a deadly stare as they turn and walk away.

"Why did you have to be rude?" asks Bianca. "One of them was kind of cute."

"Je suis désolé chérie - I'm sorry darling. If you want to go talk to them instead, you're free to indulge yourself."

"Laisse tomber - Never mind; it's no big deal. You seem on edge tonight."

"It's just that this thing with Guy has been on my mind. Perhaps, I'm also nervous about the sale of the painting in Monaco. Guy's been pushing me for a commitment and it's distracting me from focusing on making plans to sell the painting. A lot could go wrong during the trip. Jacques is right about me, albeit for the wrong reason. I'm going to be a lot more stressed on this trip than I have ever felt working at the club."

"Oui, c'est vrai – Yes, that's true. Why don't you go home and get some sleep."

"Oui, I should." Then, you can go after your man, or both men for that matter, without feeling guilty. I know you just want to get laid, you little bitch."

Bianca gives Valerie a devilish smile.

"Do you blame me?"

Valerie and Bianca kiss goodbye. Then, she leaves the bar alone, but not without several eyes in the room following her to the door. She puts on her helmet, fastens it under her chin and mounts her motorbike. Feeling the soft leather between her thighs, she pumps the kick-starter, and the engine comes to life. She slides her visor over her face in a determined fashion, then revs the motor a few more times before releasing the clutch and speeding away.

Valerie is still feeling frustrated and confused. Her feelings for Guy are getting in the way of her normal routine and her plans for selling the Rembrandt. She must find a way to solve her problem, short of breaking off their relationship entirely. She can think of no solution at this moment, so she decides to give things more time to settle down.

During their trip to Nice, Valerie needs to find a way to keep the Rembrandt hidden from Guy and keep him from becoming involved in her business in Monté Carlo. These are the things that are cluttering her mind, presently.

I'm not going to think about this now, Valerie says to herself.

She spontaneously revs the throttle and lifts the front wheel of her bike high into the air and rides off into the night toward home.

XII. Rendezvous on the Blue Train

The next morning around 11 am, Valerie calls her buyer.

"Hello, Alejandro," says Valerie.

"Si," a voice replies on the other end of the line.

"I have your package. I'm planning on bringing it with me to Nice next week. I can meet you in Monté Carlo at L'Hôtel de Paris to make arrangements for the exchange."

"Bueno - Good! What day will you arrive in Monaco?"

"A week from Friday."

"Bueno. Call me before you leave Nice. I will let you know the suite number I'm staying in.

"D'accord - Agreed," says Valerie. "Don't forget the price we agreed upon. I'm taking a big risk by bringing you this painting, so don't stiff me and try to renegotiate."

"Don't worry. I will have all your money."

"Bon alors, au revoir – Good then, goodbye," says Valerie.

Valerie hangs up the phone. The stakes are very high because there's so much money involved for such a rare work of art by a famous artist. Valerie and Bianca's lives are also at risk. She knows people are willing to kill for a stolen painting like the one she plans to sell to Alejandro de la Cruz. Valerie is trying to think of every possible scenario of how things could go wrong, but there's always an x-factor.

I will have to tell Guy that I have business in Monaco and that I need to go alone. I just won't tell him what business I'm conducting and hopefully he won't ask too many questions.

Valerie nervously paces back and forth in her living room before pouring herself a glass of Courvoisier to calm her nerves. She looks up at the clock and sees that it's almost noon.

"Fafa, it's time for your afternoon walk and maman needs to think."

Fafa's head bobs up out of his basket. He trots over to his master eagerly, oblivious to what she's been planning. If he knew what she's up to, he would be thinking – *Don't go maman – stay with me!*

It's been a difficult week for both Guy and Valerie. They haven't seen each other at all because they've both been trying to work hard and get things done prior to their trip to the south of France. Both Valerie and Guy are nervous about going away together, but for different reasons. Guy is stressed because he believes there is a lot riding on this trip, in terms of his relationship with Valerie. She is anxious mainly because of her business in Monaco.

They planned to meet at La Gare de Lyon in Paris and take the train from there to Nice. The Blue Train, also known as The Millionaires Train, is an overnight line, which originally made its debut in 1886, as one of the world's first overnight lines. It typically stops in Dijon, Lyon, and Marseille before reaching its final destination in Nice. It begins in Calais, next to the English Channel, and ends in Menton, a little town northeast of Nice, just before the border with Italy. It's not far from Eze, which is also known as the Village in the Sky.

The Blue Train got its nickname from its dark, blue-colored sleeping cars, adorned with gold trim. All the cabins have a comfortable place to sleep, and passengers enjoy a five-star dining experience. When this overnight train first came on the scene, passengers were assigned personal attendants, who took care of all their needs. Only the rich and famous could afford the high price of this luxurious form of transportation, similar to the Orient Express. Now, there are second- and third-class compartments so more people can afford to travel on this line.

The French Riviera has always been the playground of the rich and famous. Writers, musicians, and artists like Pablo Picasso, F. Scott Fitgerald, Gertrude Stein, Coco Chanel, and Cole Porter in the 1920s all took the Blue Train from Paris, seeking out the soothing, turquoise waters of Le Côte D'Azur – The Blue Coast.

Guy and Valerie will be traveling First Class and will disembark in Nice, where they have booked a room at the famous Hôtel Le Negresco. This luxury suite hotel opened its doors in 1913 to the aristocratic society of Europe. It was built along the Promenade des Anglais, overlooking the Mediterranean Sea. Its pink dome, along with its stained-glass windows and marble floors, gives the hotel a classically French Bourgeois complexion.

Le Negresco is also well-known for its fine art collection and opulent décor, which changes with the current fashion. Not far away, there is a museum dedicated to Pablo Picasso, the famous Spanish artist, who is best known for his unique, avant-garde style.

Valerie intends to visit the Picasso and Matisse museums while in Nice, but she dares not attempt another art heist before she tries to sell the Rembrandt. The Dragon Princess will have to wake up earlier than usual to catch the train on the morning she departs. However, first, she must take Fafa for his walk before dropping him off with her neighbor. Then, she will stop at a café to have a quick espresso and croissant before taking the train from Courbevoie to meet Guy at La Gare de Lyon.

The previous night, Valerie removed the Rembrandt from its frame and packed it with her luggage. Then, she replaced the empty space in her bedroom with Bianca's nude portrait. If all goes as planned, she will be ready to embark on her journey to the Blue Coast by Monday morning.

Valerie knows she will need a certain amount of luck to leave the Riviera with a suitcase filled with cash, while evading discovery by Interpol. She wishes she had Guy's lucky coin, but since she doesn't, she will bring a deck of Tarot cards with her to predict the outcome of future events. Despite being highly intelligent, Valerie still has superstitious proclivities. She does believe in fate and chance, but still adamantly resists the lure of true love.

*

The time has finally arrived to make the journey south. Fafa has been properly taken care of and Valerie has finished her espresso. She walks down the street with her luggage in tow to board the train from Courbevoie to Paris. She takes a seat and removes the Tarot cards from her purse. She begins to flip one of the cards and places it in front of her. It is the fool, upright – meaning a new beginning, having a free spirit. It perhaps refers to Valerie's new course in life once she sells the Rembrandt. The next card is the lovers. Perhaps, foreshadowing her relationship with Guy. Finally, she flips the card of death, which greatly disturbs her mind.

Who could this be referring to and when?

She will have to wait and see what destiny is being carved out for her and her friends. Only time will tell. She feels excited and anxious at the same time because of what the cards have revealed. Perhaps, her destiny is to die on this trip.

As her train finally enters la Gare de Lyon, Valerie sees Guy standing on the platform, waiting for her with his hat on and his coat draped around one arm and his valise is in his other hand.

How gallant Guy is to wait for me here, instead of meeting me inside by the ticket counter.

As the train comes to a complete stop, and the doors open, Guy searches for Valerie among the hordes of people disembarking. Suddenly, he sees her rolling her luggage across the platform. She's wearing a red beret, tight black leather pants, patent red leather heels, and a white silk blouse. She spots Guy walking toward her and waves. As they come together, they kiss and exchange greetings.

"Salut Guy," says Valerie, as she smears her cherry red lipstick all over his mouth.

"Salut Val. Ça va?" Guy replies.

"Merci de m'avoir attendu ici. C'est très gentil – Thank you for waiting for me here. It's very sweet of you."

"It's my pleasure."

"Have you been waiting long?"

"No, not at all, because I had to stand in line for a while to buy our train tickets."

"Oh, you have them already - superb! You're a doll, merci.

The two begin walking in the direction they need to go, in order to catch their train on time.

"That looks like a lot of luggage you have there, Val," says Guy.

"Well, you know we are going to be away for a week. I need to tell you that I have some business in Monté Carlo I need to take care of while we're in the south. I must pop over there toward the end of the week, so I can get it settled, if you don't mind. I was hoping to fit in a little gambling too while I'm there too."

"I don't gamble."

"Oh, well, that's alright because I want to go alone anyway. I won't be too long – not more than a day."

"Really, Valerie - you're telling me this now!" Guy replies, caught by surprise again.

I wish Valerie would stop doing this to me!

"Oui, Je suis désolé - Yes, I'm sorry, but this came up at the last minute. I need to take care of this while we're there. I'm sure you can survive one day without me."

"I suppose I can, but I wasn't expecting that this was going to be anything but a romantic get-away for both of us. And, about your intention to gamble while you're there - I hope you don't end up losing a lot of your money."

"N'inquiète pas Guy – Don't worry Guy; I play the odds. I like card games like Blackjack, Baccarat and Poker. Those games involve mental stimulation and skill. I can remember almost every card that's been played in any game."

"Isn't counting cards cheating?"

"Why is it cheating to have a good memory? It takes a lot of skill not to get caught. I admit that I made a mistake once, staying at one table too long. I had to sleep with the owner of the casino just to keep from having my legs broken and being blacklisted."

"That would definitely have ended your dancing career."

"Don't I know it! Anyway, I learned my lesson not to be too greedy. Although, I do expect to win just enough this time to have a little fun and pay for some of our expenses on this trip."

Guy smiles at Valerie and rolls his eyes.

"You don't need to worry about that. I'll have everything covered. I don't want to rush you, since I have our tickets already, however, we should still head over to the platform where the Blue Train departs."

"Oui, d'accord – Yes, agreed."

"Have you taken this line before?"

"Oui, parfois - Yes, a few times. How about you?"

"Jamais - Never. Gabrielle wanted to take this train to go away for our honeymoon if we were to have been married. However, I never proposed, so I never had the opportunity. I wouldn't consider going to the Riviera on my own, so this is my first time visiting the south of France."

"Oh wow! You are a Blue Coast virgin. Well, we will have a big adventure together then. We will have much more fun than if you had gone with Gabrielle, I think."

"I don't doubt that for a minute," Guy replies.

"Our train is coming now," says Valerie.

Guy and Valerie board, along with dozens of other passengers. Unknown to Guy, Bianca is also embarking at the other end of the platform. During the trip, Valerie will transfer the Rembrandt to her for safe keeping. Valerie knows that she might be a target for the police as well as thieves, but to her knowledge, Bianca is invisible to everyone.

Valerie and Guy pass a few compartments, until they see theirs. The space itself is relatively small, but luxurious all the same.

"I wonder how quiet these walls are," says Valerie. "We might be making some noise tonight when we christen this compartment's bed."

Guy looks at Valerie and smiles.

Valerie often makes statements meant to provoke a reaction in me. Most of the time she's only teasing, but some of the time, she means exactly what she's saying. That's when I need to pay attention.

As the pair settles in, Valerie notices that champagne, strawberries, chocolate, and flowers have been gifted to their sleeping quarters by the conductor.

"Genial!" exclaims Valerie.

"Guy, let's open the champagne and have a toast to our journey."

"You love having any excuse to drink, don't you?"

"Oh Guy, don't be a killjoy!"

Guy holds a napkin over the bottleneck and pops the cork, causing a flood of bubbles to rush toward the opening. He holds a crystal champagne glass in one hand, while pouring Valerie's drink, before filling his own cup.

"To good fortune!" exclaims Valerie, thinking about the business exchange she will soon be making in Monaco.

They touch glasses and take their first sips, sealing the wish with a kiss, just as the Blue Train gets underway.

"Guy, I must confess that this trip is as much for business as it is for pleasure. I'm happy to be having some fun with you, but don't mistake me for Gabrielle. This vacation won't be exactly like the honeymoon you never had, considering it being strictly romantic. However, I guarantee that you will have an exciting and memorable time. I can promise you that much!"

"Je te comprends. Tu n'es pas amoureux de moi - I understand you. You're not in love with me. You enjoy my company, and you have business to take care of in Monaco. I get it!"

165

"Oui, but it doesn't mean that I would rather be alone on this trip or with someone else. You are important to me. However, I must keep my head on my shoulders and my feet underneath me. I hope you understand."

"Oui, je t'ai compris – Yes, I understood you."

"Let's go to bed, and I will make you forget everything."

Valerie kisses Guy sensually on the lips, which has the desired effect. They finish drinking their champagne, then Valerie slowly undresses her lover, so he can slip into bed and watch her undress in the dim light. She will make love to him like never before, albeit within the confines of a small bed.

This time, Valerie will be gentle and sweet, like she is normally with Bianca. She will take her time, savoring every moment and make him wait for almost 20 minutes before she allows him to enter her. She will make this night one he will not soon forget. Over an hour later, they end their love making by climaxing together to the sound of spinning wheels and the train whistle blowing, until Guy drifts off to sleep for an afternoon nap.

Now that Guy's asleep, Valerie slips out of bed, collects the painting, and hurries down the corridor to where Bianca is staying in second class. When Valerie arrives, she knocks gently, and Bianca opens the door.

"Salut - Hi Valerie," says Bianca and kisses her friend.

"Voici la peinture - Here is the painting. Now, I must go right away, before Guy wakes up and finds out that I'm not there."

"Je comprends, au revoir – I understand, goodbye. I'll see you in Nice."

Valerie scurries back down the corridor towards her compartment. She slips back inside quietly, then into bed without interrupting Guy's slumber. Everything is going smoothly and according to her plan.

XIII.   Hide and Seek

The Blue Train makes a stop in Lyon before continuing to
Marseille. Unknown to Guy and Valerie, another international art thief
by the name of Sylvain Bonnet, also known as The Cat from Brussels,
has just boarded the Blue Train in Lyon. He suspects that Valerie is
carrying a very valuable painting. Sylvain aims to steal it from her if he
can find it before the train arrives in Marseille, so he can depart the
train there.

It must be in her compartment if she's carrying it, Sylvain thinks.

He must first discover which cabin Valerie is staying in and then try
to search for the prize, while she's occupied in the dining car. Sylvain is
acting on a rumor only, so he's aware that he may find nothing at all.
He will have to wait at least until dinnertime before he can make a
move. However, he can't do anything until he knows her cabin number,
so he goes in search of the passenger roster before heading to his cabin.

While still on-route to Marseille, Guy and Valerie leave their
quarters, as expected, to have dinner. Sylvain spots their movements
and watches them as they disappear around the corner. He proceeds to
their door, picks the lock, and enters their compartment.

Sylvain knows he only has about 30 minutes at best to find the
painting if it's there, and remove it from its hiding place, without being
seen. He moves with great efficiency while searching Valerie's room.
He looks under the mattress, in their luggage, the drawers, etc., but he
can't find anything. He even searches the overhead bunk bed, but

there's still nothing there.

Valerie may not be carrying it with her, or perhaps she may not have anything to sell at all, The Cat thinks to himself.

Sylvain had received information from a good source that Valerie is planning on meeting a buyer in Monaco to unload a priceless work of art. Unfortunately, time is running out before the train arrives in Marseille, before continuing to Nice. He does his very best to put the cabin back exactly the way he found it. He obviously doesn't want Valerie to be alerted to the fact that someone has been in her cabin. He exits her compartment unnoticed by any passengers or crew members.

Where can it be, I wonder? Perhaps in the luggage compartment. Maybe she's mailed it to herself in Nice. She could not have taken it with her to the dining car - could she?"

Frustrated, Sylvain decides to go to the dining car to satisfy his curiosity. He will keep a close eye on his rival, hoping she will give him a clue as to where the valuable cargo might be. Sylvain surmises that Valerie might leave the train for a while in Marseille during the layover to stretch her legs and have some lunch before reboarding. However, it's pure speculation on his part, but he's hoping for a lucky break.

Guy and Valerie are currently enjoying their dinner, unaware that they have a thief on their trail. Sylvain finds a free table and sits down close enough to Valerie, so he can overhear her conversation with the gentleman sitting with her. He orders some supper, so that he doesn't draw too much attention to his presence.

Sylvain is wearing a bronze, suede leather chapeau and grey sunglasses to conceal his face from their view. He's not certain whether Valerie would recognize him, but he doesn't want to take any chances.

"So, Guy, how are you enjoying our little adventure?" asks Valerie.

"So far, so good, Guy replies."

"Bon, ça me fait heureuse - Good, that makes me happy."

"I must admit, I didn't think you would agree to come along with me on a vacation trip, but I suppose since you told me that you have some secret business to take care of in Monaco, that's why you agreed, n'est-ce pas? – Isn't that true?"

"It's not just that, Guy. You must know I adore you and enjoy our time together."

"You say that, but I still have the feeling that if not for your business in Monté Carlo, you might not have agreed to take this trip with me."

"Eh bien, tu te trompes, Guy - Well, you're mistaken, Guy. Now, finish your dinner and stop over-thinking everything. I'm here with you, and it shouldn't matter what other reasons I have for coming, should it?"

"I suppose not. I just wish you wouldn't keep me in the dark about your plans. You won't even tell me who you're going to meet next weekend or for what purpose exactly."

"You don't discuss your business with me either, Guy. I don't ask about your work because it's really none of my business."

"Well, I don't talk about my job with you, besides the fact that it's boring, is mostly because when I'm with you, I don't want to think about work."

"C'est la même chose pour moi, mon chéri – It's the same thing for me, my darling."

The conversation Guy and Valerie are having confirms to Sylvain that he's on the right track concerning the painting. Still, he asks himself… *Where is the merchandise she's carrying, I wonder? She won't even tell this man she's traveling with, so how will I ever find out?*

"You should stop fretting about things that aren't important," says Valerie.

"Fine, I promise I'll behave." Guy replies.

"When we arrive in Marseille, we will have about a two-hour break. We can get off the train there for a little while to have an early lunch, if you like. We can eat some bouillabaisse – the dish Marseille is best known for," says Valerie.

"That sounds tempting. Let's do it!" Guy replies.

"There's your smile. I thought you'd lost it for a moment," says Valerie.

"When I'm with you Val, I'm always happy," Guy replies.

Sylvain smiles after hearing this plan. He'll have another chance to look for the painting when the train stops, and now he has more evidence that Valerie plans to sell whatever she's carrying in Monté Carlo.

Valerie winks at Guy and puckers her lips to blow him a kiss. She removes one of her shoes and rubs her toes up against Guy's leg to get a rise out of him.

"Are you ready for another little frolic after dinner?"

"You mean you've already recharged your batteries after the last time?"

"Oui, mon chéri – Yes, my dear," Valerie replies, as she swirls her tongue, wetting her lips.

"Allons-y alors – Let's go then."

Guy and Valerie exit the dining car with Guy's arm held affectionately around Valerie's shoulders. As they approach their cabin, Valerie notices her hair pin that she wedged between the opening of their door, had fallen to the floor. She looks at Guy in an alarmed manner.

"Guy, someone's been in our cabin!"

"How do you know? We haven't even gone inside yet to see if anything has happened."

"I know because after putting a Do Not Disturb sign on our door, I put one of my hairpins in between the opening before we left this morning. It's now on the floor, which means someone entered our compartment."

"Could it have been a porter or a maid, perhaps?"

"I doubt it, but we can ask. I don't think the staff would have entered our room with that sign displayed. Guy, open the door; I want to look around."

Guy complies with Valerie's request, and they walk into their cabin together. Valerie scans the room, looking for any sign that something is out of place.

"Guy, there are several things in the room I can tell have been moved. I know it doesn't look like it because it's very subtle, but I can tell. Someone has been here searching for something."

"What should we do?"

"I'm not sure yet, but whatever they were looking for, I'm sure they didn't find it. However, I believe that whoever was sneaking around here will likely be back again. I'm going to talk to the conductor to ask him to have his staff keep an eye out and to contact the police if they see anything suspicious. That's all we can do. If we are to catch this thief, we need to be clever about it."

"Valerie, what is it that you're not telling me? Why is there someone on the train looking for something in our cabin, when perhaps no one else's room has been disturbed? What do you have that someone wants?"

"C'est rien; tu dois faire confiance à moi - It's nothing; you must trust me."

"Are we still going to leave the train in Marseille for brunch?"

"Oui, I won't let this miscreant ruin our enjoyment on this trip. Don't worry now, I will have everything under control. Nous allons attraper ce conard - We are going to catch this jerk!"

Valerie had thought about mailing the painting to their hotel just in case someone tried to steal it on the train, but she ultimately dismissed the idea. She didn't want to take a chance on the painting getting lost or confiscated. She considered hiding it in one of the panels of their sleeping compartment, but she thought that would take too much time. Guy would probably discover what she was doing. Valerie finally decided that she would let Bianca keep it and have her hide it discreetly inside her bed roll pillow, in her sleeping compartment. No one would think to look for it there.

Now that Valerie put the conductor on the trail of the thief, she feels more confident that this criminal will no longer be a threat to her. She won't allow a sewer rat to interfere with her plans.

While she is in Nice, Valerie will look for a flat to buy, overlooking the Mediterranean Sea. Nothing extravagant – something modest that won't draw too much attention to herself. However, it still needs to be chic enough to be a comfortable holiday destination, where she can relax whenever she needs a rest. Eventually, it will be her retirement home.

Performing every night can be stressful at times, and occasionally it's nice to be able to take a break from it to recharge her batteries. Valerie wants to have a tranquil place to paint in a beautiful setting by the sea and the money she will receive from the Rembrandt will give her what she desires.

Valerie thinks that Guy is the perfect man to help her look for a condominium, since he's a real estate investor and can advise her to make a good decision. She doesn't like keeping secrets from him, but she has decided that Guy is too strait-laced to keep quiet about her illegal side-business. She can't take a chance on revealing the truth to him, because he might turn her in or insist that she give up the merchandise.

Guy is becoming more curious about what Valerie is keeping from him. However, she has taken great risks to acquire such a rare piece of art and she dares not allow her scheme to unravel by letting her new beaux in on her secret. Still, Guy hasn't given up trying to find out what she's up to. Every minute the painting remains in Valerie's care is a risk, but it's one which she must take until she can sell it.

The next morning, the Blue Train begins to slow down as it approaches the Marseille station. Valerie's instincts tell her that the thief will make a second attempt to find what he's looking for, but she is still one step ahead of him. Sylvain is unaware that Valerie is wise to the break-in. She already has a good idea concerning his identity, but at this point, she can't be certain. Valerie is taking a risk by involving the police, however her hand has been forced. With any luck, by the time she and Guy have finished their early lunch, the fiend will be in police custody and her prize will be safe.

As the train finally comes to a halt, many passengers board and leave the train. Valerie and Guy are among the crowd who are departing. Valerie takes notice of what appears to be several plain-clothed agents boarding the train in search of the burglar. They take a seat for the moment to be less conspicuous, so that the culprit won't immediately try to run. Sylvain waits about 15 minutes before making his move. However, the moment he tries to pick the lock on Valerie's door, he is seen by one of the agents who blows his whistle, alerting the other officers.

Quick as lightning, Sylvain scurries down the corridor in search of a way to escape. He sees two other officers racing toward him from the adjacent car. He acts quickly and climbs through an open window and swings himself up onto the roof of the train. Police officers follow him in hot pursuit. The Cat begins to race along the top of the train, jumping from car to car, until he can slip back out of sight, through another open window.

Sylvain must think fast to evade capture. He looks around and sees a woman's coat and hat hanging on a hook. He quickly puts them on and exits the train casually, so he doesn't draw too much attention to himself. Soon, Sylvain begins to blend in with the crowd of people heading away from the platform and disappears. He is safe for the moment.

Valerie has out maneuvered him this time, but in the end, The Cat has avoided being captured. Sylvain will need to find another way to get to Nice, so he can make another attempt before the painting is sold. It will be several hours after the Blue Train reaches the Blue Coast, before he will be able to catch up to his target.

The Rembrandt is also safe for the moment, but Sylvain is still on the prowl, and he won't give up the chase so easily. For the moment, Valerie is unaware that The Cat has escaped her little mouse trap.

During all this excitement, Valerie and Guy were on their way to l' Epuisette for some of Marseille's famous fish stew, along la rue du Vallon des Auffes – a very chic French bistro, overlooking the Mediterranean.

"Deux pour le déjeuner – Two for lunch?" asks the hostess.

"Oui, merci – Yes, thank you," Guy replies.

"Right this way," says the hostess.

Valerie and Guy are seated outside at a table overlooking the seashore. The sun reflects upon its many miles of turquoise coastline, which sparkles like stars in the night sky across the surface. A misty grey sky creates the canvas for what appears to be a beautiful painting by Monet or Renoir.

The scenery almost appears to be too picture-perfect to be real. The squawk of seagulls and splash of the tide upon the jagged rocks below interrupt the silence of this blissful morning, creating an allusion of peace and tranquility. The aroma of fish and sea salt permeates the warm breeze and whets their appetites.

"Alors, Valerie, aren't you going to tell me what's going on? Why was someone rummaging around in our cabin and why are you worried about them coming back again? Clearly you have something somebody wants. What is it that you're hiding from me?"

"Ne t'inquiète pas, mon amour. Tout verra bien – Don't worry, my love. Everything is going to be fine."

"What do you mean? Everything is not fine."

"By now, whoever it was, has probably already been arrested by the police and on his way to jail, I think."

"I hope that's the case Val. However, I'd still like to know what this man or woman is searching for."

"S'il te plaît - Please, Guy, just sit there and look pretty. Let your Dragon Princess take care of squashing this bug."

"Oh, all right then - if you insist. I will stay out of it. However, I hope there is no one else coming after whatever it is you're trying to conceal. This is supposed to be a peaceful and fun vacation for us, and so far, I don't feel relaxed."

"Reste tranquille, mon chéri – Stay calm, my dear. You're by the sea now with me. Listen to the sound of the waves and breathe the fresh air. You will be at peace in no time at all – Je te promis - I promise you."

Valerie removes one of her cigarettes from her case and Guy lights it for her – this time, more smoothly.

"Perhaps, after I order some food, I will feel better," says Guy.

"Oui, c'est ça - Yes, that's it," Valerie replies. "Garçon!"

The waiter comes to their table with some sparkling water in hand and his notepad to take their order.

"Have you both had a chance to look at the menu?" asks the waiter.

"Oui," Guy replies.

"Qu'allez-vous prendre pour le déjeuner - What will you have for lunch?"

"We will have two dishes of your bouillabaisse, s'il vous plaît – please."

"Also, bring me a glass of champagne," Valerie chimes in.

"And for you, monsieur. What would you like to drink with your meal?"

"Une tasse de Chablis, s'il vous plaît - A glass of Chablis, please."

"Merci, I will return in a moment with your beverages. In the meantime, please enjoy some refreshing sparkling water," says the waiter.

"Merci," Valerie replies.

Guy reaches for Valerie's hands to hold and stares into her eyes.

"This is very romantic here - don't you agree?"

"If you say so, Guy. However, you must realize by now – I'm not the romantic type. Je suis désolé – I'm sorry. I hope you're not falling in love with me, Guy. If so, you'd better be careful, because you might get burned. I am a dragon, after all."

"I know that you're gifted at putting up a strong defense, but I think you are just hiding behind your armor. If there is a way to penetrate it, I will find it. I'm certain that underneath it all, you have a soft interior."

"Guy, you're either a hopeless romantic, a fool or perhaps both. Perhaps, they are the same thing. I don't fall in love easily. In fact, I can say for certain that I have never been in love, and I doubt I ever will be. I'm a practical and simple woman with expensive taste – that's all. Once I have what I want – I'm done. It's best if you don't get too attached to me. I have never been involved in an affair for very long. And, we have only known each other for a very short period of time."

"You're going to fight your feelings to the bitter end, aren't you?"

"I don't enjoy fighting, Guy - not even with myself. So, let's not argue."

The waiter returns with their drinks, and the pair lift their classes to make another toast.

"Santé – To good health," says Guy.

"A la bonne fortune - To good fortune," Valerie replies.

XIV.   The Riviera

When Valerie and Guy return to their train, they find several police officers standing in a circle on the platform discussing their plan to find and apprehend the thief that got away. The commander will leave some men around the train station as a precaution, in case the thief returns and attempts to board another train. As they begin to fan out, Valerie stops one of them to ask what's happening.

"Pardon, monsieur agent – Excuse me, mister policeman, but can you tell me if you have caught the burglar, and do you know who it was who broke into my cabin?"

"Unfortunately, mademoiselle, the culprit has escaped, but it was a man we believe. We have alerted more of our officers in the area, and we are creating a dragnet to try and trap him. We don't know his identity yet, but don't worry, we'll find him."

"Merci," Valerie replies.

"Is there anything else you can add, mademoiselle? Do you know why someone might be interested in your compartment? Do you have anything of value that this criminal might be searching for?"

"Non, je n'en sais rien du tout – No, I know nothing at all."

"Alright then. We're checking to see if anyone else's cabin was disturbed. We will place a couple of officers on board to keep watch until your train arrives in Nice."

"Merci, monsieur."

Valerie looks at Guy with disappointment, while biting her lip. She can't believe the incompetence of the French police, who ride around on bicycles, unarmed. She handed The Cat to them on a silver platter, and they still couldn't catch him. So much for her clever plan. So much for the useless French police.

"Do you not know who this character might be?" asks Guy.

"How could I know; I haven't seen him," Valerie replies.

"Well, who do you think he might be, and why is he after something that he thinks belongs to you?"

"If you must know what I think, Guy, I believe this criminal is likely a man known as The Cat. He's an international art and jewel thief, and he may think that I am carrying something valuable to sell in Monté Carlo. However, as you can plainly see, I have nothing expensive I'm carrying, other than my clothes and the jewelry I'm wearing. I am an artist, but my work is nothing of great value – not to a man like him anyway. He must have the wrong information if he thinks I have something he might want."

"Perhaps that's true, but this joker clearly believes otherwise."

"Eh bien - Well, I can't help what he thinks. He's just going to be disappointed, I'm afraid. If we are lucky, the police will catch him and that will be that."

"Let's hope so."

Valerie and Guy return to their compartment on the train and find that their cabin has not been disturbed. The police were able to disrupt The Cat's second attempt and chased him away before he had a chance to break-in again.

"Fortunately, this time nothing has been disturbed."

"Well, that's at least something."

"Let's make love and forget about it for now. We still have a few hours before we arrive in Nice."

"I'm on board with that. Afterwards, we'll still have time to take a nap."

Valerie begins to undress, then lies on the bed waiting for Guy to take her in his arms. When Guy finally falls asleep after their love making, Valerie slips away once again to rendezvous with Bianca. She knocks on her door and lets her know who's there. The two greet each other in the usual way, then Bianca closes the door behind them.

"Salut, ma belle-fille – Hello, my beautiful girl – is the painting still safe?" asks Valerie.

"Oui, chérie – Yes, dear, it's here inside my pillow," Bianca replies.

Bianca removes the Rembrandt from its hiding place and shows it to Valerie.

"Did you know that snake Sylvain has likely been aboard the train and entered my cabin, searching for this?"

"Non, I didn't know, but I heard a lot of commotion from the police after we arrived in Marseille. Is that what it was all about?"

"Oui. I warned the conductor to notify the police that The Cat was lurking about, and to have their men waiting for him when we arrived in Marseille. They boarded the train and chased him, but unfortunately, he got away."

"Tant pis - Too bad. Now what are we going to do?"

"We can do nothing now, except be on the lookout for him, in case he shows up again in Nice or Monté Carlo."

"I'm frightened Valerie! The last thing we need is for either the police or The Cat to be on our trail."

"Ne t'inquiète pas, ma petite. Tout verra bien – Don't you worry, my little one. Everything will be alright."

"J'espère que tu as raison - I hope you're right."

"I'd better go now. Guy is a light sleeper. He's already suspicious enough."

"Oui, d'accord – Yes, agreed. I will meet you at the apartment I rented in Nice after we arrive, and you get settled. Voici, l'adresse - Here is the address."

"Merci, à bientôt – Thanks, I'll see you again soon."

Valerie gives Bianca a kiss on the lips, then slips away down the corridor. She hurries as fast as she can, so that Guy doesn't realize she has disappeared. Fortunately, when Valerie returns, Guy is still sound asleep. She removes her clothes and slides back under the covers. Guy stirs for a moment, then settles back down.

The only sound remaining, besides the movement of the train, is from Guy's respiration, as his mind returns to a dream state. She extends one arm around his chest and presses her breasts against his back before closing her eyes. Feeling his strong body against hers gives her a sense of security that she never knew she needed.

Valerie tries to relax, but her mind won't allow her to stop thinking about what else might go wrong. She tries to bring back the recent memory of her and Guy making love, but it only causes her to become more aroused, instead of it calming her mind. She notices, once again, a heightened sense of emotion that she's beginning to develop. It makes her feel uncomfortable to have any sense of vulnerability.

Valerie may even be becoming a bit possessive of her new lover. Even though she doesn't want to belong to anyone, she might be starting to feel as if Guy belongs to her. She is even developing a sense that she needs to protect and shield him from harm.

Get control of yourself Valerie. Stop overthinking things – don't drive yourself crazy!"

However, Valerie is finding it harder to stay focused while she's with Guy.

There is only about twenty minutes left before they arrive in Nice, so she gives Guy a nudge to wake him up. It won't be long before the train pulls into the Nice station.

Hôtel Le Negresco has a stellar reputation for being one of the most luxurious boutique hotels in the south of France. There's a possibility that Sylvain might come searching for Valerie there. However, the Rembrandt will be safely tucked away with Bianca at another location. The Dragon Princess is happy to play the role of decoy, as long as it means that the stolen painting is out of reach of The Cat's claws.

Valerie is not quite as concerned about Sylvain stealing the painting as much as she is with his presence drawing too much attention from the police and Interpol. Guy is already starting to become more suspicious too. She doesn't want him asking too many questions and getting more involved. There is a lot riding on this exchange, and much could still go wrong during this trip, but Valerie is confident that she's still in control.

"Réveille-toi! Nous sommes arrivés à Nice - Wake up! We are arriving in Nice," says Valerie.

"Okay, Val, une minute, s'il te plaît - one minute, please," Guy replies.

Valerie gets out of bed and begins to get dressed.

"Don't you want to kiss me first?" asks Guy.

"Later my love. Now we must get ready to depart the train. Dépêche-toi – Hurry up!"

"D'accord, j'arrive – Okay, I'm coming!" Guy replies.

Guy slowly opens his eyes. The room appears fuzzy at first, but in a moment, he can see that Valerie is already dressed and is in the process of putting on her makeup. Guy sits up slowly and forces himself to get out of bed. Then he begins to dress and puts his belongings in his valise.

"Okay, I'm ready now," says Guy.

"Bon – Allons -y – Good, let's go." Valerie replies.

The doors to the Blue Train open, just as the luxurious iron horse comes to a full stop.

"Nice Ville!" the conductor shouts.

The young lovers depart the train and head straight to the street. When they walk outside, Guy attempts to hail a cab to take them to the hotel. It's a walkable distance, but he knows Valerie will expect a ride, and not be forced to traipse through the streets of Old Nice in high heels.

"Taxi!" Guy shouts.

A black Mercedes pulls up alongside the curb in front of them. The driver gets out and opens the trunk. Guy opens the back door for Valerie, as the driver stores their luggage in the back.

"Where to folks?" asks the cab driver.

"Hôtel Le Negresco," Valerie replies.

"Tout de suite – Right away," says the cab driver.

Valerie looks out of the window to see if she can see Sylvain lurking about, but she sees no one. For the moment, she is relieved. Before they depart, Valerie catches Bianca out of the corner of her eye hailing a cab for herself. She tries to distract Guy's attention, so that he doesn't spot her by accident. Valerie scans the crowd on the street once more, just to be certain they're not being followed.

"What are you looking at Val?" asks Guy.

"Oh, nothing dear – just sightseeing. Nothing to worry about."

A few minutes later, their cab pulls up in front of the hotel. A valet approaches their car to help them with their luggage.

Hôtel Le Negresco has a beautiful view of the Mediterranean Sea and is walking distance from the marketplace in Old Nice. This unique French landmark opened its doors in January 1913. The hotel highlights an exquisite crystal chandelier, adorning the great room. This centerpiece was supposed to be a present for Czar Nicholas II, until WWI broke out. During the war, the hotel had to be converted into a hospital, which put the iconic vacation spot in the red and drove it to financial ruin.

The iconic landmark was first sold to a Belgian company and then again to a woman named Madame Jeanne Augier, who came from a family of enormous wealth and influence. She had a unique flair for extravagance and decorated the seaside retreat with lavish interior furnishings, which included expensive works of art and exquisitely crafted antiques, suited more for royalty versus the nouveau riche. The hotel restaurant, Le Chantecler, was headed by one of the finest chefs and sous chefs in all of France, dubbing Hôtel Le Negresco – 'The Crown Jewel of the Riviera.'

"Bonjour, mademoiselle et monsieur. It's a great pleasure to see you here again Valerie," greets the hotel concierge.

"Merci Jean-Pierre," Valerie replies.

"They know you here as well?" asks Guy, a little surprised and even more impressed.

Valerie looks at Guy and smiles.

"Mais oui, bien sûr, mon amour – Yes, of course, my love," Valerie replies.

"I should have guessed."

"S'il vous plaît - Please, come to my office. I will check you in personally, so you don't need to wait in line," says Jean-Pierre.

"Merci, Jean-Pierre. You're a doll."

Guy and Valerie follow the concierge to his office and sit down, while he checks the room assignments.

"It says here that you are booked in the Marie Antoinette suite for six nights. C'est juste - Is that right?" asks Jean-Pierre.

"Oui, c'est ça – Yes, that's right," Valerie replies.

"Bon - Good. You'll be on the fifth floor. All your luggage will be sent to your room immediately. Voila, la clay à votre chambre – Here you are, the key to your room."

"Merci," says Valerie, as she kisses Jean-Pierre on both cheeks.

"Allons – y – Let's go, Guy. I'm anxious to take a shower, change my clothes, and have time to relax before dinner. Perhaps, we can even have a cocktail in the meantime."

"You certainly wouldn't want to miss an opportunity to have a drink."

"Oh Guy, sometimes I wonder if you are too strait-laced for me."

Valerie and Guy head to the elevator. It has been a long and eventful journey. She takes one more look around, just to be sure no one is watching or following her. Satisfied that the people she sees are only guests, Valerie takes Guy's arm and leads him to their room. The porter will bring their luggage in just a few minutes.

"This is quite a piece of real estate," says Guy.

"You would comment on that, wouldn't you," Valerie replies laughing. "You can't stop thinking about work anytime you're near a nice building. This is a landmark hotel – one of the finest in the south of France. Isn't it enough to say it's beautiful?"

"It's more lovely now that you've graced it with your presence."

Valerie laughs.

183

"You don't need to try to butter me up, Guy. You know you'll receive plenty of attention later tonight, regardless."

"Well, it doesn't hurt to add a little cream to the mix, occasionally."

"Save your cream for later," Valerie replies, as she winks at Guy.

"You can never turn down the heat, can you Val?"

"What can I say - "I'm a dragon!""

Just then, the elevator doors open and the two lovers step onto the plush crimson carpet and head to room number 56 - the Marie Antoinette Suite. The room itself is truly exceptional. The curtains are made of fine oriental gold silk and the bed covering is a colonial blue color, made from fine satin. There is an ornate gold settee, embroidered with circular patterns, offset by two antique aquamarine chairs and a round white marble coffee table. Fresh lilacs have been placed on top of the table in a crystal vase. The aroma of their sweet scent fills the room, like fine perfume from Grasse.

On the wall behind the headboard of the bed rests a portrait of Marie Antoinette. She's portrayed glaring angrily toward the door, as if she is offended by the intrusion of anyone's presence in her royal chambers. Standing in the room, Valerie feels the presence of nobility. She has the sense that she is in a medieval castle chamber at the center of a vast kingdom.

Despite the opulent décor in the room, Valerie's eyes are lured to the balcony where the curtains have been drawn back, so she can see the magnificent view of Le Côte d'Azur – the Blue Coast.

As she looks out over the Mediterranean Sea, Valerie imagines that all of France is at your feet, as if she were Queen Antoinette.

"What a beautiful room," says Guy. "How's that for avoiding a work statement?"

"It's an improvement," Valerie replies, smiling.

"Shall we unpack and then go have dinner?"

"Oui, mais embrase moi premièrement – Yes, but kiss me first."

"So, when is your business in Monaco exactly?"

"Over the weekend on Saturday afternoon. It's not for several days, so we have plenty of time together before that happens. I want to relax for a day, then maybe look at some flats along the coast. While I'm gone, try not to get too distracted by all the beautiful young girls who will be hovering around. Remember, you're with me while we're here," says Valerie, revealing a bit of uncharacteristic possessive jealousy.

"I wouldn't dream of it," Guy replies.

Valerie gives Guy a sharp stare, just to make sure he knows she's serious. Guy catches her glance and smiles because he wants her to feel attached to him. For Guy, this is a good sign. It's something he's been wanting to happen between them for a while.

Sometimes, jealousy can lead to a good thing, but I know in general, Valerie believes it's poison. That's why I'm surprised by this unexpected rant. It's not like her.

"Where shall we eat Val? You must know a few good restaurants outside of the hotel."

"Oui, J'en connais – Yes, I know some. Would you like a crêpe or something else?"

"Un crêpe avec le fromage Swiss et jambon – A crepe with Swiss cheese and ham, sounds very good right about now, along with a good bottle of red wine."

"Who's thinking about drinking now?"

Guy smiles.

"Are you ready to go Val?"

"Oui, – Yes, but let me just change my shoes into something more comfortable to walk in. Il y a un petit restaurant s'appelle La Veille Crêpe pas loin d'ici - There is a little restaurant called La Veille Crêpe, not far from here. We can go there if you like. It's a bit of a walk to town, but after that long train ride, I think I want to stretch my legs."

"D'accord, allons -y – Agreed, let's go."

Valerie and Guy take the elevator down to the first floor. As the doors open, Valerie scans the lobby again, looking for any sign of The Cat. Instead, she sees Jean-Pierre, the concierge.

"May I call a cab for you?" asks Jean-Pierre.

"Non, merci - we're going to walk," Valerie replies.

185

"Bon, enjoy your evening."

Valerie and Guy stroll out of Le Negresco and walk arm and arm along the Promenade des Anglais. It's a beautiful evening with only a few clouds in the sky – a warm 27 degrees Celsius. The noise of cars zipping by the boardwalk is muffled by the waves crashing against the shore. Seagulls hover overhead looking for tidbits of food dropped by tourists.

A sense of calm suddenly falls over Valerie. And, for a moment, she stops thinking about the Rembrandt and focuses her attention on the picturesque scenery and background noise.

"The French Riviera really has an allure, n'est ce pas? – isn't that true?" says Valerie.

"Oui," Guy replies.

"It's so relaxing to be along the coast and break out of my daily routine."

"Oui, it's very pleasant here. However, I can't help but think about the real estate potential – Je suis désolé – I'm sorry."

"Oh Guy, save those thoughts about business for when we look at apartments in a couple of days."

Valerie smiles at Guy and holds his arm more tightly, resting her head on his shoulder affectionately, in an uncharacteristic fashion.

"So, where is this crêpe restaurant you recommended?"

"C'est juste à côté de la rue là – it's just next to the street over there."

Valerie looks over her shoulder once again, scanning the crowd for any sign of The Cat. She knows he will eventually turn up at some point. Where and when is the only question.

"Is there anything wrong ma chérie – my dear?"

"Non bébé, tout va bien. Nous sommes arrivés – No baby, everything is fine. We are here."

Valerie and Guy enter the restaurant.

"Bonjour, madame et monsieur," says the hostess, assuming they're a couple.

"Mademoiselle - Miss," Valerie corrects her.

"Je m'excuse, mademoiselle – Excuse me, miss. Please take a seat over here and a waiter will be with you momentarily," says the hostess, as she points to a table outside, just in front of the restaurant.

"Merci," Guy replies.

"This is my favorite crêpe restaurant in Nice. The ham and Swiss cheese crêpe here is legendary. You will love it!"

"I'll take your word for it.

Valerie calls the waiter over to their table.

"Garçon!"

"Oui, mademoiselle what can I get for you," says the waiter.

"We would like two savory crêpes with ham and Swiss cheese, and two glasses of red wine, s'il vous plaît," says Valerie.

"Tout de suite, mademoiselle."

"Merci," Valerie replies.

"Well Guy, here we are in Old Nice. How do you feel?"

"Wonderful! I'm especially happy to be here with you."

"That's sweet of you to say," Valerie replies, as she looks over her shoulder once again.

"Did you see someone you know, Val? I noticed that you've been looking over your shoulder a lot, ever since Marseille. Are you still worried about that man on the train? I'm sure the police have caught up with him by now."

"Don't be so sure, Guy. That man is a slippery fish."

"Try not to worry about him anymore. Let's just try and enjoy our dinner."

"Je suis désolé, mon chéri – I'm sorry, my dear. Listen darling, I want to pick up a few items after dinner. I know you will be bored going shopping, so why don't you go back to the hotel and change into your beach attire, so you can relax on the beach. I'll even give you permission to look at all the beautiful women while I'm gone. I won't be too long - I promise. Then afterward, I will meet you for a drink. Reserve a couple of lounge chairs for both of us."

"Are you sure you don't want me to come with you?"

"Oui, I'm certain. I just want to buy a few things I require for the room."

"You mean like some perfume and whisky?"

"It's like you can read my mind."

"Oh, very well, but don't be too long – okay."

Oui bébé, Je te promets – Yes baby, I promise you.

Telling Guy that she is merely going shopping is obviously just a ruse, so she can rendezvous with Bianca. Valerie needs to discuss the details of her plan with her for the exchange in Monté Carlo.

The heist in Boston had made world headline news and Valerie knows she must proceed with extreme caution. The Cat is still chasing her, as far as she knows, so his presence adds to the risk she's already facing.

As the young duo enjoys their wine, the waiter returns with their supper.

"Bon appétit," says the waiter.

"Merci," Valerie replies.

Guy and Valerie raise their glasses once more in another toast.

"To good fortune," says Valerie.

"To romance," Guy replies.

XV.   Cat and Mouse

Sylvain has been on the run from the police since the train stopped in Marseille, thanks to Valerie's quick thinking. However, that didn't deter The Cat with nine lives from his quest to steal whatever work of art Valerie is planning to sell in Monté Carlo. Sylvain's narrow escape from the law only made him more convinced that Valerie is up to something grand. Reboarding another train, or even taking a bus from Marseille now is out of the question. He knows the police will have men looking for him at those stations.

The Cat decides to do the only thing he can do, which is to rent a car and drive to Nice, but he will first need to take a cab to a neighboring town because the police will still be looking for him in Marseille. Even though Valerie will have a head-start, Sylvain's intuition tells him that she won't make a move until the weekend, since the Formula 1 race will have law enforcement preoccupied. If he's lucky, Sylvain should be able to catch up with her before she leaves for Monté Carlo.

Sylvain's plan involves trying to ascertain who the buyer will be, and then steal the painting either before Valerie has a chance to sell it or during the exchange. If he is unable to make any progress identifying either the buyer or the place of the transaction, he will consider kidnapping Valerie's travel companion and hold him in exchange for the merchandise. The Cat can only hope that Valerie cares enough about the gentleman she is traveling with to give up her valuable cargo, in exchange for his life. Sylvain knows this is a big gamble because from what he has learned about Valerie, she isn't the sentimental type. She may be willing to sacrifice her knight during this game of chess.

Sylvain successfully makes an appearance in Nice on the same day that Valerie's train arrived, but not until early evening. He has an inclination that Valerie might be staying at Hôtel Le Negresco, but it's only a guess. He's tempted to go there that evening to scout out the lobby, but he decides to lay low for now. He can't take the chance of being seen by Valerie, who he believes was responsible for his run in with the police.

She will only alert the authorities again if she spots me surveilling her.

So, Sylvain collects the key to the apartment he's rented in Villefranche-sur-Mer, a little fishing village minutes from Old Nice, and sets up his base there. Sylvain decides he needs help, so he calls on a colleague living in the area. She goes by the name of Vanessa St. Pierre. Her mother was active during WWII as an underground secret agent. She passed along some of her knowledge and skills as a spy to her daughter.

Vanessa has become proficient with a pistol and is accomplished in martial arts. Her black hair, and grey-blue eyes coupled with her athletic figure is enough to manipulate any man into doing her bidding.

"Hello, Vanessa, it's Sylvain."

"Sylvain, ah oui, ça va – yes, how's it going?"

"Ça va - I'm doing okay. Look, I need your help."

"Qu'est ce qui se passe – what's happening?" asks Vanessa.

"Something big is going down in Monté Carlo this weekend. I think Valerie Fontaine has a stolen painting in her possession that she's trying to sell. She put the French police on my trail to knock me off the board, but I was able to evade capture. I searched her cabin on the train from Lyon, but I came up empty. She seems to be traveling with a boyfriend or bodyguard or something of that nature. I don't think I will discover by myself what she's carrying or where she's planning on making the exchange. I need you to be my eyes and ears, especially since the police and Valerie are on to me. I may also need your help dealing with that man who is accompanying her."

"Je comprends - I understand. Where and when do you want to meet to discuss your plan?"

"So, you'll help me?"

"Oui."

"Bon. How about at 9 am tomorrow morning, at my flat in Villefranche-sur-Mer?"

"Oui, d'accord, donnes-moi l'address - Yes, agreed, give me the address."

*

Meanwhile, Guy is paying the check for dinner.

"Okay Valerie, I guess I'll let you go for now. Try not to be too long, okay?"

"N'inquiete pas, mon chéri - Don't worry, my dear. However, if I am delayed, don't be upset. I'll be coming along in no time - you'll see."

"Okay, à tout à l'heure – I'll see you later."

Guy kisses Valerie goodbye and walks back toward the hotel alone. As soon as Guy is out of sight, Valerie breaks away from the marketplace and heads to Bianca's flat.

"Valerie!" says Bianca happily, as she opens the door.

"Is everything all right? asks Valerie.

"Oui, ça va – Yes, everything's fine." Bianca replies.

"Let me see the Rembrandt again please."

"Wait just a minute. It's in the bedroom."

Bianca brings a cylinder from the other room. She opens the lid and removes the painting.

"C'est magnifique - it's magnificent! It gives me chills. M'écoutes – Listen to me… The Cat is probably in Nice by now. It's likely that he doesn't know what we have or where we're keeping it, but he seems determined to take whatever it is he thinks we have. I doubt he knows anything about you. We must find a way to distract him long enough to make the exchange this weekend. He may have recruited help by now. So, we not only have to be on our guard and watch out for him, but we need to keep an eye out for any accomplices he may have hired as well. Tu m'as compris – You understand me?"

"Oui, je comprends. Yes, I understand. What's your plan?"

"I painted a very good forgery of the Rembrandt and I'm going to keep it as my ace in the hole. The Cat is a thief, but he's not an art expert. I am setting another trap for him at L'Hôtel de Paris in case he tries to make another play for our prize. If he's successful in stealing the fake from me, he won't discover that he's been duped until days later when he can have a professional examine it. By then, we will be long gone with our cash."

"Brilliant darling! That's why I adore you."

"Tell me more - the time, place, and the name of the man I'm meeting with in Monté Carlo."

The man's name is Alejandro de la Cruz. I'll let you know the time and place for the rendezvous by the weekend. The rest of the plan includes heading up to Monaco on Friday afternoon. I plan to do a little gambling in the evening before meeting with the buyer to discuss the time and place for the exchange. Then, you'll meet with him Saturday afternoon, while I set the trap for Sylvain at L'Hôtel de Paris. Afterwards, we'll lie low for a little while before heading back to Paris. The Cat will be chasing his tail, while we get rich!"

Bianca and Valerie laugh gleefully, knowing that their payoff for all their hard work is close at hand.

"Do you really have to rush off so soon?" asks Bianca.

"Oui, I need to get back to the hotel before Guy starts wondering where I am."

"I'd better hurry now. I still need to pick up some things from the market before meeting Guy back at Le Negresco."

"Okay, kiss me again before you leave."

"A bientôt - see you soon." says Valerie.

"Au revoir mon amour – Goodbye my love," Bianca replies.

Valerie hurries down the stairs from Bianca's apartment and through the marketplace. She quickly buys some lavender perfume and a bottle of Glenlivet whisky before walking back toward Le Negresco.

Vanessa has been enjoying an espresso at le Café du Port, while waiting to spot any sign of Valerie. Suddenly she sees her target walking across the square near the Opera House. She drops some money on the table and follows Valerie through the crowd of people, who are buying fresh fish, fruit, and souvenirs.

Vanessa pauses for a moment at one of the fruit stands, pretending to look them over, just as Valerie turns her head to see if anyone is following her. Valerie sees nothing out of the ordinary, so she resumes her journey back toward the hotel. She is keeping a sharp eye out for Sylvain, not knowing that he has already recruited a partner to join him in his quest for the painting.

I'm sure Sylvain must be watching me. He will never give up until he has what he's after.

In an attempt to make sure she's not being followed, Valerie quickens her pace and takes a detour down Le Boulevard Victor Hugo. Vanessa is aware that Valerie is looking for Sylvain, so she's not too worried about being exposed, as long as she's careful. She has never been seen by The Dragon Princess before, however, she doesn't want to increase her pace too much or get too close because that would surely draw Valerie's attention.

Vanessa attempts to see if Valerie looks like she's carrying something that resembles a painting, but as far as she can tell, she appears only to be holding a designer purse and a small shopping bag. Nothing that resembles a work of art. As Valerie disappears behind a building, Vanessa pursues, but she must not risk being seen. So, she decides to take a shortcut to Hôtel Le Negresco and wait for Valerie to arrive, guessing that's where she's headed. Vanessa circles around her mark and travels at a faster pace down side-streets.

She arrives at the hotel ahead of her target and keeps an eye out for the Dragon Princess' appearance. Valerie had previously warned her concierge friend to have his staff keep an eye out for The Cat and instructed him to alert the police if he's seen. Jean-Pierre is looking for a man, not a woman, so the chances of Vanessa being discovered as a spy are very remote, as long as she remains discreet.

Sylvain's accomplice is wearing a black dress with red Stilettos, a red Louis Vuitton purse and dark Ray-Ban sunglasses. As she enters the hotel, she seems to blend in with the other wealthy guests. She walks through the lobby confidently and heads out onto the veranda, virtually unnoticed, except for a few young men whose heads were turned, as she walked by them.

Vanessa checks her purse which houses her weapon of choice - a silver and black Beretta. She doesn't expect to have to use it, but she must be prepared for anything. Where Vanessa is seated, she has a good view of the lobby, so she can see Valerie when she arrives. She pulls a platinum lighter from her handbag and ignites a clope and blows her first puff of smoke into the air. She is aware that Valerie is a clever woman, but thinks to herself… *Perhaps this elusive, dark artist has finally met her match.*

In the next moment, a woman with a hand-knit ivory skirt and gold colored silk blouse enters the hotel lobby. Her smokey colored Maui Jims and wide rimmed Christian Dior hat provide cover for her face, but Vanessa knows the identity of the woman. It's The Dragon Princess, returning to her nest. Jean-Pierre is there to greet her with a kiss.

"Salut, mon ami – Hello, my friend. Have you seen The Cat prowling around today by any chance?" asks Valerie.

"Non, mademoiselle. Je n'ai rien vu – I have seen nothing," Jean-Pierre replies.

"I'm not sure if that concerns me more, or less. He must be in town by now, I should think."

"Do you have any valuable jewelry that you wish me to keep safe for you?"

"Non, merci Jean-Pierre."

"Well, let me know if I can be of any further assistance."

"Oui, bien sûr, merci – Yes, of course, thank you."

Valerie looks around scanning the lobby to reassure herself that she isn't being watched. She sees nothing out of the ordinary, so she decides to go upstairs to her room to change. Afterwards, she will meet Guy on the beach for a cocktail. Vanessa slips back into the lobby after the elevator doors close and watches for the ascending numbers.

Top floor, aye? That's going to be a problem. I will need a passkey to get to that level, but even if I could steal one, I still won't know what room she's staying in. I'd better go before that pompous concierge comes back snooping around asking questions. I'll probably need to find another way to accomplish my mission.

As Vanessa exits the building, Valerie starts to get undressed in her luxury suite. She removes her blouse and lays it on the bed. She opens the curtains and stares out of the window. She unfastens the hooks on the side of her skirt, then unzips it, allowing it to fall to the floor. She stares in the mirror at herself, admiring all her curves and soft pale flesh. Valerie places her hands on her hips, absorbing a panoramic view of her form, turning sideways to view her profile.

"Not bad – not bad at all!" she whispers to herself, as she turns a little more, peering over her shoulder to get a better look at her back side.

Valerie opens the wardrobe, pulls out a periwinkle sundress, and slips it on before slipping her feet into a pair of silver beach sandals. Afterwards, she goes into the bathroom to baste her hands and face with a generous portion of coconut scented moisturizing lotion, then sprays her neck and wrists with some of the perfume that she just bought at the marketplace.

The Dragon Princess returns her sunglasses over her eyes, grabs her purse, takes one more peek in the mirror, then locks the door on her way out. Valerie expects to find Guy comfortably relaxing, reading a book on one of the lounge chairs on the sand, overlooking the sea. Valerie feels a mild sense of satisfaction, as she steps in deliberate fashion along the boardwalk, leading out to the pebble beach, in front of the hotel.

The open umbrellas near the shoreline look like white sails out on the sea, fluttering in the breeze, creating an illusion of peace and tranquility. The moon is just beginning to make an appearance, when Valerie finally sees her lover. At this moment, Guy is ordering another cocktail from a young blonde waitress dressed in a lemon-colored mini-skirt and a white sleeveless blouse.

Formidable - Great! Now he'll be preoccupied and won't ask me many questions. I'll put him on his heels instead by asking him if he's been flirting with that young salope.

"Hey baby, how was shopping?" asks Guy.

"It was fine. I bought some perfume – do you want to smell it?" asks Valerie, stretching her neck in front of Guy's nose.

"Mmm – that's nice."

"Tu l'aimes bien - You like it?"

"Oui - Yes."

"What are you drinking?"

"A Rum Collins."

"Mmm, sounds delicious – garçon!"

"Oui, mademoiselle," a male waiter replies.

"Whisky on the rocks, s'il vous plaît - Johnny Walker Black."

"Tout de suite, mademoiselle – Right away miss."

"You're looking lovely honey," says Guy.

"Merci. I see you are taking in the beautiful sights," Valerie replies, hinting at all the sexy women in view, including Guy's waitress."

"Nothing like the lovely vision in front of my eyes right now."

Valerie blushes and laughs, appreciatively.

"Guy, you're getting smoother with your quips. However, don't think I didn't catch you ogling that waitress, just a minute ago."

"Was I?" Guy asks, innocently.

"Oui, et tu le sais – Yes, and you know it. Don't worry; I don't mind. I'm just having some fun at your expense."

Valerie removes her cigarette case from her bag and places a smoke between her lips. She feels satisfied that she has successfully distracted Guy from asking about what else she might have done in the marketplace.

"I could use a spark."

"I'm sorry dear; I didn't bring my lighter with me this time."

"Don't worry, I have one in my purse."

Valerie pulls hers out, and ignites the tip of her fag, before releasing a cloud of smoke from her nostrils.

"So, how are you enjoying the Riviera Guy?"

"I love it! I'm thinking of opening a real estate office down here, so we can spend more time by the sea together."

"Well, I will be your first client, because I'm looking for a property to buy here."

"Ah, yes, you did say that. I wasn't sure if you were serious."

"Of course, I'm serious. When have I ever been otherwise?"

"I thought you didn't want me to think about work while we're here?"

"Well, I can make an exception this once, if you can help me find a two-bedroom condo with a nice view of the sea, like the one we have from our room."

"We won't have too much time to search for a place this trip I'm afraid. We're only visiting for a short while."

"Well, we can certainly look at a few places as a start. I was thinking of looking in Villefranche-sur-Mer."

"Why there?"

"I heard there are no real estate taxes."

"How did you find that out?"

"I have my sources, Guy."

"I'll investigate it for you further. However, you'd better make sure that I'll receive at least half the commission on your new place, as your buyer's agent. Otherwise, I may have to reconsider our business relationship."

"Oh Guy, you make me laugh. When it comes to me, our relationship is all personal, and you know it."

Guy smiles because he knows she's right.

"Well, sometimes, I feel like one of your clients Val because you always remind me who's in charge."

"I won't let you forget that dear."

Guy grins.

"I honestly want you to come with me to see some top-level apartments tomorrow. I know we're going to need to recruit a local real estate agent to have access, but you can still split the commission between yourselves if I find one that I like. Since this is your business, I will leave it up to you to find somebody to open some doors for me."

"Oui, bien sûr – Yes, of course. I will do that for you."

Just then, the waiter returns with Valerie's drink.

"Merci, monsieur. Can you bill it to our room please?" asks Valerie, as she tells Guy to tip the waiter.

"What shall we toast to this time?" asks Guy.

"I always toast to good fortune."

"To good fortune then."

"La mer est tellement belle, n'est-ce pas? – The sea is so beautiful, is it not?" Valerie proclaims.

"Oui, and it is not something I have ever had the pleasure of appreciating, until now. I'm beginning to understand better all the accolades concerning this place."

"I'm so pleased you like it, Guy. I had a feeling you would if you gave it a chance. It takes me away from my daily routine. It allows me to just relax and reflect on my life in a way I can't do in Paris. The only negative thing for now is that I miss my little Fafa. That's why I want to buy a flat, so my pumpkin can accompany me on my trips here."

"Je comprends ce que tu veux dire - I understand what you mean to say."

"I want to show you a few other places in the region as well, like Menton, Antibes, and Eze. Menton is a little town, not far from the

Italian border with quaint little shops and restaurants. It's not as touristy as it is here in Old Nice. It's a bit cozier with more locals. The beach there has sand instead of pebbles. It's also an easy train ride to Portofino if one has the time to visit the Italian Riviera. I would even consider buying a place there because it has a small-town atmosphere. It's also quite picturesque and tranquil."

"Eze, on the other hand, has a mountainous medieval village, which looks like a fortress. There, you can find some shops, luxury hotels, and wonderful restaurants. From the top you can see the most spectacular view along the Riviera. Antibes is another small town, not far from Cannes. It also has a local vibe and not a lot of tourists. It has wonderful pastry and coffee shops and crêpe restaurants. I like it there too."

"You're sparking my interest Val. It sounds like I'll have my work cut out for me."

"Don't I always stimulate your curiosity?"

"Oui, that's the problem."

"Oh, it's not a problem for you - It's your pleasure."

Guy smiles.

"We're going to have such fun together, aren't we darling?"

"Doing anything with you Valerie is always exciting."

"Kiss me baby but be discreet.

Guy kisses Valerie, smearing her freshly painted smile a little.

"Where would you like to have dinner tomorrow evening Valerie?"

"Well, I haven't thought about it much, but since Old Nice used to be part of the Roman Empire, like Provence, how about dining at Chez Acchiardo, which serves authentic Italian cuisine? They have the most delicious pasta dishes there."

"Italian it is then."

"Now that we have that settled, tell me - what did you buy at the market today?"

Valerie cringes, hoping that this will be Guy's first and last question concerning their time apart earlier.

"Well, uhm, I bought a bottle of whisky and some perfume from Grasse, like I told you."

"Okay. Did you see anyone you know? You always seem to be acquainted with people everywhere."

Valerie bites her lip this time, hoping that these questions go no further.

"You mean like a male acquaintance, perhaps? Guy don't be jealous! You know how I disapprove of that!"

"No, that's not what I'm implying. I was simply making conversation," Guy says.

"How about you, Guy? Did you meet anyone today? Remember, I noticed you flirting with that sexy young waitress earlier," Valerie replies, deflecting Guy's intrusive questions.

"Didn't I deny it?"

"Oui, you did, but you know you were - you letch. I told you – I don't mind you flirting, if it puts you in the mood to devour me later."

"Val, I don't need any extra stimulation to be in the mood to make love to you."

"How about if I do one of my dance routines for you later?" Valerie teases.

Guy smiles.

"That is something I will never discourage. However, won't dancing feel too much like work for you?"

"Non, not if it's for you, mon chéri – my dear."

"You're incredible!"

"Oui, je sais - Yes, I know," Valerie replies, smiling.

"You're getting a nice bronze tan already, Guy. You're going to make me look like Moby Dick in comparison."

"I assure you that you don't look anything like Moby Dick."

"Truthfully, I prefer my skin color the way it is – milky white. I don't like looking like a boiled lobster, because that's what will happen if I'm out in the sun for too long. I need to be careful tomorrow."

"Just wear plenty of suntan lotion – You'll be fine."

"I'm ready for bed. How about you?"

"Oui,"

"Es-tu prêt? – Are you ready?"

"Oui."

Guy suddenly begins to think about what his life might have been like if he were married to Gabrielle. She is a lovely woman, and he adores her as a friend, but now he realizes that he needs more stimulation and excitement in his life. Little does Guy know that he's about to get exactly what he wished for and become entangled in the biggest dramatic scene of his life. It may just prove to be more than he can handle.

XVI.   Love & Lust

The next morning, Vanessa arrives in Villefranche-sur-Mer. She knocks on the door of Sylvain's apartment. The Cat peers through the window curtain before unlocking the door.

"Dépêches-toi! Entrez, vite! - Hurry, come in quickly. You weren't followed, were you?" asks Sylvain.

"Non, tout va bien – No, everything's fine," Vanessa replies.

"Dis moi -Tell me, what did you discover?"

"Only that Valerie is in fact staying at Hôtel Le Negresco with that gentleman, on the top level. I believe he is her boyfriend and not a bodyguard. Unfortunately, I would need a passkey to advance to their floor. There is also a security guard stationed in front of the stairs checking room keys, so I couldn't find out what suite they're staying in. It's almost impossible to get to their room without drawing attention from the staff. There's not even a way to enter from the outside, without being seen, even if I could climb that high."

"I think it's unlikely she would have anything extremely valuable in her room because she wouldn't trust that it would be safe with a maid rummaging about. She probably wouldn't try to store it in the hotel safe either because that would also mean losing control over it. If it's a valuable painting that she's carrying, it probably wouldn't fit in a hotel safe, anyway. Whatever she's planning to sell, it must be stashed somewhere else. I need to follow her to see where she goes and see who she meets."

"Je suis d'accord – I agree. I doubt she would put a priceless painting in a hotel room or safe. Those strong boxes are meant for jewels and cash, which don't take up a lot of space. It's more likely that she's hidden it somewhere nearby - but where, I wonder. It could be anywhere I imagine. Where did you see Valerie today exactly?"

"I saw her in the marketplace. Unfortunately, I couldn't tell where she had come from exactly - only that she was doing some shopping before heading back to the hotel."

"That's interesting. What did she buy - anything unusual?"

"I couldn't tell exactly because I saw her only after she finished shopping. It wasn't much, and there was nothing she was carrying that resembled a rolled-up painting. I didn't see her talking to anyone either. I was lucky to spot her at all among such a crowd of people. She had on a hat and sunglasses, so it wasn't easy to be sure it was her – but it was her. I overheard her talking to the concierge later."

"Okay, good work. At least you've confirmed where she's staying. I only wish I knew when she's planning on leaving for Monté Carlo and who her buyer will be. I need you to try and find out more today if you can."

"I'll do my best."

"I'd like to be able to make a move before Valerie leaves for Monaco. That would be ideal. Once she's there, it's going to be more difficult to track her movements and interrupt her plans, I think. However, that will be the time when she will be most likely to have the merchandise in her possession. It's also more likely that there will be bloodshed. I just wish I knew more - merde!"

"Don't worry Sylvain, I will find out what you need to know soon. I will do whatever it takes!"

"To be clear, I don't want you to kill anyone. That's not why I hired you!"

"Je comprends - I understand. We are playing a high stakes game though - it's difficult to predict what might transpire. I must be prepared for everything. I will do my best to avoid violence."

"Just try to stay undercover and don't do anything that might alert the authorities. Tu me comprends – You understand me?"

"Oui Sylvain."

"On your way then."

Vanessa is disenchanted that Sylvain wants her to leave so soon. All this talk about espionage and theft has triggered her sexual appetite.

"Don't you want me to stay a little while longer to help you relax?" asks Vanessa seductively, as she slowly begins to unbutton her blouse. "I can pour you a drink and we can get naked."

"Not now Vanessa! We have work to do and so little time. I don't want to mix business with pleasure. I'm paying you to do surveillance, not to sleep with me. We can't afford to become distracted. You're a very alluring woman Vanessa, but this is not the moment to fool around."

Vanessa scowls with displeasure.

"Well, if that's how you feel, then I guess I'll be off."

Vanessa buttons up her blouse reluctantly. She's visibly annoyed after Sylvain's unexpected rejection.

"Call me if you discover any new information," says Sylvain.

"Oui, boss. Anything you say," Vanessa replies, sarcastically.

The tone in Vanessa's voice conveys her sharp dissatisfaction with her longtime acquaintance. She collects her purse which cradles her Beretta and then she slinks away down the stairs to the street. Her motorbike is parked just on the other side of the road.

I've got to find out where this exchange is going to take place in Monaco, and who her buyer will be," Vanessa says to herself, as she mounts her black and silver Yamaha.

Vanessa kick-starts her bike and revs the throttle before speeding away, back in the direction of Old Nice.

The exchange is only days away and neither Vanessa nor Sylvain have much to go on yet. She needs to get closer to Valerie somehow and cause her to provide clues to either the buyer of the merchandise or to the venue and hour of the exchange. She needs time to think and come up with a plan before she arrives back in the old village.

"Damn that Sylvain for dragging me into this! If only I didn't need the money.

The end of May is always the time for one of the most famous events in the world – The Formula 1 race in Monaco. Almost as well known in certain European aristocratic circles is a wealthy sport enthusiast and art collector by the name of Alejandro de la Cruz from Barcelona, Spain. He is often seen in public at fancy parties, escorting exotic women half his age, and driving high-priced automobiles, like Ferraris and Lamborghinis. Besides having an eye for fast cars and fast women, he also has a keen eye for fine art.

The young millionaire has already made Valerie a generous offer for the Rembrandt, despite its status as a stolen item. Alejandro knows that Valerie will not likely receive a better offer for it, anywhere in the world. The fact that the merchandise is hot makes acquiring it more desirable to Alejandro.

It's just afternoon, and at this moment, the young playboy is already throwing money around in Monté Carlo playing craps at L'Hôtel de Paris. There are no less than four beautiful women in their twenties, flanking him on both sides. They're currently indulging themselves with champagne and caviar. They are being well paid for their company, as well as for their bodies. Win or lose at the tables, De la Cruz will still come out ahead.

"Come on six!" Cruz shouts, as one of the women blows on the dice in his hand before letting them fly.

"The gentleman has won 6,000 francs," the Boxman announces.

The young ladies clap their hands and smile with delight, as the other spectators cheer Alejandro's recent victory.

"This is going to be my lucky weekend!" Alejandro announces.

The Spanish millionaire owns one of the Formula 1 cars in the race. He's already placed a large bet that his car will cross the finish line first. It's not a bad gamble since he has recruited one of the most successful drivers in the world to get behind the wheel of his Maserati.

"Bring me a drink Francesca," Alejandro demands from one of the ladies standing beside him. She strolls over to the bartender in a sultry manner and asks for a cognac.

"Tout de suite, mademoiselle - Right away, miss. It's for the gentleman at the craps table, n'est-ce pas – is it not?"

"Oui," Francesca replies.

"There is no charge," says the bartender.

"Ah bon, merci – Oh really, thank you."

The moment she turns around, there are screams and applause. Alejandro is on a winning streak. Francesca knows this will mean good fortune for her as well, but at the expense of her body and her soul. However, she is willing to sacrifice her dignity to ride the wave Alejandro is taking her and his other female companions on. Francesca knows very well that she and the other women mean nothing to señor de la Cruz, and that he is just using them for sex and appearances. She doesn't care, as long as her purse is full by the weekend.

As Francesca approaches the craps table, she hands Alejandro his drink, and kisses him on the cheek. Tonight, the five of them will party until dawn, after many hours of sex, alcohol, and cocaine. At least through the weekend, they will all dine in five-star restaurants and drink expensive French champagne and sleep in a luxury suite – a stark contrast from roaming the streets of Pigalle in Paris.

"Eight, another winner," exclaims the Boxman.

"I think I ought to quit while I'm ahead. Come on ladies, let's cash out and go upstairs," says Alejandro.

Each of the women will receive their cut, but not until the weekend is over and the Formula 1 race has finished. Francesca and the other girls have already done most of their shopping at an exclusive lingerie boutique called La Fleur du Mal, and are wearing nothing but silk and lace underneath their cocktail dresses, compliments of señor de la Cruz. Pearls, gold, and diamonds are the only other objects touching their soft velvety skin. However, everything comes at a high price in Monté Carlo. The champagne and caviar are merely aphrodisiacs for Alejandro's four course meal, served up by his ladies of the night, under satin sheets and over naked flesh.

"Come on ladies, the party has only just begun," Alejandro announces, as he places his arms around his late-night companions and walks to the elevator door with a pocket full of cash.

*

At this same moment, Guy and Valerie are heading back inside their hotel after having a late breakfast and an early swim. The warm sun and sea air, along with a little alcohol, have stimulated their lustful appetites. As Guy unlocks the door to their room, Valerie, always vigilant, peers down the hallway to make sure they're not being watched.

"Guy, would you like some of the whisky I bought yesterday?" asks Valerie.

"Non, merci. I usually don't drink this early. You don't want me to disappoint you in bed, do you?" Guy replies.

"Non, absolument pas! – No, absolutely not! Let me just have a quick shot before I let you undress me."

Valerie fills a shot glass to the rim before pouring it down her throat. Drinking helps to relieve her stress and puts her in the mood for sex. To her surprise, her feelings for Guy have continued to grow stronger by the day and she finds herself daydreaming about a future together. She's aware that she's been feeling more possessive of him lately, and it's unsettling. The idea of falling in love makes Valerie feel uncomfortable and it's causing her to become distracted. This is a sentiment that she detests and thinks to herself that she must do something about it soon before it's too late.

Valerie will arrange for the painting to be exchanged on Alejandro's private yacht, around 1 pm on Saturday, just before the Formula 1 race, while most of the city of Monté Carlo, including the police, will be preoccupied. She will also set up a fake exchange at L'Hôtel de Paris during the same time and will make it obvious in what room and at what time it will occur, so that The Cat will know and be lured into her trap. The stage will be set to allow Sylvain to attempt to steal the replica, while Bianca and Alejandro rendezvous on his yacht.

Valerie will also have the hotel manager in Monaco alert the local police to keep an eye out for Sylvain and any of his accomplices. Hopefully this time, the authorities will catch him in the act, while she gets away with a suitcase full of money. No one currently suspects Valerie of any criminal activity, as far as she knows, so she doesn't anticipate being followed by Interpol or even by the local police when she makes her move.

The exchange, which will take place on Saturday, is not just a big deal because of the money involved, but also because the Rembrandt is a stolen, priceless item. Valerie and Bianca could go to prison if they're caught, so Valerie needs to stay focused and tells herself not to become sidetracked by her feelings for Guy. Giving in to her carnal desires is another story.

Come on Guy, I'm ready!

Valerie allows Guy to unfasten and open her robe, until it slides off her shoulders and drops to the floor. She snakes her right arm and leg around Guy's neck and waist, then kisses him on the mouth. She pulls Guy's Polo-shirt over his head and runs her sharp claws across his exposed flesh, as she is in the habit of doing. He winces just a little from the pain, which makes Valerie smile with satisfaction. Guy gently removes Valerie's crimson bathing suit, one shoulder strap at a time, kissing her soft, exposed skin beneath the elastane material.

*

Back in Monaco, Alejandro is being entertained in a hedonistic manner by his four high-priced prostitutes. The cocaine he's been snorting for the past half-hour has energized his body and stimulated his mind. The crack of a horse whip and a woman's screams set fire to his dark desires.

Francesca is blindfolded and has her wrists tied. She wears only a garter belt, fine silk stockings, and high heels. She senses two women's hands touching her breasts, while a third kisses her on her neck and mouth. Alejandro stands behind Francesca with a riding crop in his right hand, while grabbing her by the hair with his left. She submits to her master's dominance, as he continues to mark her backside. He puts the whip down so he can enter her from behind.

The other women and Alejandro's bodyguards watch this spectacle with crazed delight. Alejandro is forceful and sadistic, thinking only about his own pleasure. While the other women seem to be enjoying themselves, like children in an amusement park, Francesca feels like she has sold her soul to the devil. She can't wait for the Spaniard to fall asleep, so that she can take a shower and attempt to wash away her shame.

No amount of money can be worth this, Francesca tells herself, as she squeals in pain, while tears form in her eyes. However, the more Francesca resists, the tighter Alejando's grip becomes around her hips and hair and his fingers press ever deeper into her body. As he reaches a climax, she reaches the height of her humiliation.

*

In Nice, at Hôtel Le Negresco, the dragon tattoo around Valerie's breast has already made its appearance, after stripping the Dragon Princess of her bathing apparel. This time, their love making has taken on a different characteristic. Valerie's touch has become uncharacteristically softer and her kisses sweeter. Her caress is refined and more delicate than before and her embrace has become more sensual and gentler. Instead of taking control as she usually does, Valerie allows Guy to lead this dance for the first time.

Guy immediately notices the difference in Valerie's approach but says nothing. He doesn't want to spoil the moment. He takes this cue from the Dragon Princess to express himself more freely. He lifts her up, cradling her in his arms, before gently placing her on the bed. He puts his hands on top of hers before closing his fingers, locking them into a firm grip.

Valerie lies underneath Guy's powerful physique and offers no resistance, as he cautiously attempts to infiltrate her emotional defenses. She closes her eyes and opens her legs wider, inviting her lover to bond with her in a way they have never experienced in the past. For the very first time, Valerie gives in to her sentiments, as they slowly make love, eventually reaching a climax in unison.

It seems like hours have gone by, but it has only been about 45 minutes since they disappeared under the covers. Valerie slowly opens her eyes and looks up at Guy who is gazing down upon her in a way he never looked at Gabrielle. The Dragon Princess knows she's let her guard down and now feels a sense of regret and vulnerability that she's never experienced before now. Strangely, she also feels happy and fulfilled – even uplifted. Her combined feelings clash and create a sense of confusion within her.

"I'm not sure what just came over me," says Valerie.

"What do you mean?" asks Guy.

"I wasn't myself just now. Je suis désolé – I'm sorry."

"There's no need to apologize. I loved how you were with me."

"Vraiment - Really?"

"Oui, bien sûr - Of course. I don't understand what you mean."

"Laisses-tomber – Never mind - It's not important."

Valerie gets out of bed and puts her robe on, without getting dressed. She grabs a cigarette from her case and her lighter, then opens the curtains, before walking out onto the terrace. She stares out at the sea and tries to ignore her feelings. She lights the tip and blows smoke through the air to relieve some of her anxiety.

"Is everything okay Val?" asks Guy.

"Oui, mon chéri – tout va bien – Yes my dear, everything is fine."

XVII.   Plotting and Planning

As Vanessa arrives in Nice, she stops at a local Irish pub called the Snug and Cellar to have a beer, while collecting her thoughts.

"What'll you have, mademoiselle?" a waiter demands.

"Guiness," Vanessa responds.

"Tout de suite - Right away," says the waiter.

Of course, in France, right away means in about 10-15 minutes. No one ever seems to be in a hurry here, especially in Nice. While she's waiting, Vanessa thinks to herself about what her next move should be.

What if Valerie hasn't told her boyfriend her plans or even what she's carrying? Even if I get close enough to overhear her conversation, there may be nothing valuable in it, and I will just be wasting more time. I may find more clues if I go to Monaco early and try to get a feel for who Valerie's buyer might be. There are plenty of rich folks in Monté Carlo, so it may not be obvious who has the ability and desire to buy such an expensive item.

However, not all of them are known to be fine art collectors. I need to narrow the possibilities down, if I am to have any chance of discovering the identity of the buyer. If I get a list of guest names from my friend who works at L'Hôtel de Paris, then I could go through it and try to match them with known art collectors. Perhaps that's where I should start.

The waiter finally approaches her table with her beer.

"Voila, mademoiselle," the waiter says as he places her bottle of Guiness on the table, along with a frozen glass."

"Merci," Vanessa replies.

Just then, a man approaches her table. He is medium-built, athletic looking with dark hair and brown eyes. He's dressed in a clean pair of jeans with a white button-down dress shirt with no tie, underneath a sport jacket.

"May I join you?" the man asks.

"Well, uh…" Vanessa replies, stumbling over her words.

Before she has a chance to finish her sentence, the man sits down next to her.

"Allow me to introduce myself. Je m'appelle André Bouchard - My name is André Bouchard. I'm on vacation, traveling alone, trying to make a few new friends while I'm staying here in Nice."

"Well André, enchanté - it's a pleasure meeting you. However, I'm kind of busy right now. You see, I already have a date - with Monsieur Guiness here." Vanessa replies, slightly shocked by this man's boldness.

"Well, I'm sure Monsieur Guiness won't mind the intrusion. You seem like you're just sitting here without having a care in the world. I thought that maybe you could use some company. No woman as beautiful as you should have to drink alone."

Vanessa blushes.

"You're very charming Monsieur Bouchard, but…"

"Please call me André," the stranger interrupts again.

"Okay, André, but I really…"

"S'il vous plaît - Please, mademoiselle, I'm here by myself and I'd enjoy a little company. I promise you that I am a gentleman. I only wish to have someone to talk to for a while and perhaps show me around."

Vanessa gives André a skeptical look. She begins to wonder if this man is just hitting on her or if he has an agenda beyond a hook-up.

"You're very persistent André. You must be in sales of some type, I'm guessing. You know, there are at least a dozen other good-looking single women here at this bar, so why did you choose to sit at my table?"

"Tout simplement – Quite simply, because you are the best-looking woman here, and you have a motorbike, which I find exciting."

Vanessa laughs and blushes again.

"Ha, you are very suave indeed, aren't you. Well okay, you have convinced me to have one drink with you, but I'm afraid you will be buying."

"That's fair – garçon!"

"Oui, monsieur," the waiter replies.

"Un coca avec glaçon, s'il vous plaît – A coke with ice please, and bring the lady another beer when she's finished with this one."

"What, no rum in that coke?" asks Vanessa suspiciously.

"It makes me sleepy during the middle of the day. I have been doing a lot of walking already, so I'm a little tired. I prefer to preserve my energy, so I can stay alert. You would think it very rude of me if I sat next to you and fell asleep at your table while we were chatting - wouldn't you?"

"Hmm, oui, je comprends – yes, I understand," Vanessa replies, while not buying his excuse entirely.

"So, are you also just visiting Nice, as I am?" asks André.

"Non, J'habite ici – No, I live here."

"Ah bon - Oh good. Perhaps you can show me around later?"

"Je suis désolé – I'm sorry, but I'm really very busy this week. Perhaps some other time."

"Is that because of your work?"

"Oui," Vanessa replies.

"What is it that you do?"

Vanessa thinks for a moment about how to respond.

"Research, and you?"

"I work for an insurance company."

"So, where are you visiting from exactly?"

"Brussels."

"Ah, très bien – Oh, very good."

Vanessa is still annoyed with Sylvain for rejecting her earlier. She almost feels spiteful. However, she knows she shouldn't become side-tracked from her mission. Although, André is giving her the attention she craved earlier. The wound is still fresh, and André is stroking her bruised ego. She may not have the time to satisfy her sexual desires right now, but this stranger's attention is helping her to cover up the emotional scar she received in Villefranche-sur-Mer.

So, Vanessa decides to entertain André's advances. She calculates that she can still remain focused on her mission, while taking a short break from the pressure she's under.

"Will you excuse me just a moment," says Vanessa.

"Oui, bien sûr – Yes, of course," André replies

Vanessa leaves the table for a few minutes to call her friend in Monté Carlo. She will ask her to prepare a list of hotel guests for her, so she can try to find Valerie's buyer.

"L'Hôtel de Paris, may I help you?"

"Oui, is this Chloe?"

"Oui, ah Vanessa, ça va?"

"M'écoutes – Listen to me...I want you to do me a favor. I need a list of your guests' names. I can't tell you why I need it yet, except to say that something big is happening there this weekend and I must find out who is involved. Once you put the list together, I'd like you to call me at home, d'accord - agreed? I know you're not supposed to do this, but believe me, it's very important."

"Oui, bien sûr – Yes, of course. Anything for you dear. Give me a few hours. I'm very busy right now. Guests are pouring in from everywhere for the big race."

"No problem. I won't be home for a couple of hours anyway. I met this guy at a bar and he's making it difficult for me to shake him loose."

"Is he good looking?" asks Chloe.

"Oui, but that's not the point," Vanessa replies.

"Okay, well, now I must go. I'll ring you later, okay?"

"Oui, merci, au revoir – Yes, thanks, goodbye."

Vanessa hangs up the phone and returns to her table where André is waiting for her.

"Everything all right?" asks André.

"Oui, but I need to go shortly." Vanessa replies.

"So soon? Aren't you at least going to give me your number?"

"Okay, I will, but keep in mind that I'm very busy this week. I won't be free to do much. Even having dinner will be challenging. How long will you be in town?"

"I will be in Nice through the weekend."

"Okay, voici mon numéro de téléphone – here is my telephone number. Appelle-moi quand tu veux – Call me when you want. Merci pour la bière - Thanks for the beer. Now, I must be going. It was a pleasure meeting you André."

"The pleasure was all mine."

André does have a secret motive behind his interest in Vanessa, and it's not about sightseeing or sex. Exactly what his agenda is remains to be seen for the moment. Vanessa walks away without looking back in her usual sexy manner. She puts her helmet on, mounts her motorcycle, and kick-starts the engine. She revs the throttle a couple of times before speeding off down the avenue. She knows she needs to find some answers as soon as possible.

André watches her as she disappears from his sight. He suddenly realizes that besides his interest in her professionally, he has a strong physical attraction to her. He's aware this could cause him to lose sight of his purpose for meeting her. So, he clears his mind and pays the check before driving back to L' Hotel Victor Hugo, where he's staying. He has business of his own to take care of there.

That gal is going to be trouble for me in more ways than one - I just know it, André says to himself.

About a half-hour after Vanessa arrives home, she receives a phone call from her friend Chloe who has the list of names. Vanessa sifts through them, until she comes across the name of Alejandro de la Cruz.

Hmm, I've heard of this character before. He's a player and a patron of the arts. I'd be willing to bet he even has a stake in the Formula 1 race. Now, he's someone I think I should investigate.

Vanessa picks up the phone and calls Sylvain.

"Allo, Sylvain?"

"Oui," he replies.

"I came across a name just now who I think might be Valerie's buyer."

"Qui - Who?"

"Alejandro de la Cruz. Tu le connais? - Do you know him?"

"Oui, he's a Spanish playboy who has expensive taste in priceless art and high-priced hookers."

"Exactement - Exactly!"

"Is he in Monté Carlo now?"

"Oui. He's staying at L'Hôtel de Paris."

"Then, he's likely our man - good work Vanessa. I'm going to pop up there to see what I can find out."

"Okay."

"I want you to stay in Nice for now and keep an eye on Valerie. Try to see if you can discover any details of her plan."

"Je comprends – I understand. Au revoir – Goodbye."

"Ciao," Sylvain replies.

I should probably return to Hotel Le Negresco and try to follow Valerie and her boy-toy wherever they're planning on going for dinner tonight. Perhaps, I can bribe the waiter to be seated at a table near them."

Just then, Vanessa's phone rings.

That better not be Sylvain again with another job for me.

"Vanessa?" a voice inquires on the other end of the phone.

"Oui, c'est qui – Who is this?" asks Vanessa.

"C'est André - It's André."

"Ah, André," Vanessa replies, surprised. "Comment ça va – How are you?"

"Ça va bien, merci – I'm fine, thank you. Listen, I'm sorry to bother you so soon after we just met, but as you know, I'm not in town for very long. I just wanted to see if you'd like to have dinner together tonight. If you say no, I'll understand."

Vanessa's first instinct is to reject his offer, but then she thinks to herself that maybe she would be less conspicuous trying to surveil Valerie, if she had a dinner companion. She thinks for a moment about how to work it out. She obviously can't let André know that she's planning on spying on someone during dinner. Then, she has an idea.

"M'écoutes, André – Listen to me, André, I would love to have dinner with you tonight, but I'm not sure exactly what time I'll be free. So, why don't you give me your number and I'll call you later. I'll tell you when and where we can meet, okay?"

"Oui, d'accord – Yes, agreed. I thought you were going to turn me down, so I'm happy that you said yes. Here is my number…"

"Merci, à tout à l'heure - Thanks, until later," says Vanessa.

"Au revoir – Goodbye," André replies.

I've got to get changed and head over to Le Negresco. I will try to catch Valerie on her way out of the hotel, and then follow her to whatever restaurant she and her male companion have chosen. Hopefully, they will be on foot, but if they take a cab, I will be prepared. Valerie is a bit of a prima-donna, I imagine. She'll probably get dressed up and go to a nice restaurant in a taxi. I guess I'll have to wait and see. I should probably dress nicely, take a cab to her hotel, and tell the driver to wait while I watch for them to make an appearance outside the hotel.

Vanessa proceeds to get changed and moves her Baretta to a fancier purse, which matches her shoes. Then, she calls for a cab to pick her up at her apartment to take her to the Hôtel Le Negresco. Only minutes after Vanessa arrives, she spots Valerie and Guy walking arm in arm in front of the hotel, on their way out. Sure enough, they hail a cab.

"Follow that cab," Vanessa commands.

"Oui, mademoiselle," the driver replies.

Just as Vanessa suspected, Valerie doesn't like to walk when she's in a fancy dress and high heels. Only a few minutes later, both cabs arrive in front of Chez Acchiardo. Guy and Valerie exit first and go into the restaurant. After they're out of sight, Vanessa pays the cab driver and walks to a nearby phone booth to call André.

"Allo, André, c'est Vanessa – Hello André, it's Vanessa."

"Ah, Vanessa, bonsoir – good evening."

"Can you meet me at Chez Acchiardo, as soon as you can?"

"I can be there in about 20 minutes."

"Wonderful. I will ask for a table and wait for you inside. Hopefully, I will have one by the time you arrive, since I don't have a reservation."

"Bon alors – Good then, I will see you soon," says André, excited.

"I'm looking forward to it," Vanessa replies.

André is quite pleased that things are going his way.

Vanessa hangs up the phone and walks to the restaurant. She asks the host if she can have a table for two next to Valerie's when her guest arrives. Fortunately, there's one available where she will be able to listen to their conversation. Vanessa tips the host and walks over to the bar to order a drink, while she waits for André to arrive.

Valerie may not reveal anything valuable, but perhaps I may pick up some clues concerning the location and time of the exchange and where she will be staying in Monaco.

In the back of her mind, Vanessa contemplates kidnapping Valerie's male companion to force her hand and give-up the painting. However, this tactic may cause the whole scheme to unravel. This would not only expose her identity, but she would also risk involving the police. The penalty in France for kidnapping with a deadly weapon is steep, so it would be a tremendous risk. Sylvain will become enraged if she blows this operation. Then, she won't even get paid. So, she decides to play it cool and just keep Valerie under surveillance.

A few minutes later, André arrives and greets Vanessa with great enthusiasm.

"I'm excited to see you," says André, sincerely.

"It's good of you to come at the last minute," Vanessa replies.

"I wouldn't miss it. I hope I haven't kept you waiting too long."

"Non, pas de tout – No, not at all."

"Now that your party has arrived, mademoiselle, you may follow me to your table," says the host.

"Merci," Vanessa replies.

As André walks with Vanessa to their table, he immediately

recognizes Valerie. He can't believe his luck.

"Your waiter will be with you shortly," says the host.

"Merci," André replies.

"I didn't really expect you to accept my dinner invitation, however I'm quite pleased that you did. At the café this afternoon, I had the impression that you weren't really interested in seeing me again, even though you gave me your number. I must confess - I wasn't confident that the number you gave me was any good."

"Eh bien – Well, a woman can change her mind, can't she?"

"Oui, I suppose it is your prerogative. In any case, I'm very grateful to be here with you."

"Shall we order some wine?" asks Vanessa.

"Oui, absolument – Yes, absolutely. We shall toast to our chance meeting," André replies, knowing that it's a white lie.

Vanessa blushes. She is beginning to be drawn in by André's charismatic personality. She almost forgets why she's there, but only for a moment.

He's certainly a charmer, Vanessa says to herself.

In the meantime, the waiter has already brought a bottle of Prosecco to Valerie and Guy's table and is about to take their dinner order.

"For the lady, what will you have this evening?" demands the waiter.

"I will take the lobster ravioli and a goat cheese salad," Valerie replies.

"And, for the gentleman?"

"I will take your homemade lasagna, s'il vous plaît - please."

"Excellent choices," says the waiter.

"So, Valerie, can tell me a little bit about the weekend you have planned in Monaco. Are you sure that you don't want me to go with you?" asks Guy.

André and Vanessa both suddenly pay close attention, the moment they hear the word Monaco.

"Je suis désolé, mon chéri – I'm sorry, my dear, but I prefer if you stay here in Nice, while I conduct my business."

"Why is it such a big secret that you can't tell me anything or allow me to go with you?"

"Je ne peux pas te dire - I can't tell you. S'il te plaît, mon chéri, laisse tomber – Please, my dear, just drop it."

"So, you're leaving on Friday, and you'll be back Saturday evening sometime?"

"Oui, J'espère – Yes, I hope so."

"And, this is all business, nothing personal, right?"

"Oui, exactement – Yes, exactly."

"Will you at least tell me where you're staying?"

"Oui – I will be staying at L'Hôtel de Paris."

"Okay, will we are going back to Paris on Sunday morning sometime?"

"Avec un peu de chance, oui – With a little luck, yes."

"Okay, then I'd better savor the time we have left together. Friday will be here in no time, and then I won't see you until it's almost time to leave."

"I promise to give you all the attention you wish for until then."

Vanessa and André have been hanging on to every word that has left Valerie's lips. They have been so caught up trying to listen in on Valerie and Guy's conversation, that even though they have both been looking at the menu, they haven't said a single word to one another. André realizes why Vanessa accepted his invitation to dine with him this evening.

This can't be a coincidence, André surmises.

It seems that both he and Vanessa have both orchestrated this rendezvous for professional reasons. Despite that fact, the two of them are genuinely attracted to one another.

"Are you ready to order Vanessa?" asks André.

"Huh? Oh, I'm sorry, oui. I apologize for being distracted. Please forgive me."

"Oh, it's all right. I'm also distracted by your beauty."

221

Vanessa blushes, flattered by André's most recent compliment.

This man is so gallant. Is he deliberately trying to seduce me? If he is — it's working.

Vanessa kicks herself under the table.

Don't get distracted, don't get distracted, don't get distracted, Vanessa warns herself repeatedly.

"Guy, no more talk about my business now, okay? Let's just enjoy our dinner." says Valerie.

"D'accord - Agreed," Guy replies.

The two of them continue to enjoy their dinner, while Valerie changes the subject to the type of flat she's looking for in the region. She knows Guy likes discussing real estate and hopes that talking about it will satisfy him.

In the meantime, Vanessa and André put in their drink and dinner orders and discuss touristy things to do in Nice. It's almost a relief to Vanessa that Valerie and Guy have stopped talking about Monaco because it allows her to enjoy her dinner and get to know André better. She has learned enough valuable information already tonight to keep Sylvain satisfied. Now, she can finally enjoy herself.

Perhaps later, I can finally get laid! Vanessa says to herself.

About an hour later, Valerie and Guy have finished their desserts and Guy is paying the bill.

"Garçon, can you call us a cab please?

"Oui, monsieur."

Valerie and Guy get up to leave the restaurant without noticing the couple who are sitting behind them.

"Would you like coffee or dessert Vanessa?" asks André.

"Non, merci. Thank you for your company. I enjoyed being here with you, but I think I'd just like to go home now," Vanessa replies.

"Okay, I'll ask our waiter for the bill. How did you get here?"

"I took a taxi."

"Oh, would you like me to drive you home? I have a car I rented while I'm visiting."

"Say no, say no, say no," Vanessa repeats to herself.

"Oui!"

Oh, mon Dieu – Oh, my God, what did I just do? He is so handsome! It won't hurt to have just a little bit of fun tonight, will it? I can give Sylvain a call with the news in the morning. This is all his fault anyway.

"Okay, let me just pay for dinner and then we can go."

"Merci, tu es très gentil - you are very kind."

This guy is trying very hard to get into my pants, I think. Well, he doesn't know it yet, but he's going to get what he's after tonight. He must be as horny as me because he's been staring at my chest all night. I'm going to give him a night he'll never forget. I just hope he loses some of that gentlemanly behavior when I get him into bed.

In the morning, Vanessa will call Sylvain to tell him when Valerie plans to leave for Monaco, where she plans to stay, and what day she will make the exchange. The pieces of the puzzle are finally coming together. Tomorrow, she and Sylvain will discuss in more detail how they will attempt to steal the painting.

However, that business will have to wait until morning because Vanessa has other plans for tonight. If she only knew who she's about to take home with her to bed, she might have decided to go home alone, instead.

"Es-tu-prêt, Vanessa? – Are you ready Vanessa?"

"Oui, you have no idea!"

XVIII.   Monté Carlo

Friday morning finally arrives, and Valerie is feeling nervous. She's also excited that she's getting close to her goal of finally cashing in on the Rembrandt. She has mixed emotions about the upcoming events of the weekend because she's also an artist and appreciates the incredible workmanship and significance of the painting. She also wants to eventually retire from dancing and make a new life for herself in the south of France.

Valerie and Guy had found a beautiful three-bedroom condominium in Beaulieu-sur-Mer, overlooking the bay, near the Hotel Le Versailles. After Valerie receives the money for the Rembrandt, she wants to make an offer and put a deposit down. She would be able to afford an even nicer place than the one she's chosen, but she doesn't want to attract too much attention to herself, after the sale is complete.

There is a park nearby for little Fafa to play and a café and boulangerie just down the street. Also, she will be only about 20 minutes from Old Nice by motorbike, whenever she wants to socialize or shop at the open street market.

This is the life Valerie has dreamed about for years. She will be able to paint every day and spend time writing poetry. She'll also have more time for traveling. Valerie has wanted to experience life in Asia and the Dark Continent, and perhaps even paint some scenery or people while she's over there. The money she will receive from the painting will easily finance these excursions, in addition to her new flat.

In one sense, Valerie will miss living in her little town of Courbevoie every day. However, she will still be able to afford to live along the Riviera and spend the tourist season up north. She will miss the adoring crowds and the attention she receives from the men and women at Le Théâtre Coquette, but she hopes she will find similar satisfaction creating and selling her art in Old Nice.

Due to her increasing age, fewer younger patrons will be clamoring for her to remove her clothes on stage in the future. Valerie knows it's only a matter of time before her current life is completely over, and it becomes time to set the wheels in motion toward achieving her next dream.

It's almost time to move on to a new life, but first I need to get out of bed and have a cup of coffee.

"Guy, wake up! Let's go downstairs and have breakfast on the veranda. Then, I'm going to finish packing and take a cab to catch the train."

"Do you want me to go with you to the station?" asks Guy.

"Non bébé – No baby, I'll be fine. Let's just go have some coffee and a croissant together, and then I'll be off." Valerie replies.

"Okay."

"Let me just put my face on and dress myself."

Guy is still feeling uneasy about Valerie going away to Monaco alone while he stays back in Nice. However, he knows he can't change her mind at this point. He's not worried that she's going there to see another man. Guy is confident that the rendezvous this weekend will only be for professional purposes. However, he still wishes he knew exactly what type of business she has herself mixed up in. He suspects it might involve something illegal because of this business involving The Cat.

She must have a good reason for being so secretive.

While buttoning his shirt, Guy looks up and catches a glimpse of Valerie topless, slipping on a fresh ivory colored lace bra, which distracts him from his present thoughts.

225

How magnificent she is! I never had this same kind of feeling with Gabrielle. She has a nice body and a beautiful face, but she was always so focused on being a wife and mother - she forgot how to simply be a woman. Valerie is all woman! She exudes sexual energy and confidence. I love that about her.

Guy is finally beginning to realize why he's so drawn to Valerie and lost interest in Gabrielle. After about another 15 minutes, Valerie and Guy are finally ready to head downstairs to have breakfast.

"Je suis prêt – I'm ready," Valerie announces. "Don't worry Guy, everything's going to be fine."

Valerie takes Guy's hand, smiles at him, then kisses him on the cheek for reassurance.

After breakfast, Valerie and Guy return to their room so that Valerie can collect her traveling case. She doesn't want Guy to go with her to the train station because there's a chance that he might spot Bianca and become even more suspicious.

Valerie plans to rendezvous with her friend once the train starts moving. Bianca will not only be the one carrying the painting, but she will also be the one selling it to Alejandro on his yacht. The Dragon Princess must continue to be careful not to be seen with Bianca. If she's being followed, their eyes will be on Bianca as well, and her anonymity will be blown, putting both of them and their scheme at great risk.

"Kiss me goodbye Guy."

Guy gives Valerie one of those kisses that says - *I wish you weren't going.* She looks at him afterwards, as if to say - *Don't worry, I'll be back soon.*

Guy watches with sadness as the door shuts behind her and only her footsteps can be heard walking down the hallway. Once she's downstairs, Valerie asks Jean-Pierre to call a cab for her to take her to la Gare de Nice-Ville - the Nice train station, where Vanessa awaits her arrival. Sylvain has already gone ahead to Monaco and has booked two rooms at L'Hôtel de Paris for himself and Vanessa.

As Valerie arrives at the train station and steps out of the cab, Vanessa tosses the coffee she's been drinking and moves inconspicuously in the Dragon Princess' direction. She heads to one of the counters near where Valerie is purchasing her first-class ticket to leave on the next train to Monté Carlo. Vanessa purchases her own ticket and follows Valerie to the train. A few minutes later, Bianca can be seen waiting at the other end of the platform, where she will mount one of the other cars in second class.

At this point, things are still going according to Valerie's plan. However, she's unaware that an agent of Sylvain has been following her for the past several days. Valerie peeks over her shoulder to see if she can spot The Cat, but overlooks Vanessa, who wears her hat well below her profile.

Ironically, Vanessa is so preoccupied watching Valerie, she doesn't realize that there is someone following her as well. A man in a trench coat wearing a brown hat and dark sunglasses is trailing both she and Valerie. He steps onto the train with a first-class ticket in hand.

Vanessa recalls what happened to Sylvain after he searched Valerie's compartment on the Blue Train, so she doesn't want to take any risks which would draw the same kind of attention to her. For now, she will just watch, wait, listen, and follow Valerie wherever she goes. As the train moves away from the station, the wheels are set in motion for what is to become a collision course with fate.

About an hour later, the train rolls into Monté Carlo station. Bianca will be staying close by at L'Hôtel Azur, but just far enough away from the action at L'Hôtel de Paris. Valerie, Bianca, Vanessa, and the man in the trench coat all deboard the train, on their way to their destination of fortune. Valerie is the first one to step into a cab.

"Where to, mademoiselle?" asks the cab driver.

"L'Hôtel de Paris, s'il vous plaît, et dépêchez-vous - The Paris Hotel please, and hurry, Valerie replies.

As Valerie's cab pulls away from the curb, Vanessa and the man in the trench coat follow closely behind in separate taxis. Other than Valerie, no one else notices Bianca walking alone, carrying the Rembrandt over her shoulder. As Valerie arrives at L'Hôtel de Paris, a bellman offers to take her bag. Since she is not carrying the real Rembrandt, she gladly allows the young man to take her valise and enters the hotel with just her purse in hand.

"Valerie, it's so good to see you again," says the concierge, as he kisses her on both cheeks.

"Salut Jules, ça va - how are you," Valerie replies.

"I'm sad to see that you are only staying with us for one night. Are you sure you don't want to stay with us on Saturday night as well? We're having the winner's party here after the Formula 1 race."

"J'aimerai bien, mon ami – I would love to, my friend, but unfortunately I need to get back to Nice as soon as my business is finished here."

"Je te comprends – I understand you. Anyway, if you change your mind, please let me be the first to know so I can reserve your room. I'm going to send up some flowers and champagne - on the house."

"Merci Jules, tu es trop gentil – Thank you Jules, you are too kind. I appreciate all that you do for me."

"C'est mon plaisir - It's my pleasure."

As the elevator doors open and Valerie heads to her room, Vanessa walks through the front door of the hotel, soon followed by the man in the trench coat, who Vanessa still hasn't noticed is shadowing her. Vanessa catches a glimpse of Valerie as the elevator doors begin to close and keeps an eye on which floor it stops at before checking-in. After receiving a key to her room, Vanessa heads upstairs, while the mysterious man in the trench coat follows her to the elevator.

L' Hôtel de Paris is buzzing with spectators, Formula 1 drivers, dignitaries, ambassadors, oligarchs, well-known actors and actresses, sports icons, and even royalty. They are all focused on tomorrow's prized race. Anybody who is anybody is there for one of the greatest events in the world. The guests are dressed to the nines, while gambling, drinking and dancing. Even though it's not quite noon yet, the champagne is flowing like the Seine River. There is a white, pearl-colored Steinway in the grand ballroom where classic show tunes are la soupe du jour. If you didn't know better, you'd think it was the roaring twenties, all over again.

Valerie chose the following day to make the exchange deliberately because no one besides she, Bianca, and Alejandro will be thinking about anything else but the race. All eyes and ears will be focused on the streets of Monté Carlo. The police force will be stretched thin and maintaining security for the event will be a nightmare.

Valerie still needs to speak with Alejandro before the night is over. However, the press is currently all over him. She will have to wait until she can talk with him alone. She has a good idea what to expect from him, based on his reputation as a ladies' man.

The Dragon Princess knows that Alejandro will probably attempt to mix business with pleasure, but she isn't about to let that happen when she sees him. This is one time that her head must stay clear, and her clothes must remain on. There's too much at stake to become distracted by Alejandro's boyish exploits. She can't afford to screw things up now. She must stay focused on her mission.

By this time, Bianca has already arrived at her hotel. She opens the door to her room, pleased that she and Valerie will finally be able to shed themselves of this burden and make a healthy profit.

Valerie's protégé knows that she needs to prepare herself for anything that might happen tomorrow. So, she checks to make sure that the Derringer pistol she has brought along with her is loaded, before returning it to her purse.

Bianca looks at the clock on the wall and sees it's almost time for lunch. Unfortunately, she can't be seen in public with Valerie or Sylvain, so she must eat alone. She expects to get a call soon from her colleague to let her know the exact details for the time and place of the exchange tomorrow. Thinking about all this makes her begin to feel anxious.

She runs her fingers through her hair and then shakes it out before glancing at herself in the mirror. Bianca likes what she sees, but her lipstick needs freshening. She grabs a tube from her purse and twists it until the rouge protrudes from its gold cylinder. She watches herself once again in the glass, as she glides the pigmented waxed tip laced with cocoa-butter, across her puckered lips.

Similar to Valerie, when Bianca feels stressed, sex is her go to response to relieve the pressure. Being alone will not be an issue for her. She begins to unbutton her blouse and unfastens her bra from the front. She allows them both to fall off her shoulders and guides them onto a chair. Still watching herself in the mirror, she crosses her arms and cups her breasts, rubbing her nipples gently between her fingers to create arousal. She unzips her skirt and steps out of the leather material which had been surrounding her hips.

Bianca sits on the bed and slides her silk stockings down below her knees and ankles. She looks down and stares at her body, before sliding one hand underneath her rose-colored lace panties. She closes her eyes and creates an image in her mind, daydreaming about three men ravishing her.

The young dancer lies back on the bed and tries to relax, moving her fingers back and forth, ever so slowly at first, and then in a circle with increasing speed. She gradually begins to feel a flowing warm sensation throughout her quivering body, until she senses an oncoming surge.

Bianca opens her eyes for just a moment before her release and tries with great difficulty to keep her screams silent. She closes her eyes once again and grips the bed cover tightly with her free hand, just at the height of her climax. In the next moment, she lies still on the bed completely satisfied, still breathing heavily, released from her tension. Bianca begins to gradually lose consciousness, until she falls asleep. Lunch will have to wait.

XIX.   Setting the Stage

After Vanessa unpacks her clothes, she phones Sylvain from her room. He has been waiting for her call.

"Oui, hello," says Sylvain, after he picks up the phone.

"C'est Vanessa - It's Vanessa."

"Ah bon! Are you here in the hotel now?"

"Oui."

"We should meet right away. I have something to tell you."

"Okay, come to my room. We can talk while I finish unpacking," says Vanessa.

"Okay, I'll be right there," Sylvain replies.

Sylvain grabs his Walther PPK and takes the stairs so that he won't run into Valerie in the elevator by accident. As he arrives at Vanessa's door, he knocks gently.

"Is that you Sylvain?" demands Vanessa, holding her Baretta in one hand.

"Oui."

Vanessa lowers her weapon and puts it down on the console table, as she opens her door.

"Viens vite - Come in quickly," says Vanessa.

Sylvain notices the Baretta, lying on the table.

"You should at least wait until I pay you before you shoot me," says Sylvain.

"Don't be ridiculous!" Vanessa replies.

"I'm just trying to lighten the mood a little. You don't seem to be in very good spirits," says Sylvain.

"That's because I'm the only one in this hotel other than you, who's not having any fun. Everyone else is partying their asses off."

"Stop complaining. You have a job to do for which I am paying you very handsomely. Once we have the painting, you can celebrate as much as you like. Now, listen to what I must tell you. I was able to overhear some chatter downstairs at the tables. Apparently, Valerie is planning to sell a painting that's worth a few million US dollars. Although, no one seems to know what painting she's selling."

"You were right - Alejandro de la Cruz is the buyer. I believe the exchange will happen first thing in the afternoon in his suite on the top floor, just a couple of hours before the race begins. Most everyone will be out on the street by then, and few people will be focused on anything else. Unfortunately, even if we could break into Valerie's room ahead of the sale to conduct a search, that still wouldn't give us enough time to get away before the hotel security guards come looking for us. More importantly, the painting might not even be in her room. So, it's best to pounce during the exchange."

"Je comprends - I understand. Alejandro will likely have bodyguards with guns, so we will need to surprise them and take them out quickly and quietly. We should use silencers. There may be at least one man guarding the door, and possibly a few more inside the room."

"I agree that we may have to use our guns, but I want to avoid killing anyone if possible. Is that understood?"

"Oui, boss."

"There is only one way I think this can work. First, we will need to steal a pass key from one of the maids, take out the camera in the hallway, then wait for Valerie to arrive with the painting. Once she's inside, we'll take out anyone guarding the door and use the key to enter the room. We'll try to catch anyone inside by surprise and hold them at gunpoint, until they give up the painting. Afterwards, we set off tear gas to facilitate our escape. Hopefully, we won't need to kill anyone, but we must be prepared to shoot anyone who tries to stop us, if necessary."

"In what suite is Alejandro staying?" asks Vanessa.

"2112," Sylvain replies.

"Bon, how about if we meet in your room tomorrow at noon and then go together. Do you have your weapon?"

"Oui, d'accord, c'est ici – Yes, agreed, it's right here."

Sylvain shows Vanessa the gun he's carrying.

"What about Valerie's boyfriend – is he here in Monté Carlo too?"

"I don't think so. Valerie got on the train alone, so I assume he's still back in Nice. I don't think she wants him involved in this. As far as I can tell, she hasn't told him anything. He's definitely her lover and not a bodyguard or accomplice."

"Okay, then we won't have to worry about him interfering in our business."

"J'espère pas – I hope not."

"There is one more detail that we need to consider," says Sylvain.

"What's that?" Vanessa replies.

"Alejandro has hookers around him all the time. They could be in the room when we break in. I don't want them getting caught in the crossfire. They're not part of any of this and I don't want them getting hurt."

"I doubt Alejandro would expose himself in that way to a handful of whores who could blackmail him after the sale. It's a safe bet they won't be in the room tomorrow afternoon."

"You're probably right, but just be prepared, in case you're wrong."

"D'accord – Agreed."

"Is there anything else we should consider?" asks Sylvain.

Vanessa thinks about André for a moment, but then dismisses it from her thoughts.

"No nothing," she replies.

"Bon - Good, then we won't meet again until tomorrow at noon in my room, unless something important comes up."

"Okay, à demain – until tomorrow."

Sylvain returns to his room and stays out of sight for the remainder of the evening. He will order room service later, instead of eating out. The less risk he takes being seen, the better.

Valerie still must meet with Alejandro to go over her plan for the following day. She has the operator at the front desk call his room.

"Buenas noches," says Alejandro, a little out of sorts, as he answers the phone.

"It's Valerie," she replies.

"Ah, Valerie, como estas - how are you? Are you here at the hotel now and do you have my package with you?"

"Oui, I am here, and your item is safe in Monté Carlo. We should meet to make arrangements for the exchange. Do you have my money?"

"Si, come to my suite now and we can discuss the details for tomorrow."

"I don't think that's a good idea. You're not alone, are you?"

"No, but it doesn't matter. My girls are blind, deaf, and dumb when it comes to my business."

"Well, I don't know anything about your salopes, but I don't trust them. For all you know, one of them could be a spy. I would prefer it if you came to my suite alone instead. Additionally, you must behave – this is a business meeting, not one for pleasure."

"All right, fine, don't get testy! Eres una diabla – You are such a devil!"

"Non, Alejandro – I am a dragon, so you'd better be on your guard."

"I see you understand Spanish."

"Si, just enough to comprehend when I'm being toyed with."

"I wouldn't dream of deceiving you, Valerie."

"You'd better not! Meet me in 15 minutes. I'm in suite 2216."

"Muy bueno – Very good, but I need to get dressed, so make it 20 minutes."

Alejandro hangs up the phone and announces to his harem that he needs to go to a meeting.

"Have some more champagne girls. I'll be back in time to take you all out to dinner in my limo."

The ladies squeal with delight, as the Spaniard puts on his suit and tie and heads out the door to meet with Valerie. After hearing Alejandro's knock, The Dragon Princess peers through the peephole to make sure who's outside her door.

"Entra, date prisa por favor – Come in, hurry please," says Valerie.

"Buenas noches – Good evening," Alejandro replies, as he waltzes casually through the entryway. "You look ravishing my dear."

"Please have a seat, señor de la Cruz. Can I get you something to drink?"

"Si, Tequila with ice would be nice."

Valerie walks over to the bar in her suite and places two glasses on the counter. She dips into the ice bucket and drops two rocks into Alejandro's glass before pouring her own drink. After handing her guest his poison, she opens her purse and pulls out a cigarette. Before she has time to grab her lighter, Alejandro speaks.

"Allow me," Alejandro says, as he lights her cigarette, trying to be gallant.

Valerie inhales, then releases a large cloud of smoke through her nostrils, habitually.

"Merci," says Valerie. "Now, let's get down to business."

"I have no objection. However, I had heard that you French women are supposed to be a little more romantic."

"Never mind that!" snaps Valerie. "Now, listen to me… I've had a thief on my tail before I arrived in Marseille. He is likely here in Monté Carlo, as we speak. I need to act as a decoy to throw him off the trail, so we can complete the transaction."

"What do you have in mind?"

"I want to stage a fake exchange in your suite. I will be there, but you will be meeting with my agent instead, at 1:00 pm tomorrow. That will give you plenty of time to get back to the race. After midnight tonight, I want you to sneak away from the hotel and stay overnight on your yacht, until the transfer takes place the following day. Do not bring your bimbos with you, but you may bring along whatever security personnel you deem necessary."

"My agent will hand the Rembrandt over to you, but only after you have presented her with the cash, and she's satisfied that the money is all there. You will tell no one what you're doing or where you're going, nor will you mention to your bodyguards exactly what's in the tube my agent gives you. Lo entiendes – Do you understand?"

"Well, it seems like you have this all worked out, Valerie. What does this agent of yours look like and what is her name?"

"Her name is Bianca, and here is her photo."

Alejandro studies the photo for a moment before handing it back to Valerie.

"Wow! She is almost as beautiful as you?"

"Never mind that. She is commissioned to make the exchange for me - and that's all! So, don't get any of your perverted ideas into your head!"

"Why do you have to take all the fun out of everything, Valerie," Alejandro says with a smile.

"I will arrive at your suite for the fake exchange while you will be meeting with Bianca at 1 pm. Have one or two of your guards there to meet me, but no one else. Is that clear?"

"Si, entiendo - I understand."

"Bon - Good. This will be the last time you'll ever see me. By tomorrow, you will have your prize and I will have my money."

"Let's drink to good luck – cheers," says Alejandro.

"To good fortune," Valerie replies.

The two of them touch glasses.

"If my car wins the race, I will have recouped all my money and then some. Plus, I will have the Rembrandt. A lot is at stake tomorrow!"

"Bonne chance et bonne nuit – Good luck and good night," says Valerie.

"Gracious, buenas noches – Thank you, good night," Alejandro replies.

Valerie opens the door for Alejandro. He walks out a little disappointed that Valerie gave him no opening for a romantic interlude, but he is content knowing that he will likely have most of his wishes come true by tomorrow afternoon.

It's okay, I'll have almost everything I want very soon, Alejandro says to himself.

Almost as soon as Valerie closes the door to her hotel suite, the phone rings.

Now, who could that be, I wonder? I told Bianca not to phone me, unless it was an emergency, and that I would contact her after making the arrangements with Alejandro.

"Allo, oui," says Valerie.

"Valerie?"

"Oui, oh, it's you!"

"Well, that's not exactly the warm reception I expected. I just called to see how you were making out," says Guy.

"Oh, je suis désolé, mon amour – I'm sorry, my love. I didn't expect your call. Everything is going smoothly so far. I should be finished with my business by around 2 pm tomorrow. Then, I plan to leave Monté Carlo afterward. Hopefully, we can enjoy our last night on the Riviera together before going back to Paris on Sunday."

"Are you sure you're alright?"

"Oui, n'inquiète pas mon chéri, tout va bien – Yes, don't worry my dear, everything is going well."

"Eh bien, j'ai confiance en toi - Well, I trust you, but give me a call tomorrow when you have time, just before you're ready to leave."

"I will try. How about you - how are you doing?"

"I'm fine Val, just a little bored. Tu me manques - I miss you."

"Tu me manques aussi, mon chéri – I miss you too, my dear."

"You're only spending one night alone, so try to make the best of it. I'm sure you can find someone to have dinner with. There are lots of beautiful women at the Riviera this time of year."

"Is that what you want me to do?" asks Guy, a bit confused.

"I don't want you to do anything, except what will please you. I'm just telling you, if you're lonely and not happy because we aren't together, then you are free to do what you want to entertain yourself."

Guy spends a minute trying to absorb the implications of Valerie's statement.

I wonder - is she telling me that she doesn't care if I spend the evening having dinner with another woman? How far does she expect me to go with it? Is she also saying she won't mind if I sleep with another woman, as well? What game is she playing with me now? I thought she told me earlier not to look at other women while she is away. I'm confused. I'm not sure if I'm comfortable with Valerie's thought process. Whatever she's doing in Monté Carlo, it must be a big deal, because it's obviously taking priority over our romantic week together.

"Okay Valerie, I'll see what I can arrange."

"Alright Guy, I need to go now. Prends soins de toi – Take care of yourself."

"Toi aussi – You also."

Guy feels a little strange after their conversation. He knows that many people in France have very liberal sexual habits, but he's not one of those people. For a moment, he contemplates whether he's made a mistake by leaving Gabrielle, who has more traditional ideas concerning relationships. He's beginning to have second thoughts about his decisions lately. Perhaps, this is the wake-up call he needed.

Perhaps I'm not cut out for this type of lifestyle after all. Maybe this time, I bit off more than I could chew. Perhaps, I should just chill out and stop being so uptight and invite some lady to have dinner with me. It doesn't mean I have to sleep with her. Maybe, I'm overthinking things, as usual. However, I do feel kind of silly dressing for dinner to eat alone at La Rotonde. Perhaps, I should just let fate decide again.

Guy takes out his lucky coin, ready to let fate decide again.

Heads, I have dinner with some random lady I meet downstairs at the bar or tails, I order room service and eat alone.

Guy flips his coin and catches it with both hands. Slowly, he opens his palms and allows himself time to absorb the outcome.

After hanging up with Guy, Valerie leaves the hotel to make a call from the outside to Bianca, to tell her more details of her plan. Vanessa notices that her target is on the move and follows her to a phone booth near the hotel. She knows she won't be able to hear what Valerie is saying, but perhaps the Dragon Princess will meet with the person she calls and possibly reveal where she's hiding the painting. Vanessa assumes that the call Valerie is making must be important.

"Allo, oui," says Bianca as she answers the phone.

"C'est Valerie."

"Ah, Valerie, ça va?"

"Oui, tout va bien – Everything is going well. M'écoutes – Listen to me. I need you to meet Alejandro on his yacht tomorrow at 1:00 pm."

"What's the name of his yacht?"

"C' est appellé – Orgullo de España – It's called the Pride of Spain."

"Okay, Je le trouverai - I'll find it."

"How's everything going with you? Are you nervous about tomorrow?" asks Valerie.

"Oui, un petit peu – Yes, a little bit," Bianca replies.

"N'inquiète pas, tout ira bien - Don't worry, all will go well.

"Okay, je te fais confiance – Okay, I trust you."

"Remember this one last thing… We will do the same dance tomorrow that we performed for Guy at the club. Do you understand me?"

"Oui, je t'ai compris, très bien – Yes, I have understood you very well."

"Bon, je vais aller maintenant. Bonne chance – Good, I'm going to go now. Good luck!"

"Merci, Valerie, je t'aime – Thanks, Valerie, I love you!"

"Je t'aime aussi, au revoir – I love you too, goodbye."

Valerie hangs up the phone and crosses the street back to the hotel. Vanessa is disappointed that Valerie is not going anywhere, other than back to the hotel, but she still follows her from a safe distance.

The Dragon Princess is still mainly looking out for Sylvain, so she's still not suspicious of anyone else who might be following her. Ironically, Valerie wants Sylvain to follow her now, so he will be lured away from the real exchange.

The stage is set for tomorrow. Now, all there is to do is wait. Valerie will have all morning to wake up late, have a leisurely breakfast, and then put her plan into action.

What could possibly go wrong, Valerie thinks to herself.

XX.   The Game Begins

The day of the big race has finally arrived, and the streets are lined with thousands of spectators. The press is there in spades, along with everyone who's anyone. Since early morning, the champagne has already begun flowing, bookies are taking bets, and people are dressed as if the royal family is hosting a wedding. A plethora of limousines and luxury automobiles of every type have created a bottleneck around the city.

The odds are currently 5-1 that Alejandro's speedster will take the checkered flag. All the top Formula 1 drivers are here, so the competition will be fierce. It seems that every police officer in Monaco is present. Despite it being such a small country, the eyes of the world descend upon Monaco every year for the grandest race of them all.

It's the perfect cover for the sale of the Rembrandt. At this moment, Valerie is enjoying breakfast alone at a café across the street from L'Hôtel de Paris. Vanessa is watching her from a newspaper stand nearby, while The Cat remains in his room, loading his gun and sipping his morning espresso.

Valerie has planned to leave the country by the time the race is finished with a suitcase full of cash. Under normal circumstances, she would have placed a bet on the race, but she wouldn't be sticking around to collect any additional money, even if she did win. She has her mind focused on another prize, which is a sure thing. While the whole city of Monté Carlo is buzzing with Formula 1 frenzy, Valerie is simply

241

enjoying her croissant and her morning fix, trying not to think about the events which will unfold during the afternoon.

*

Back in Nice, Guy is not feeling so relaxed after having dinner in his room, then tossing and turning in his bed all night. Something about this whole situation has made him feel very uneasy. He senses that something might go terribly wrong today. So, once again, he decides to take out his lucky coin and flip it, letting fate decide whether he travels to Monté Carlo or stays in Nice.

He tosses the coin in the air and lets it fall to the floor. It turns up heads this time, so that means he will take the next train out of Nice to Monaco. He knows Valerie's room number at L'Hôtel de Paris, so he expects that he can track her down there. However, if she's not there, it will be like looking for a needle in a haystack because of the number of people gathered for the race.

The next train to Monté Carlo leaves at 11:45 am, so Guy should arrive around 12:45 pm. He knows it's a risk surprising Valerie at the last minute, but if he lets her know ahead of time that he's decided to come to see her, she'll likely tell him to stay in Nice - and that is not an option for him anymore. Something has been eating away at Guy inside which compels him to go find Valerie, as soon as possible. He will leave everything in fate's hands.

*

Valerie is just finishing her breakfast, but instead of walking back to L' Hôtel de Paris like Vanessa expects, she hails a cab and heads over to Bianca's hotel. This action catches Vanessa off guard. She can't react fast enough, and now Valerie is gone - but where? Vanessa starts to panic.

Merd! Where is she off to now? Valerie must be going to retrieve the painting! However, she must be coming back later because this hotel is where the exchange will be – won't it?

Vanessa decides that the only thing to do now is to head back to L'Hôtel de Paris and wait for Valerie to return. She will contact Sylvain to tell him the bad news.

Hopefully, he won't be too upset with me.

At this moment, Alejandro is on his yacht, anchored in the Port de Monaco. He's annoyed Valerie talked him into sleeping alone.

Why did I agree not to have my girls with me last night? I could hardly sleep a wink. Damn that Valerie!

Alejandro opens the suitcase full of money, just to make sure it's still all there.

This is a lot of money for a painting. Anyway, I hope it's worth it. It's going to hang right next to my Van Gogh in my secure room. Valerie had better arrive on time because I need to get back for the start of the race. This whole ordeal is making me a bit stir-crazy. I'm going to be glad when it's all over, so I can concentrate on watching the race. I have a lot riding on that too!

"Do you men have your guns loaded? I hope you won't need to use them, but I want you to be prepared, just in case something unexpected happens. There's a lot of money in this suitcase and the merchandise I will be receiving is irreplaceable. So, keep your eyes and your ears open, so I can wrap this up in plenty of time before the start of the race," says Alejandro.

"Si Jefe – Yes boss," his men shout.

In the meantime, Vanessa knocks on Sylvain's door to update him on the situation.

"Vanessa! Viens, dépêche-toi - Come in, hurry."

Sylvain looks both ways down the hallway and spots a maid entering a room several doors down.

"Qu'est ce-que tu fais la maintenant - What are you doing here now? You're supposed to be tailing Valerie."

"Je suis désolé – I'm sorry, but I lost her after she finished breakfast. I wasn't expecting her to jump in a cab. I thought that she would walk back to the hotel instead because she was on foot when she left. I still believe that she will make the exchange this afternoon, here in the hotel, but now I can't be certain. Perhaps she went to retrieve the painting and will come back with it."

"If that's true, it would have been a better opportunity to try to steal it from her while she's in the process of retrieving it. Merde!"

"Je suis désolé, encore – I am sorry, again," says Vanessa.

"We'll just have to make the best of it and stick to our original plan, that's all. Just go back downstairs and make sure you spot her when she returns. Instead of meeting up with me here, follow Valerie instead, and then I will meet up with you in front of Alejandro's suite. Give me a call the moment she arrives - d'accord - agreed?"

"Oui, d'accord – Yes, agreed."

"Now get going - I don't want to blow this!" says Sylvain.

"Oui, patron – Yes, boss," Vanessa replies.

Sylvain opens his door for Vanessa, peering out into the hallway once again to see if anyone is there. He doesn't see the maid this time.

She must be in one of the rooms cleaning, Sylvain thinks.

He spots a bellman with a cap and mustache, who appears to be pushing a luggage cart toward the elevator.

Vanessa decides to take the stairs on her way to catch up with Valerie. The bellman takes notice of her movements. As he looks up, she sees a glimpse of his face. For just one moment, Vanessa has the sense that she has seen this man before, but she can't quite place him. However, she can't get this thought out of her head.

That man seems familiar to me, yet how could I possibly know some bellman from L' Hôtel de Paris?

She puts the thought out of her mind for the moment and heads to the bar to wait for Valerie to return.

I need a drink - a Bloody Mary perhaps. I think I'll make it with a double shot of vodka. This whole business is starting to wear on my nerves.

*

It's now approximately 11:10 am. Guy steps outside the front of Le Negresco with an overnight bag, just in case he needs a change of clothes for later.

"Taxi monsieur?" says one of the drivers.

"Oui, la gare, s'il vous plaît – Yes, the train station, please," Guy demands.

"Hop in."

Guy is still a little nervous about surprising Valerie on the same day she's supposed to be returning to Nice. However, he has a gut feeling that tragedy make strike soon.

Perhaps it's jealousy or insecurity or the feeling that I'm not in control. Maybe that's all it is. No, damnit -something is wrong; I know it! I must get to Monaco as fast as I can to try and prevent something dire happening before it's too late!

When Guy arrives, he tips the driver and heads straight to the ticket counter.

"Un billet, aller au retour à Monté Carlo, s'il vous plaît – One round trip ticket to Monté Carlo, if you please," Guy demands.

"That will be 100 francs," says the man behind the window.

The agent passes him his ticket, after he gives the attendant the money. Guy is so engrossed in his thoughts about Valerie that he hardly notices the swarm of people all around the station. Guy also doesn't notice a woman dressed in black, wearing a beret and dark sunglasses, watching him. She had been sitting alone at the bar in the lounge of Le Negresco the previous night, nursing a scotch and soda. She might have said yes to a dinner invitation if Guy had asked her.

Guy has been shadowed, ever since Valerie left him behind, without knowing it. As he takes his seat on the train, he pulls out a Figaro newspaper and begins to look at the real estate section, trying to distract his attention from his purpose for being on there. The lady in black takes a seat on the other side of the same car, keeping watch over Guy's every move.

*

Back in Monté Carlo, swarms of people continue to pour into the city from all over Europe. The streets are now mobbed with sport fans, party goers, dignitaries, celebrities, and politicians. The gaming tables are full, and bets are being placed on the outcome of the race. The Formula 1 drivers are giving one last look over their cars and talking to their pit crews.

It appears that Valerie is now on her way back to L'Hôtel de Paris, which will be to Vanessa's relief, as she waits for her in the hotel lounge. Alejandro looks at his Rolex to check the time, then tells one of his bodyguards to pour him a glass of bourbon to help calm his nerves. At the same moment, a taxi pulls up in front of L'Hôtel de Paris. Her misty sunglasses and wide brimmed chapeau shield her eyes and face, as she steps out of the cab. The woman tips the driver and walks through the revolving doors with a midnight blue cylindrical container strapped to her shoulder. Vanessa immediately spots the woman with silvery blonde hair as she enters the hotel lobby and darts over to the house phone to alert The Cat.

"Allo, Sylvain, c'est Vanessa – Hello Sylvain, it's Vanessa. Valerie is back and she's carrying the painting. I think she must be headed to Alejandro's suite right now."

"Je comprends – I understand. I'll meet you there in just a few minutes. Let Valerie enter the room, then wait for me."

"Okay," Vanessa replies.

The wheels are in motion – there's no turning back now.

*

Guy's train has just arrived at the station in Monté Carlo. As he exits the car, he is followed by the woman in black. As Guy approaches the street, he hails a cab. A moment later, a grey Citroen pulls up to the curb behind the taxi and the woman in black steps into the car.

"Bonjour Céline," says the driver.

"Follow that cab and don't lose him!" Céline commands.

The car pulls away from the curb in haste.

At the same moment, a gentle knock can be heard on the door of Alejandro's suite, just as another taxi pulls up at the Port de Monaco. A woman with dark hair gets out of the cab and asks the driver to wait for her. She walks toward Alejandro's yacht with the real Rembrandt in hand, checking over her shoulder to be certain no one has followed her. She smiles briefly, believing she is only moments away from discovering the pot of gold at the end of the rainbow.

Back at L'Hôtel de Paris, the door to Alejandro's suite opens and one of his bodyguards motions to the woman with blonde hair to enter the room. Surprisingly, there are no guards in the hallway, which

Vanessa is grateful to see. A maid walks out of one of the rooms, just as Sylvain arrives on the scene. He motions to Vanessa to deal with her.

As the maid enters another room, Vanessa follows her and knocks her on the back of the head with her beretta, once they are out of view. The maid falls to the floor, unconscious. Vanessa quickly gags her mouth and ties her wrists behind her back. Then, she steps over her body and closes the door behind her.

"Es-tu prêt, maintenant – Are you ready, now?" asks Sylvain.

"Oui," Vanessa replies.

At that same moment, the woman with dark hair wearing a red silk scarf and dark sunglasses steps on board Alejandro's yacht. She is escorted by two armed bodyguards.

"Are you Valerie's girl?" asks Alejandro.

"Oui," the woman responds with a deep voice.

"Can I offer you a drink?"

"Non, merci – No, thank you. Let's get down to business. I'm on a tight schedule."

"As you wish. You sound just like your boss," Alejandro replies.

"It appears that you brought the item - may I see it?"

"Show me the money first," says the woman with the red scarf.

Alejandro motions to one of his bodyguards to retrieve the suitcase full of cash.

"Your manner reminds me of Valerie a little too much, I think. She's all work and no play, just as you are now," says Alejandro.

"We're more alike than you might imagine," the woman with dark hair replies.

Back at L'Hôtel de Paris, Valerie has pre-arranged with the concierge to have the police on alert, since she expects The Cat to make a play for the Rembrandt. Unfortunately, most of the police resources are already stretched very thin, so they don't have the manpower to have officers waiting in the hotel lobby. However, they will be on call and can arrive within a moment's notice.

Sylvain and Vanessa have now positioned themselves in front of Alejandro's door with their guns raised. The camera in the hallway has been disabled, but even though they can't be seen, security will come to check to see why it's not working in no more than 15 minutes. So, they need to move fast.

Sylvain quietly places the key he's stolen in the lock and turns the handle, before abruptly pushing the door open. Both Vanessa and The Cat leap into the room without warning, shouting to everyone to get down on the ground and throw away their weapons. The bodyguards whirl around and make a move to draw their guns, but they're too late.

"Put your pistols on the floor and kick them over to us – now! Then, get on the ground with your hands on your head. You, (speaking to the blonde woman), hand over that painting!"

"Watch the door!" Sylvain shouts to Vanessa.

The guards slowly bend down to place their guns on the floor, when suddenly one of them points his weapon at Sylvain and shoots him in the arm. The Cat flinches in pain but returns fire and kills the man on the spot.

In that moment, Vanessa's eyes focus on the other bodyguard, but out of the corner of her eye, she sees the woman she assumes is Valerie pointing a Derringer in her direction. She turns and fires two shots, hitting the woman twice in the chest. Blood begins to pour out of her open wounds, and she collapses on the floor. The second bodyguard exchanges fire with Sylvain, but he loses the battle and drops to the floor beside the others.

Sylvain spots the blue cylinder with the replica inside resting on the sofa, and shouts to Vanessa.

"Grab the painting and let's get out of here! The hotel staff must have heard those shots."

Before Vanessa can reach for it, the door swings open, and a man dressed in a janitor's outfit and three police officers race into the room with their guns raised.

"Hands in the air; you're under arrest," the janitor shouts, flashing his badge. "My name is Inspector André Bouchard, and I'm with Interpol."

Vanessa looks at him in shock, after she recognizes her weekend lover from Brussels.

"André!" she shouts.

"You know this man?" Sylvain demands.

"Oui," Vanessa replies, looking on in disbelief.

At the same instant, Guy and Céline are just arriving in front of L'Hôtel de Paris. Guy rushes inside and heads straight for the elevator and immediately notices lots of commotion, along with an increasing police presence in the lobby. As he waits for the elevator door to open, he sees several officers racing up the staircase.

Guy's worst fears have come to fruition. He's frightened about what could be happening upstairs. The elevator finally arrives, and Guy presses the number to Valerie's floor, just as the woman in the black beret slips inside the elevator beside him.

Upstairs in Alejandro's suite, the officers try taking the pulse of the victims on the floor. They look up at André shaking their heads.

"They're all dead, Inspector," one of the officers says.

"Cuff those two and take them away," says Inspector Bouchard, as Vanessa stares into his eyes, trying to make sense of everything.

As the suspects are being led out of the room, Guy and Céline arrive on the top floor where the shootings took place. He is about to walk in the direction of Valerie's suite when he sees and hears the activity at the other end of the hallway.

Guy abruptly runs to Valerie's door and knocks furiously, but there is no response. Fearing the worst, he quickly walks down toward Alejandro's suite, where there are now at least a dozen police officers. The woman in black now approaches him holding out her badge.

"Monsieur Martin, I am Sergeant Céline Garnier with Interpol. We would like you to answer some questions and help us to identify a body."

"A body! What body?" Guy demands.

Guy is now in a state of panic and is sure that something terrible has happened to Valerie.

"If you will just come with me, please," says Céline.

Sergeant Garnier escorts Guy into Alejandro's suite where he sees three bodies lying on the floor immersed in blood.

Inspector Bouchard looks up as they walk through the door.

"Who is this?" asks the inspector, looking straight at Céline.

"This is Monsieur Guy Martin – Valerie Fontaine's male companion."

"How do you know my girlfriend?" asks Guy.

He freezes when he views the woman with blonde hair lying on the floor, dressed in Valerie's clothes.

"Oh, mon Dieu! Est-ce-que c'est Valerie – Oh, my God! Is that Valerie?" Guy cries out.

"We're hoping you can tell us," Sergeant Garnier replies.

"I can't see her face, but I recognize her clothes," says Guy.

"Officer, turn her head," Inspector Bouchard commands.

"Oui, Inspector."

The officer turns the blonde woman's head and pulls back her hair, which turns out to be a wig. The officer removes it, revealing her natural dark brown hair color underneath. Both Guy and André look at each other, surprised.

"That's Bianca! Guy exclaims.

"You know this woman?" asks the inspector.

"Oui," Guy replies, gazing upon the young woman in utter astonishment, but relieved that it's not Valerie lying there.

"Who is Bianca?" asks Sergeant Garnier.

"Bianca is my girlfriend's colleague from Le Théâtre Coquette – a nightclub in Paris," Guy replies.

"Sergeant, open that tube on the couch and see what's in it," Inspector Bouchard demands.

Céline opens the tube and removes the copy of the Rembrandt, which Valerie painted herself.

"It's a painting sir."

"Well, it will need to be analyzed and logged into evidence."

"Oui, Inspector."

André is familiar with the Isabella Stewart Gardner Museum art theft, but he doesn't recognize this copy of the Rembrandt, which is connected to the famous Boston heist, on March 18, 1990.

"May I look at that more closely?" asks Guy.

"Do you recognize this painting?" asks Inspector Bouchard.

Guy looks at the painting carefully and recognizes it as a work of art, similar to the one he had seen in Valerie's bedroom recently. Somehow, it seems different, but he's not sure why. Guy ponders the implications if he were to respond in the affirmative.

"Uh, non, je suis désolé – Uh, no, I'm sorry." Guy replies.

Guy believes that if he admits what he knows, it may cause Valerie, no end of grief. He's sure that if he speaks up now, The Dragon Princess will view it as a betrayal and their relationship would be over. Inspector Bouchard absorbs Guy's response suspiciously.

Just then, the hotel concierge appears in the hallway, along with two hotel security guards.

"Whose suite is this anyway?" asks Sergeant Garnier.

"It's the suite of señor Alejandro de la Cruz," the concierge replies.

"So, where is he and where is Valerie Fontaine?" asks Garnier. "I'm willing to bet we'll find both of them together on his yacht," Inspector Bouchard replies. "On-y va – Let's go! There's no time to lose!"

XXI.   Vanishing Act

The woman with the red silk scarf is satisfied that all the money is in the case. She removes the Rembrandt from the tube she's carrying and presents it to Señor de la Cruz.

"What a thing of beauty this is. It's worth every penny I'm paying for it," says Alejandro.

"I'm glad you like it. It was nice doing business with you. However, I fear that the authorities might be on our heels by now. I think it would be a good idea to order your crew to take your yacht out of the harbor and lure the police away from the Riviera. I also suggest that you put the painting on a speed boat and point it in the direction of Spain. Then, get back to the raceway as soon as possible, so you can not only watch your car win, but also not get caught sitting here with a stolen painting."

"You're a very clever woman – like your boss. I think I will comply with your recommendation. José, set a course for Corsica and get underway as soon as we disembark," Alejandro commands.

"Si Señor Cruz," José replies.

"Well, now I must be going."

The dark-haired woman leaves the ship with the suitcase full of cash and walks back to her cab, which has been waiting for her to return.

"Take me to the train station, tout de suite – right away."

When she arrives, instead of getting on a train back to Nice, the woman in the red scarf takes another taxi to Eze to lay low for a day. This way, if her original cab driver is questioned, he will tell the police he dropped his passenger off at the train station. They will assume that she took the first train leaving Monaco back to France, and the authorities will be off on a wild goose chase.

Alejandro will be heading back to the raceway as soon as he gives his crew further instructions. He orders two of his men to take the painting with them on a fast boat to his villa on the island of Menorca, off the coast of Spain. Then, Alejandro instructs his captain to take his yacht to Corsica to lure the police away from himself and the boat where the Rembrandt is stashed.

As the two boats get underway, Alejandro gets in his Mercedes and tells his driver to take him to the start of the race. By the time any police arrive at the dock, everyone will be gone. It will appear as if nothing has happened.

"Step on it driver; we need to get out of here and get to the raceway in good time," Alejandro commands.

About fifteen minutes later, Inspector Bouchard, **Sergeant Garnier**, and the police arrive at the dock in great haste, only to find that Alejandro's yacht has left port and is headed out to sea. The large vessel is still in sight, but the speedboat is long gone.

"Merde! They're getting away!" Bouchard shouts.

The inspector grabs a two-way radio from his car and demands to have a helicopter sent to the docks, so he can board the chopper and pursue them.

"Dépêchez-vous – Hurry!" Bouchard shouts.

Sergeant Garnier interrupts the inspector for a moment to ask for clarification.

"Sir, when we catch up with them, are you planning to interrogate them or formally charge them? As far as we know, they haven't done anything wrong that we can prove. The only crime that's been committed, as far as I can tell, is what's happened in that hotel room, and we've arrested the two people responsible for it already," says Céline.

"N'inquiète pas - Don't worry sergeant, I'll think of something. Alejandro de la Cruz and Valerie Fontaine must be involved in all of this somehow. I'll eventually get to the bottom of this. We are going to have another crime on our hands if that painting winds up having been stolen. I'll just say for now that they're both wanted for questioning, d'accord - agreed?

"Oui, I just don't want to have to answer for making a false arrest."

"Je t'ai compris – Understood, Céline. I want you to stay behind while I go after Alejandro's yacht in the helicopter. Find out if either Alejandro or Valerie have gone back to the hotel or to the racetrack. If Alejandro is along the raceway, he will probably be near his pit crew. I believe he owns car number six. I have alerted the harbor police patrol to be on the lookout for his ship."

"Understood, inspector."

"Sergeant, see if you can also track down Monsieur Martin again. He may be able to lead us to Valerie. If you find him, don't confront him - follow him instead and see where he goes. Take a couple of officers with you."

"Oui, Inspector – I'm on it."

"Here comes the helicopter. Let's move out!" shouts Bouchard.

As Inspector Bouchard and Sergeant Garnier attempt to hunt down their targets, the woman in the red scarf arrives in Eze. She checks into L'Hôtel Château de la Chèvre d'Or under the name of Colette Gilbert. For the moment, Colette keeps her disguise in place, until she enters her room. Her suite has a breathtaking view of the Mediterranean Sea since it's situated high above ground. It's unlikely that the police will come looking for her here, for the foreseeable future.

Back at L'Hôtel de Paris, Guy has been waiting to hear any word from Valerie, worried about where his lover could be. Impatient and frustrated, he decides to call over to Hôtel Le Negresco and speaks to the concierge personally just in case Valerie has returned or left a message for him.

"Hello, Jean-Piere, this is Guy Martin. I'm calling to see if Valerie

255

Fontaine has returned to the hotel or if there are any messages for me."

"Oui, monsieur, there is a message for you. You are to meet Colette Gilbert at L'Hôtel Château de la Chèvre d'Or in Eze this evening. You are to tell the front desk manager that your name is Louis Savard, and you will be given a key to her room. Take care that you're not followed and tell no one where you are going or who you'll be meeting. After taking the train to Eze, you are to take a cab to La Taverne d'Anton near the base of the mountain village. Then, walk up to the hotel on foot. Comprenez-vous, monsieur – Do you understand, sir?"

"Oui, J'ai vous compris, merci – Yes, I have understood you, thanks."

Guy is relieved that Valerie is alright, and he knows where to find her.

At least I know Valerie is still alive, but what the hell is going on? What has Valerie got herself into, and what has she gotten me involved in?

Guy steps outside and hails a cab to go to the train station. He gets in the car and drives away. Only two minutes after he leaves, Sergeant Garnier shows up in front of the L'Hôtel de Paris and hurries inside, only to find that both Guy and Valerie are nowhere in sight. She confirms with the hotel manager that Valerie had already checked out of her room earlier that morning.

So, Céline decides to look for Alejandro, instead. As she makes her way through the crowd, she spots him talking to one of his crew members. The race has just started and the noise on the street is intense, between the cars' engines and all the people cheering.

Meanwhile, Inspector Bouchard's helicopter has finally caught up to Alejandro's yacht, on route to Corsica – a vacation paradise for the rich. André and two other agents climb down a rope ladder from the chopper and jump aboard.

"I am Inspector Bouchard with Interpol. I want to speak with Alejandro de la Cruz - immediately!" André shouts.

"Lo siento señor – I'm sorry sir, but Señor de la Cruz is not on board - he's at the racetrack."

"Well, I have a warrant to search this vessel. Turn this ship around and head back to the port of Monaco – now!"

"Right away, señor."

As the Orgullo de España turns around, Alejandro's speed boat is well on its way to reaching its destination off the coast of Spain, unfettered by any law enforcement. Back at the racetrack, Sergeant Garnier is busy interrogating Alejandro.

"Señor de la Cruz?"

"Si."

"I am Sergeant Céline Garnier with Interpol. I'd like to speak with you about the event that occurred in your suite this afternoon."

"What event? I don't know anything about it. Can't this wait? I'm very busy right now. I have a car in this race!" Alejandro protests.

"No, it can't wait! I'm sorry sir, but three people were shot and killed in your hotel suite this afternoon, a little over an hour ago. Can you explain what was going on for something like that to happen?"

"What! Who was killed? I don't know anything concerning what you're talking about. I haven't been in my suite since yesterday evening. I spent the night on my yacht and came here directly."

"We also found a painting in your room, which we believe was brought by a nightclub dancer from Paris. It seems to be at the center of it all. Do you know anything about that?"

"What painting are you referring to? The only paintings I know of in my suite are the ones the hotel decorators put there for their guests. I doubt any of them are especially valuable – they're all copies. I have my own."

"Concerning your yacht – Where is it headed and why did you order it to leave port?"

"I asked my captain to take it to Corsica because I didn't want it exposed to this massive crowd. Fans go crazy when their favorite car wins or loses - you understand. I didn't want my ship exposed to mayhem. Now please tell me, who was killed?"

"Apparently, this cabaret dancer named Bianca Dubois and two of your bodyguards."

257

"Dios mio – My God!"

If she's saying that woman in my suite was Bianca Dubois? Then, who did I meet with on my yacht earlier? I better not have been swindled! However, the painting looked authentic to me. If it was a replica, it was a damn good one. That woman must have been Valerie in disguise. No wonder she spoke like her. But, why the deception, I wonder?

"Can you tell me who shot them and why?" asks Alejandro.

"Oui, we know who shot them – they're in our custody. Their names are **Sylvain Bonnet, also known as The Cat, and Vanessa St. Pierre**. Are these names familiar to you?"

"No, I've never heard of either of them before now," Alejandro replies.

"Sylvain is a known art and jewel thief, and his accomplice is apparently just a hired gun. We're having the painting analyzed as we speak to identify the origin and its value. You must know something about this painting. You're a well-known fine art collector."

"It's true that I collect fine works of art, but I don't know what piece you're referring to. I have never heard of the woman who has been killed or the two people you say killed her. I have no idea what any of those people were doing in my suite."

"I must confess that I don't know half the people who come and go in my room. I've been doing a lot of partying this week and people just seem to drift in and out at all hours of the night. That's all I can tell you. I don't know anything more."

"Well, Señor de la Cruz, I don't think you're being honest with me. I'm sorry for the inconvenience, but I'm going to have to take you in for further interrogation. It was your suite where three people died, after all."

"But I had nothing to do with it! I have a car in this race! I will miss the finish!" Alejandro protests. "You have no right to detain me further!"

"I do have the authority to detain you. I'm sorry señor, but you'll have to come with me."

"This is outrageous! I must be allowed to call my lawyer!"

"As you wish."

Sergeant Garnier leads Alejandro to her police car, as the race continues. Alejandro's car is currently in the lead.

Damn you Valerie and your stupid plan! Alejandro curses to himself.

When Guy finally arrives in Eze, from the opposite direction, he tips the cab driver generously and tells him to forget his face. He sees the small mountain he must climb and then notices a teenage boy sitting on a motorbike. He walks up to the youth to ask him if he'll give him a ride up the mountain.

"Bonjour young man. Can I persuade you to give me a ride up the mountain? I'll pay you 50 francs now and another 50 when we arrive at the top, if you'll forget you ever saw me," says Guy.

"It's a deal, monsieur - hop on," the young man replies.

Guy mounts the back of the motorbike, and they start on their way. The last time he rode on the back of a bike was with Valerie in Paris, on their way to her flat from the club. He's not especially comfortable, but he is anxious to see Valerie and not so excited to walk up that steep hill.

Guy has the boy drop him off a distance from the hotel, so he doesn't see exactly where he's going. Then, he hurries to find Le Château de la Chèvre d'Or through the winding village maze, sprinkled with shops and restaurants. When he finally arrives at the hotel, he walks through the lobby and rings the bell at the front desk, giving the concierge his assumed name.

"Oui, monsieur. May I help you?" says the hotel manager.

"Je m'appelle Louis Savard - My name is Louis Savard. May I have my room key, please?"

"Oui, monsieur. Voila – Here you are."

Guy walks cautiously through the corridor in the direction of the room and stops in front of the door. He inserts the key and turns the handle. When he steps into the room, a bright light from the late afternoon sun shines in his eyes. He holds his hand up to his face to shield himself from the sun's blinding light. He sees a woman dressed in black with long, silvery blonde hair standing out on the terrace, overlooking the sea. She is smoking a cigarette and has her back to him. For a moment, there is an eerie silence as she turns around. Then, she speaks.

"Guy, c'est bon de te voir – it's so good to see you!" says Valerie, with a smile.

Then, she notices the stone-cold pale expression on his face and the sadness in his eyes.

"Qu'est-ce qui s'est passé – What's happened?" asks Valerie.

Guy stands there for a moment longer before opening his mouth to talk. Then, in an abrupt fashion, he blurts out - "Bianca's dead!"

Suddenly, a dark cloud eclipses the sun's piercing rays that were shining through the glass window, just a moment ago. The joyful expression plummets from Valerie's profile, as her complexion turns dark. A veil of silence permeates the chamber, and the Dragon Princess collapses on the floor.

A WORD FROM THE AUTHOR

The concept for the story 'Twilight in Paris' came from some of my experiences while living in and visiting several regions in France. Laurence was one of the French women whom I met at a cabaret in Paris the night before I went home to New York. She used the name Valerie when she first introduced herself to me while working as a hostess and dancer, close to the famous Moulin Rouge in Pigalle.

Laurence and I kept in touch, sending letters and audio tapes, until I decided to go back to Paris to live with her a few months later. She and I shared her apartment together in the town of Courbevoie, until I returned to the United States again. Approximately twenty-two years into the future, Laurie and I reconnected.

Laurie currently lives near the city of Tours in the region of Amboise in her mother's house along with her stepfather, working as an elder care aid. She and I have remained close friends to this day. Perhaps in the future, we will see each other again to reminisce about the past and talk about our lives in the present.

Some of the descriptions I write about in this book reflect true events that happened during the time I lived in France, as well as during the three other trips I took there over twenty years later. The character of Valerie is based on Laurie's personality, but the events in this novel are fictional. This story is only roughly based on her life and experiences in one of the most romantic cities in the world.

I hope you enjoyed reading my novel and will recommend it to a friend. Also, pick up a copy of my first book - 'Love Affair with a Circus Girl,' a true-crime romance story, if you haven't read it already.

www.ingramcontent.com/pod-product-compliance
Lightning Source LLC
Chambersburg PA
CBHW060533260626

47161CB00003B/887